# OUT OF THE LION'S MAW

by
Witold Makowiecki
*and* Tom Pinch

MONDRALA
PRESS

©Ringel & Esch, S.A.R.L.-S

Mondrala Press is an imprint of
Ringel & Esch, S.A.R.L.-S
www.mondrala.com
Originally published in Polish in 1946 as *Przygody Meliklesa Greka*

Editing by InkScroll Editing
Cover Design by rock_0407

Publisher's Cataloging-in-Publication Data
provided by Five Rainbows Cataloging Services

Names: Makowiecki, Witold, author. | Pinch, Tom, author.
Title: Out of the lion's maw / by Witold Makowiecki and Tom Pinch.
Description: Ringel, Luxembourg : Mondrala Press, 2022.
Identifiers: ISBN 978-99987-916-7-1 (hardcover) | ISBN 978-99987-916-6-4
(paperback) | ISBN 978-99987-916-3-3 (ebook : EPUB) | 978-99987-916-4-0 (ebook :
mobi) | ISBN 978-99987-916-5-7 (PDF) | ISBN 978-99987-916-8-8 (audiobook)
Subjects: LCSH: Adventure and adventurers--Fiction. | Civil war--Fiction. |
Adventure stories. | Historical fiction. | Polish fiction. | BISAC: FICTION /
Historical / Ancient. | FICTION / World Literature / Poland.
Classification: LCC PN849.P72 M35 2022 (print) | LCC PN849.P72 (ebook)
| DDC 891.85--dc23

*In the Year 572 B.C. the god of the Israelites*
*spoke to his prophet Jeremiah:*

Behold, I will send Nebuchadnezzar,
the Old Mountain Lion,
the king of Babylon, my servant.
And when he cometh,
he shall smite the land of Egypt,
and deliver such as are for death to death;
and such as are for captivity to captivity;
and such as are for the sword to the sword.

*Jeremiah 43:10-11*

# TABLE OF CONTENTS

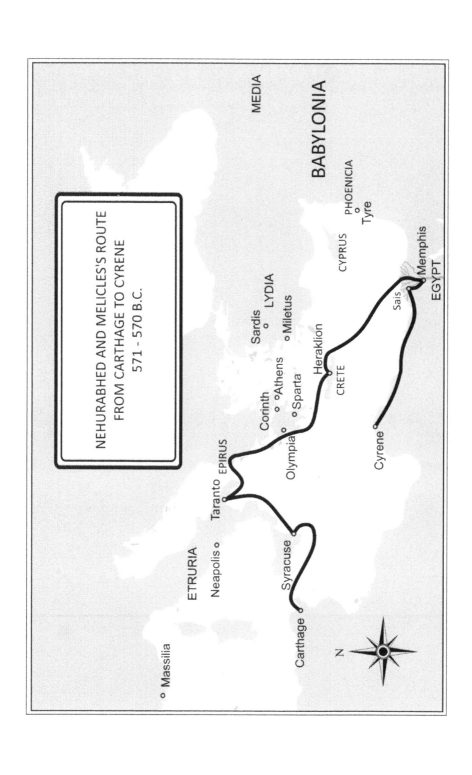

NEHURABHED AND MELICLES'S ROUTE
FROM CARTHAGE TO CYRENE
571 - 570 B.C.

Massilia

ETRURIA

Neapolis

Taranto

EPIRUS

Corinth

Olympia

Athens

Sparta

Sardis

LYDIA

Miletus

Heraklion

CRETE

Syracuse

Carthage

Cyrene

Sais

Memphis

EGYPT

CYPRUS

PHOENICIA

Tyre

BABYLONIA

MEDIA

N

# PART ONE

## Chapter One
# Fleeing Carthage

Quick, subtropical twilight descended upon the world; on the vast, luminous sea, on the great Phoenician port city of Carthage, and on this quiet, suburban garden of lofty palms, cypresses, cedars, tangled rose, vine, and oleander. The towering trees linked their branches overhead and cast deep shadows on everything below; on the small villa, on the garden paths, on the decorative fountains and statuary, on the enclosing wall. The web of shadows thickened, the shades grew darker, the silhouettes of the trees turned black. Night – humid, stifling, heavy, African night – swallowed the world.

Nehurabhed stood at the open door of the villa. He watched the darkening garden and sky overhead, still glowing with the last remains of the day. He waited. Faint traces of expiring daylight illuminated his face: long and narrow, wrinkled, and swarthy, his dark complexion contrasting sharply with the whiteness of his beard and bushy eyebrows. His face seemed aged at first glance, but his eyes, set deep under the eyebrows, were penetrating and quick, and his posture was alert and supple. His movements seemed infused with hidden and perfectly controlled energy.

He was dressed in the eastern fashion; he wore a black cloak which fell to his ankles, sandals on his feet, and a hood on his head. The hood and robe emphasized his height, lending him an air of lofty dignity.

He stood there for a long time, watching and listening. When the night had grown dark enough, he pulled the hood tighter over his eyes, tucked a small, brocaded bag and a short, fine dagger into the folds of his robe, glanced once more at the sky now darkening fast, and stepped outside.

Making not the slightest noise, he plunged into the tangled, sweet-scented darkness of the garden.

He walked quickly, purposefully, along a path he had memorized during the day. Shortly, he came to a place where a tall plane tree, broken by a recent storm, leaned against a garden wall. With agility and strength surprising in a man his age, he used the branches of the fallen tree to raise himself onto the wall, and he sat there for a while, listening. He looked around carefully, but the darkness was already total. Once he assured himself that no one had followed him, he slid down the other side of the wall into the street below and set out briskly towards the city center.

It was not as dark in the streets of Carthage as it had been in the garden. There was bustle and commotion here, with people coming home from work and slaves driven back to their pens from their work at the port. Small groups of people stopped to eat and drink at outdoor stalls while cries of reveling soldiers could be heard from a distance. Here and there was shouting, laughter, and music. Unsteady light of oil lamps spilled from open doors and windows onto the narrow street.

Having reached an intersection, Nehurabhed stopped to look around. Reassured that no one was following him, he turned into a street descending towards the shore. After leaving the residential quarter, he passed by the great workshops, where magnificent

Phoenician ships were built: sailing ships, barges, galleys, and the world-famous, terrifying, gigantic war triremes powered by hundreds of oars. Then, walking along the shore, he reached the fishing port. Here, the beach was littered with small sailing boats hung with nets and ropes under which he now and again had to duck.

Voices came from all directions. Poor fishermen, not wanting to leave their belongings unattended at night, camped near their boats and nets. They slept in tents improvised from sails or right under their boats turned upside down. Numerous shadowy figures gathered around campfires at which they fried their evening meal of fish and barley cakes and chatted in voices animated by wine.

Nehurabhed moved slowly from one fire to the next, listening to the conversations. He walked for a long time before he heard the sound of Greek. He stopped, watched, and listened. In front of him, three men sat by a small fire, lost in conversation. The man in the middle, apparently the most important of the three, talked the loudest, gesturing widely, frequently bursting out in thunderous laughter. In a grand gesture of ownership, he leaned his back against the side of a beached boat. He must have been her owner: a sailor or a fisherman. Noticing the stranger, he fell silent.

Nehurabhed walked up to him.

"You're Greek?" he asked.

The Greek nodded.

"And a sailor?"

"Yes."

"And the owner of this boat?"

"Yes."

"I want to talk to you alone."

He said this in the tone of a man accustomed to issuing commands.

Surprised, the Greek rose to his feet. His beautiful face, framed by a luxurious black beard, did not express concern: it was calm and composed. Nehurabhed inspected that face carefully. They walked some dozen or so steps away from the fire to the very edge of the sea –

silent, black, licking the beach with lazy waves. Nehurabhed looked around once more and, seeing no one, explained his purpose.

He meant, he said, to hire a good boat with a good pilot and sail to the Greek colonies in Sicily. Soonest. Tonight. Now, if possible. Two conditions: haste and silence. And then he named his price. A very good price.

The Greek was silent. Haste and mystery – it sounded like an escape. He understood anyone who wanted to get out of Carthage in a hurry but was leery of getting involved.

He hated the Phoenicians, a nation of traders and robbers, cunning, crafty, and vindictive. He hated them, as did all Greeks who competed with them for trade all across the vast shores of the Mediterranean Sea. They fought each other often; they argued even more. They traded with each other rarely; and only the hope of big profits could get him, a Greek, to visit this hateful city. This was not a friendly place for a Greek.

Of course, he had to admit it: one couldn't get a better price anywhere else for his trading goods. Carthaginians were rich and prepared to pay for quality. And because they sailed all over the great mysterious western *Okeanos*[1] and up and down those coasts, they offered goods no one else had.

Trading with Carthaginians was one thing, but helping someone escape from the city was another altogether. Carthage was a powerful state, and her tentacles reached far and wide. No merchant would dare cross her lightly. If Carthage wanted a man, it was best to let her have him.

On the other hand... the Greek had sold all his merchandise and had already loaded his boat for the return journey. And since the weather was fair, he had planned to sail home to Syracuse the next day anyway. And now, a noble-looking stranger turned up and offered to pay him very good money to sail just a few hours ahead of schedule.

That suited him. He hated the place anyway and was happy to leave it yesterday.

---

[1] *Okeanos*: The Atlantic Ocean

The Greek calculated; this stranger was not a Phoenician, and that was a good thing. But he was not a Greek, either – a bad thing. Even though he spoke the language fluently – a good thing.

He had an honest face and noble features – a good thing. And he was clearly an important person – and therefore not some petty merchant, job supervisor, a thief in trouble, or a crook trying to set him up. All good things.

All these thoughts crossed the Greek's mind as he studied Nehurabhed, trying to guess from his words and his face the secret of this hasty departure. The conversation lasted for a while, but the Greek learned nothing beyond this: the stranger offered to pay well. Really well.

Finally, he made up his mind. His boat was ready, freshly caulked, with sail and rigging all prepared, and the weather was good. There was a light westerly wind, a bit weak but blowing in the right direction. If the wind held up, one could reach the shores of Sicily in one and a half days, two at most. He cast one more glance at the sky – calm, full of stars, foretelling no surprises – and shook Nehurabhed's hand to seal the deal. In his rough sailor's hand, he felt the firm grip of a fine, soft, manicured palm: the gentle hand of a man who hadn't done manual work in many years.

This man is a great lord, he thought.

They agreed on a midnight departure. The Greek's crew had yet to pack their belongings while he himself had to go back to the city to collect money owed to him. He would return as soon as possible, within an hour most likely, and they would then sail. Nehurabhed promised to wait for him by the boat. He asked the Greek's name. The name was Kalias.

Nehurabhed asked him to hurry and reminded him again to keep quiet about their deal.

After the Greek's departure, Nehurabhed stood lost in thought for a while, staring at the dark sea. Then, he began to walk slowly along the shore. Lazy waves rolled at his feet, whispering softly in the dark. Nehurabhed also seemed to whisper as if in prayer.

Noticing that the Greek had moved off some distance already and was about to disappear behind some campfires, Nehurabhed suddenly changed direction and set off after him. He followed some distance behind so as to see and yet not be seen. He now had to quicken his pace because Kalias was marching briskly. At times, the old man lost sight of the Greek completely, but then he saw him again – a silhouette at the next fire or in the light of a lantern carried by a passer-by.

In this way, they walked around the fishing encampments, passed the dockyards, and started climbing into the city again. The streets were winding and narrow and climbed steeply upwards. In the side alleys, surrounded by high windowless walls, darkness was complete. Occasionally, a hulking passer-by hurried past him, glancing at him cautiously; it was easy to get a knife in one's back in this darkness. Nehurabhed was on alert, too, gripping the hilt of his dagger firmly under his cloak.

He reached an intersection and stopped, unsure which way the Greek had gone. Kalias's silhouette had vanished somewhere in the shadows. It seemed to him that the Greek had disappeared through a nearby gate, but he wasn't sure. He reflected for a while on what to do. At length, he decided to wait there. Surely, the Greek should return the same way he went.

Nehurabhed now stood in the shadows, almost invisible, calm, as still as a statue. Only his eyes watched every passer-by closely. He stood in this way for a long time. The lights around him began to dim, the murmurs of conversations quieting down with ever fewer passers-by. The big city was slowly settling down for the night.

Then, from behind a nearby wall, he suddenly heard a commotion: raised voices, then a short, desperate scream of pain and terror, and then the loud noise of a quarrel. People started gathering at a nearby gate leading into a courtyard. Their silhouettes cast long shadows into the street. Nehurabhed walked over to them.

"What's this all about?" he asked.

8

This time, he spoke Phoenician as fluently as he'd spoken Greek before. Several voices answered him at once – hoarse, drunk, stuttering through laughter and hiccups.

"What is this? Why, the usual! They're flogging a slave to death!"

"For running away."

"Second time already. The pipsqueak! This time they will not spare him."

"To death! Look, look, they're starting!"

Nehurabhed shuddered and looked glumly into the depths of the little courtyard where torture was about to begin. At a well, dimly lit by the flickering light of torches, lay a young prisoner, tied with ropes like a piece of smoked ham. He was completely naked. Skinny, huddled, he gave the impression of being immature, practically a child.

A gigantic slave stood over him with a flogging rod in his hand. The condemned man lay motionless. The executioner stood motionless. Their eyes were fixed on a group of speakers – several men standing nearby. Nehurabhed also shifted his gaze in that direction.

One of the men was a bald, fat Phoenician, with cold, cruel eyes, contemptuous and resentful. He was the lord of this house, this courtyard, and this slave about to be flogged to death. The second man, lively and restless, was explaining something to the first in a raised voice, arguing fiercely in broken Phoenician, swearing at the same time in Greek, Phoenician, Egyptian, and Etruscan, invoking all the gods of the world.

"Fifty drachmas[2], fifty drachmas for a slave!" he shouted.

Nehurabhed shuddered. He recognized the voice and came closer. Yes, this man who now single-handedly filled the entire courtyard with the shouting of a dozen was none other than his new acquaintance – the Greek Kalias.

"O, good people!" Kalias cried as if to call to witness the crowd around him. "What happened to the renowned wisdom of the shrewdest merchant this great city has ever had? Look here! I'm giving him fifty drachmas, you hear? – fifty drachmas! – for a slave he wants

---

[2] *Drachma*: a silver coin

to kill – and he refuses to accept! He does not want to accept fifty drachmas! Have you ever heard such a thing? O, holy Isis[3], Astarte[4], Athena[5], Great Mother of all gods! Give this man his reason back so that he may amaze us once again with his cunning!

"O, great and wise man!" he went on. "What profit do you get from a dead slave? Even your dog won't feed on him! He is too scrawny! And here I am, giving you fifty drachmas! Think about it! Think – o, you greatest of all merchants – what you can buy with fifty drachmas!"

The Phoenician shrugged and pushed the Greek away.

"Why all this talk?" he said coldly. "Give me a hundred drachmas, or let's forget the whole thing now."

Kalias gasped in indignation and raised his hands heavenward.

"A hundred drachmas? For what? O, gods, for what?! For a dead slave? He is not worth anything to you anymore! He is as good as dead!"

The Phoenician scoffed angrily.

"Why do I want a hundred drachmas?" he growled. "Why? Because you are trying to deprive me of my revenge. This dog dared to run away from me. Twice. On Moloch[6], killing him is worth a hundred drachmas to me. Besides, he is a Greek, and you are Greek, so you will pay. Pay me one hundred or shove off."

And with an impatient hand, he pushed Kalias away and motioned to the executioner to begin.

Kalias wiped sweat from his brow and tugged at his beard in helpless rage. He was panting. The unhappy slave, a young boy, a child almost, looked at him with despair. Kalias cursed.

"Sixty drachmas!" he stammered out. "I give you sixty drachmas!"

---

[3] *Isis*: an Egyptian goddess
[4] *Astarte*: a Phoenician goddess
[5] *Athena*: Greek goddess of war and wisdom
[6] *Moloch*: a god of ancient Palestine

But the Phoenician was not listening. The sharp whistle of the rod cut through the air and was answered by a cry from the condemned boy.

Nehurabhed approached Kalias.

"I'll give you the forty drachmas," he said softly. "Redeem the boy."

Kalias looked at him, astonished as if he had just seen a ghost, but he didn't waste any time on reflection. He grabbed the merchant's arm.

"I'll give you your hundred drachmas, blast you!" he exclaimed through a choked throat. "I'm giving you your hundred drachmas, hear? Untie the slave."

Melicles, for that was his name, walked with his saviors bewildered and half-dreaming. Blood dripped from his back from the terrible blows of the rod, but he felt no pain.

He was alive! He was breathing! He inhaled the cool breeze from the sea, heard the eternal crash of the waves, and joyful sobs squeezed his chest. He couldn't understand what had happened and why; he was not only alive, but he was free! How did it happen? How *could* it have happened?! Who were his saviors? He had never seen either man before. He was dumbfounded! He was confusion itself!

After a year of terrible captivity, after two hopeless attempts to escape, after so many futile endeavors, pleas, and curses, after torture and misery and now the terror of inevitable death – now, suddenly, this.

Salvation.

Where did salvation come from?

So, gods existed after all? Zeus[7] existed? And answered prayers? So, there was goodness? There was hope? There was grace?

---

[7] *Zeus*: Greek god of thunder, king of all gods

The boy was trembling. He wanted to fall on his knees before his saviors, to kiss their feet, but he did not dare do it. They walked swiftly, in silence – only Kalias gasped with anger and agitation, then he glanced suddenly at the old man walking next to him.

"How did you get here, my lord?" he asked.

Nehurabhed didn't answer right away.

"I wanted to find out where you were going," he said at last. "Were you really going to collect your money? Or were you perhaps going to report me?"

"You didn't trust me, my lord?" Kalias felt offended and pounded his oversized fist against his powerful chest. "All Syracuse knows to trust my every word as if it were the word of the sacred Pythia[8] herself!"

The old man nodded.

"From now on, I, too, will trust your word," he said simply.

Then, pointing to Melicles, he asked:

"Is that your relative?"

Kalias jumped as if burned by a branding iron.

"My relative?! Such a lame shrimp? Such a loser? Such a weak, headless, heedless fool who allows himself to be caught into slavery? And not once but three times in a row? O, ye gods! If I had such a relative, I would cry for shame. And to think that I paid sixty drachmas for a loser like this when he's not worth a broken *obolos*[9]!

"By Hermes[10]! I swear I never made a worse deal. Never. And all of this just because my heart is too soft. And my luck is rotten. Like I really needed to get there just as they started on his back. And why? Why? Why? If only I had not turned up, everybody would now be better off! The world would now contain one fool less, and I would be sixty drachmas richer!"

He gasped angrily.

"Am I your slave, my lord?" Melicles asked softly.

---

[8] *Pythia*: a prophetess of god Apollo

[9] *Obolos*: the smallest copper coin

[10] *Hermes*: Greek god of merchants and thieves

"A slave? No! A Greek will never be the slave of a Greek! At least not in my house! No! You're free, and you can run wherever the demons take you. But if you do, you will be the most ungrateful thief in the world, and Zeus the thunderous will burn you with living fire. Do you understand?"

"I understand, my lord." The boy choked with joy. "I understand, and I will serve you as long as you want. And I will be grateful to you for the rest of my life."

"If it weren't for me, you shrimp, they'd be burying you there in the garden by now. Or feeding you to the dogs."

They walked on in silence again.

"Sixty drachmas!" Kalias muttered to himself. "Sixty drachmas!"

"Perhaps, my lord, my mother will be able to pay you back this sum."

"What? Who? Your mother?" asked the Greek in a much softer tone. "Do you have a mother? Where is your home?"

"In Miletus. All the way in Ionia. In Asia."

"And Phoenicians snatched you from there?" Kalias asked in disbelief.

"No, my lord. After my father died, my uncle took me from Miletus to Parthenope. That's the Milesian colony on the Campanian[11] shore, you know."

"Of course, I know!" muttered Kalias. "I wasn't born yesterday. Parthenope. And sometimes they say Neapolis. I've been there. There is a large volcano there, and they claim, liars, that it is the site of the forge of the great god Hephaestus[12]. Even though, of course, everyone knows that Hephaestus's forge lies in Sicily, under Mount Etna. Is that where the Phoenicians got you?"

"Yes, my lord. Not Phoenicians – pirates. They attacked us while we were on our way back to Parthenope from Massalia."

---

[11] *Campania*: region of Italy surrounding Naples

[12] *Hephaestus*: Greek god of metalworking

"From Massalia? From Neapolis by sea to Massalia? Don't lie, you little brat, tell the gods' honest truth and do not confuse matters. It's a thousand miles from Neapolis to Massalia".

"I am telling the truth, my lord."

"Well, that you are from Miletus... this could be because you sing and draw out your words like an Ionian. I have a good ear for accents and will recognize an Ionian clear across the square on a market day." And then he burst out again: "My gods! So, fates drove you all the way from Miletus here, to my misfortune!"

He fell silent, but not for long; it was evidently not Kalias's custom to remain silent.

"How long ago was that?" he asked again.

"What, my lord?"

"Your getting kidnapped, of course!"

"A year ago."

"And you people couldn't defend yourselves?"

"We defended ourselves, my lord – to the death. Six of us were left out of the crew of fifteen. But the pirates had two ships. Over sixty men. We fought hard, my lord. I myself killed two. I think. But I passed out from my wounds. Then they took me."

"And they sold you in Carthage?"

"Yes, sir."

Kalias stopped panting. His anger was slowly leaving him.

"How old are you?" he asked at last when he calmed down.

"I'm past sixteen."

"And you killed two pirates?"

"I am strong, my lord."

Kalias looked at the boy's small stature and shook his head doubtfully.

"Never mind," he muttered to himself. "In your place, I would have said three."

They arrived at the shore. The boat was ready to go – it just needed a push onto the water. Final preparations were made in silence. Everything around was asleep. There was only one light all along the shore now – the great fire in the watchtower. That light was lit each evening and kept up all night as a guide for ships far at sea.

The night was calm and moonless. Nehurabhed couldn't have chosen a better time for his mysterious departure from the city. He happily settled at the bottom of the boat, now being pushed with strong hands, slowly sliding off the sandy shore and into the sea. He heard with intense relief the splash of the water parted by the prow and the flapping of the sail.

It seemed unlikely that the harbor guards might notice someone leaving the city in this darkness or that anyone might spot a single, gray sail melting away into the night. Kalias was a skilled sailor and knew the harbor well enough to clear the entrance to the port even in pitch-dark. Half an hour passed. No one said a word; only their hearts beat anxiously.

Finally, Kalias took a deep breath as if dropping a huge weight off his chest. He looked back. The light on the watchtower faded into the distance. All around them was now only night, silence, and the deep, dark sea.

"Let's thank Poseidon[13], comrades," he said in a firm voice. "Carthage won't catch us here anymore."

Then he turned to Nehurabhed.

"Lord," he said, "I understand everything, yet there is one thing I cannot comprehend. I paid sixty drachmas to save this worthless shrimp because he is a Greek, and me, well, I am a Greek, also. But you, my lord, why did you do it?"

The old man looked up at him thoughtfully.

"Because he is a man, and I am a man also," he said at last.

---

[13] Poseidon: Greek god of the sea

### Chapter Two

# This Is a Bad Place

Night. Silence.

The immeasurable depth of the sea beneath your feet; the immeasurable depth of heavens above your head. A gust of wind hardly moved the sail. The dark masses of water shifted like a great slithering beast under the boat, rocking it softly, gently.

Rest. A moment of respite amid the dormant terror of the sea. An ordinary sailor's night.

Melicles was awake. He leaned against the mast, seeing the prow of the boat in front of him, its dark contours rising and falling steadily against the bright-burning stars. Above his head, above the square sail, he saw the great swathe of the Milky Way. He stared at the stars with such intensity that tears welled up in his eyes. He shook off the tears, but then they welled up again. Let them flow. There was too much joy. There was so much joy that one had to shed a few tears.

To see the sea and the boat and the stars and to know that one would see them tomorrow, too, and the day after tomorrow and – always. To live and to be free! O, gods! How terrible it was to die when you were sixteen. And how wonderful it was to be alive when you were sixteen!

He had been born in Miletus, a large port city in faraway Ionia, which was a swathe of Greek settlement on the western shores of Asia Minor. He spent his childhood there, grew up, and studied there right up to the age of twelve. He learned various sciences: reading and writing and rhetoric – or, rather, one should say, declamation of heroic poems; and gymnastics and swimming, just like all the other Greek boys in Miletus at the time. Miletus was then the leading city among Ionian cities, and the Ionians were the leading tribe among the Greeks. Melicles's father, Lycaon the sailor – a brave sailor and a fisherman – ensured that his eldest son was as well-educated as the sons of other, wealthier citizens. At the same time, he taught his boy one more science, above and beyond those learned by all the others: he took him along on his boat, on long journeys, on fishing expeditions, and he taught him the knowledge of the sea.

This practical study was the best and quickest way to learn. By the time he turned twelve, Melicles was already a proficient sailor. He knew the habits and vagaries of the sea and could read sunrises and sunsets. He knew how to understand the shapes of clouds, the gusts and directions of winds, the sound of the waves and the swelling of tides, how to understand their language and warnings.

Then, suddenly, everything changed. When Melicles was twelve, his father died. He disappeared in a storm at sea. His ship, the pride and mainstay of his sailing life, perished with him.

Then came the difficult times: great sorrow, great poverty.

Melicles's uncle, a sailor and a merchant, took the boy with him on a journey to Greater Greece, a string of Greek settlements at the sole of the Italian boot. And then they went farther, to the recently founded settlement of Parthenope, otherwise known as Neapolis. That journey was supposed to take six months, but his new guardian,

Melicles's uncle, was lured by the good earnings in the Tyrrhenian Sea and decided to settle in the new colony.

They spent the next three years there, taking coastal trips, carrying people and goods from Neapolis to Cumae, to Messenia, to Elea or Taranto, reaching twice the shores of Gaul in adventurous expeditions far north. This was Melicles's new life and new school. He almost forgot reading and writing. But he learned his sailing like no one else his age.

He wanted to go back to his family in Miletus more than once, but his uncle, a stern and ruthless man, enjoyed the boy's free labor and did not let him go. And so, Melicles kept putting off the date of his return. And so, years passed.

On their last trip to the recently founded colony of Massalia, on the shores of Southern France, in the middle of the night, their boat was attacked by pirates. His uncle died in the ensuing battle. Melicles saw him die.

He himself fought to his last breath. He was knocked down and overpowered. He struggled to free himself, biting his attackers like a young wolf. At last, wounded, he passed out from pain and fell into enemy hands.

And then the hellish life of a slave began.

In the next few months, he was taken from one human market to another. Floggings, chains, and hunger were to teach him obedience, fear, and blind, dog-like submission to his new masters – the Phoenicians. They intended to teach him obedience, but in this, they failed. His haughty soul snarled. His pride raised its horned head after each humiliation. Instead of asking his masters for mercy, he asked Zeus for revenge. Instead of raising his hands in supplication to his masters, he clenched his fists.

He tried to escape twice. After the first time, he was beaten unconscious, and it took him a month to recover. The second time he was sentenced to death – this death from which he had now been saved in the last moment.

Such was the story of Melicles.

Sunrise found them on high seas. The sky was cloudless but dull and hazy. The wind died down; its faint gusts now barely flapped the sail, and the boat moved so slowly that Kalias began to doubt whether they could reach the shores of Sicily before nightfall. There was nothing for it, he thought, and, tired after a sleepless night, he woke Melicles, then cursed the steersman roundly for dozing at the helm and, making himself a bed among the sacks of cargo, went to sleep.

The boat plowed on along. It was a typical Greek sailboat of those days: its prow was slightly raised, its stern was wide, and it had one mast. A broad, square sail hung from its horizontal beam, tied at the bottom corners with straps of coconut fiber to the sides of the boat. The steersman's broad rudder was at the stern, at least three times as wide as a normal oar. A pair of oars were strapped to the sides – those were used only to maneuver the boat once in a harbor.

Little boats like this were used for fishing or coastal navigation, rarely for longer expeditions. But Kalias was a bold sailor and an enterprising trader. He had hoped to earn well by trading in Carthage – and he did. And then he picked up a paying passenger into the bargain. It was shaping up to be a great trip for him.

Gradually, the sun rose higher. The sea rocked them gently, lapping their sides with lazy clapping. The helmsman looked at the sleepy sea and sky and decided that this apparent peace did not bode well. A change was certain, and within the day, and in any event, before they reached Syracuse.

Melicles was not frightened by the helmsman's predictions. He had become familiar with the sea like few others. During his short life, he had experienced many storms at sea, and he knew that for a good sailor in a strong boat, the high seas, far from treacherous reefs and shallows, were perhaps safer than land. With the sure eyesight of the child of the sea, he had already judged the boat and its master, and he knew the boat should bear the heaviest blows of weather, and the pilot would serve it well.

Besides, how could he be afraid of a mere storm – he, who had been beaten for a year, who had prayed for death and looked for it in hopeless attempts to escape? Why, he would have found his death yesterday had it not been for his unexpected deliverance. And now he was not only saved, but he was free; he was getting closer with every passing hour to the land of the Greeks, and with it to his homeland and his mother. The prospect of having to face a storm at sea did not frighten him.

Yesterday, he had been surrounded by slaves and beastly slave drivers – a fate a hundred times worse than any storm – and today, his saviors were with him. Their kindness overwhelmed him with reverence and admiration: he was deeply moved, and gratitude brought tears to his eyes. He recognized Kalias: the man reminded him of his own father, who had also concealed a noble and devoted heart under a quarrelsome mask. As for the other – the distinguished old man, silent as a statue – his figure filled the boy with reverence and dread.

"He's some great dignitary or sage," he whispered to the helmsman.

"Or a priest," said the other.

A couple of hours passed without any incidents. The wind was lazy, soft, intermittent, as if it, too, fainted in the day's rising heat.

About the second hour of the day (that is, two hours after sunrise), they woke Kalias – they noticed the outlines of some land on the far-right horizon. A strip of sandy hills just barely visible from the boat shone like a golden thread between the blue of the sky and the blue of the sea. Upon seeing it, Kalias turned the boat northeast, and the land vanished from sight.

"What was that land?" Melicles asked.

"Carthage."

"Carthage, still?"

"Yes, boy. Why, does your back smart at the mention of the name?"

Then, lifting his finger upward, he said gravely:

"Carthage, you see, sits deep in its bay like a dragon in his lair. Or better yet, like the hungry throat of a viper in its wide-opened jaws. The jaws are wide open because, you know, the throat is always hungry. What we saw was one of its jaws, the eastern arm of the bay, jutting far out to sea.

"And that arm belongs to Carthage too?"

"Who knows exactly to whom it belongs? The land is empty. It's just so much sand. But the Phoenicians have built trading posts and watchtowers all along this shore. There are pirates here, too, because they come to do business with Carthage. This is not a good place."

"Aren't they afraid of the guards?"

"Who? The pirates? Why! They and the Carthaginians work together like brothers! You should have learned it on your own hide, no? The pirates sold you to the Phoenicians, yes? Well, they prefer not to go to Carthage openly, although it does sometimes happen, too, but here on these empty, sandy banks, they can do their dark business with Carthaginians. Ho, ho! This is not a good place."

This was true. Pirates, whose nests were scattered all over the Mediterranean Sea, often came to Carthage to sell their captives and resupply their ships. Hated by sailors, these men were terrors – not only for travelers but also for smaller coastal towns. Yet, they never seemed to pick a fight with Carthage. What's more, by some strange coincidence, their attacks and robberies tended to focus on those who had displeased the great city. Especially the Greeks, whose dash, energy, and enterprise often hurt Phoenician trading profits. The Greeks suffered the most as a result of these attacks, and many thought this happened with the tacit understanding of Carthage and of the Great Phoenician Council.

Carthaginians were alarmed by the rapid development of Greek colonies in the West. Fearing an open war with them, having neither a martial population like the Greeks nor a large army, they supported pirate gangs by giving them weapons and money to fight the hated Greeks. And thus, at a stroke, they achieved two benefits: they undercut Greek trade, and, at the same time, they acquired new slaves.

The trade in slaves was one of the main sources of wealth for the Phoenicians. Their leading cities – Carthage in Africa and Tyre in the Levant – were, at the time, the largest human markets in the known world. Desperate Greeks defended themselves from pirates as well as they could. Battles raged on land and sea. And so it had been for many years throughout the western part of the Mediterranean. No sailor could sail without a shudder by places frequented by pirates.

Therefore, it was not surprising that Kalias so hastily steered clear of this "bad place."

And it was not surprising that he became alarmed when he spotted two large ships sailing in front of them. But these sailing ships came from the north, from the side of Sicily, stayed far away, and disappeared quickly over the horizon.

Seeing them, Kalias nodded his head appreciatively.

"Ordinary merchant boats. Wise, understanding sailors. Check out these tricksters, two boats going together. Together for safety – and rightly so. Heh! With even one of those ships, the pirates would have had their hands full! But with two... That's smart. I like it."

Then, pointing to his own boat, he added:

"The worst thing is this kind of a barrel. Just big enough to hold trading goods but too small to fight."

Melicles shook his head.

"It's a nice boat, lord. My father had a similar boat."

Kalias looked at him curiously.

"Your father had a boat? Was he a merchant?"

"No. He was a fisherman, but he had a boat."

"He had his own boat?" Kalias looked at the boy with a lot more respect now. "And what happened to him?"

"He died in a storm. I was twelve at the time."

Kalias nodded.

"Ordinary thing with a sailor," he muttered.

Then they started talking about different kinds of boats, barges, and galleys, about the difference in shipbuilding here and in distant Miletus. They distinguished between deep sailing ships adapted for grain transport from the shallower but rounder-bellied barges intended mainly for the transport of horses and cattle. Some of these ships, in addition to the one great mast with a huge square sail, also had a second mast, slightly tilted forward, with a more triangular sail. This was the new Phoenician invention.

Most of these big cargo ships, in addition to the sail, also had twenty to forty rowers below deck – so that their locomotion did not depend entirely on the whim of the wind. Kalias talked about the great warships with high sides, sometimes with two or even three decks, and perhaps sixty rowers per side, in two and sometimes three rows, one above the other. He had seen such ships in Athens, Syracuse, and in hated Carthage.

Melicles had never seen such ships up close, but he described the pirate vessel which had captured him, which was like a hybrid of a trading ship and a warship. It was wider, with only one row of rowers, but the prow had an underwater spur, a kind of ram with which to break other boats, and a tall, overhead platform from which soldiers could jump down on their prey. Kalias was surprised that, despite his young age, the boy knew so much of the sea and could talk about it confidently like an old sailor.

"He's one smart barley cake," he said to himself appreciatively.

Hours passed in silence.

The heat continued to rise.

Towards noon, they spotted two sails on the horizon. This time, however, it was one ship, and it came from the south, from the bad side. And it caught up with them very slowly but steadily. There was some commotion on the boat.

"That's the bad side," whispered Kalias, staring at the faint silhouette of the ship.

"Phoenicians?"

"Hades[14] knows! Could be Carthaginians. Or could be pirates. I told you, here, one meets both."

"Or maybe they are ordinary merchants?"

"Maybe. Many merchant boats run through here, many sailors."

---

[14] *Hades*: Greek god of the underground and the dead

This consoled them somewhat. But the strange ship never strayed out of sight of their boat.

An hour later, as the strange ship drew even closer, Kalias said with some anxiety in his voice:

"I don't like this. She's coming too fast. We ride on the wind alone, but they also row. Why are they in such a hurry? Who rows with wind in the back?

"A narrow, large galley with sails, just like they build them now in Cyprus and Sidon. An expensive ship. An ordinary sailing ship would not be flying so fast in this ridiculous wind. This is a government ship. A military ship. No merchant would spend that kind of money just to add a little speed to his goods. Look, in this dead wind, we can barely drag ourselves for pity's sake. And they..."

Here, he fell silent, shaded his eyes with his hand from the glare of the sun, and stared towards the approaching sails. The helmsman stood by his side. They gazed together, silent, for a long time.

"By Hades and the Erinyes[15]!" he cursed again. "Rip out my guts and eat them raw if I ever set out for another trip on this gods-blasted nutshell. Righteous Zeus! In two hours, they will be upon us."

"Or earlier."

"If the wind doesn't change."

"Or if they are chasing us at all."

"Make a sharp turn and let us see if they follow us."

Kalias shook his head.

"No. I don't want to lose the rest of our speed; we're going too slowly as it is. If they are chasing us, we will soon find out."

Nehurabhed interjected:

"Are they Phoenicians?"

"Yes."

"Ordinary merchants for sure."

Kalias shrugged.

"Not going on sail and oar like this."

---

[15] *Erinyes*: spirits sent by gods to punish great sins

As he said this, he looked sharply in the face of Nehurabhed, but the old man did not flinch. He asked:

"Where do the Carthaginian coastguard boats come from?"

"They keep boats at both ends of the bay. If they see something suspicious, or if they want to pursue, they can send those boats."

"But they couldn't have seen us."

"We saw the land, yes? So, they could have seen us too."

"So? Do they send a ship after every boat?"

"No, but if they saw us in the early morning, it would have meant that we left Carthage at night, and that is suspicious."

"All right. But it's still too little of a reason to send a large ship like this out of curiosity."

"What if they received an order from Carthage to be on their guard?"

Kalias looked intently at Nehurabhed but was disappointed again. The old man's wrinkles remained perfectly still. Nehurabhed smiled slightly.

"So, Greek, do you think this is a pursuit sent after me?"

"I don't think anything, my lord, but you would know better."

Kalias observed his passenger closely.

Nehurabhed shook his head.

"It can't be," he said. "How could the city of Carthage have notified the guards at the cape so quickly?"

"Well... horsemen can travel from the city to the trading post in a few hours."

"Then the pursuit would have begun only now."

"They go fast, those fellows on the boat."

"Yes, but to be here now, they would have had to leave port at least five hours ago."

"Well, yes. I don't know exactly how long it takes for a horse to travel from the city to the end of the bay. But people also say that the Phoenicians can send messages to each other remotely."

Nehurabhed looked up at him sharply, a little curious this time.

"Yes, my lord. People say they can signal with lights. They can send a message from one post to another as needed."

"I saw fires at night. Far behind us. To the south."

"Why didn't you tell me?"

"The light was very distant, and the day was already breaking. And I didn't think it was important."

They fell silent.

Kalias shifted uneasily. Nehurabhed walked away, sat still, his eyes narrowed into slits.

And everything was as before. The boat plowed on lazily, barely swaying on the serene waves. The water splashed and gurgled against their sides. The sail flapped lightly, then hung down impotent, then flapped a little again. The heat continued to rise. The sun had passed the zenith and was starting to lean towards the west. The strange boat was getting closer and closer.

"They'll be upon us in an hour," the helmsman said softly.

"They will catch up with us before nighttime, gods!"

Kalias paled a little and began to wring his hands.

"Maybe they are ordinary merchants, maybe they are ordinary merchants," he repeated, biting his lips.

Melicles walked over to him. He was pale. His eyelids trembled for a moment, and he seemed about to break out in tears like a child, but he controlled himself. Then his face became hard, calm.

"Do you have a sword?" he asked.

Kalias looked at him in surprise.

"Weapons are useless here," he replied slowly. "That boat has twenty maybe thirty rowers. Maybe ten crew. There are five of us."

Melicles frowned and lowered his head. His eyes darkened in anger.

"I have sworn to almighty gods," he said in a muffled voice, "that I would not allow myself to be taken again. Never again. I want to die with a sword in my hand. I prayed to all gods there, in Carthage. All gods. Gods listened to me. Give me a sword, good sir."

There was a moment of silence. Kalias examined the boy carefully. He shook his head.

*It's good that I didn't leave him there to die,* he thought, but he didn't answer right away. In truth, he wasn't even sure if these people were Carthaginians or pirates. That they were going in the same direction – well, that obviously didn't mean a thing. He recalled many such events from his own past, and, until now, all those worries had turned out to have been unnecessary.

"They might be some peaceful sailors," he said.

"What if they are not?"

"Then we think what to do. By all gods, no one ever accused Kalias of cowardice. But you can only fight when you can win. Or at least save your skin."

"I will not be taken alive again. I'd rather die."

"Don't be too hasty. We still have time. And if push comes to shove – well, the wise god Hermes created money so that we can redeem ourselves, just in case. I didn't regret drachmas for you once, yes? You think I'll try to save money this time?"

The boy fell silent and only scowled at Kalias, but it was easy to tell that he had not changed his mind.

The older Greek stared at the strange ship, still distant but growing in his eyes. It was long like a viper, low and narrow. It had two low masts with wide squares of sails. The boat was going mainly by the strength of the rowers – there were at least twenty of them.

"You can already see their oars!" Kalias shouted, stamping his foot and flushing with anger.

"A curse on this wretched boat of mine and on this filthy weather and on all of this. Curse this trip! O, gods! Look!"

The wind came to a complete stop. Their sail sagged like an empty sack.

"For Hermes! They are already upon us! If only we had a little wind! Then we could wait for the night and slip away in the dark. If only we had a little wind! Blow, you stupid thing! Blow!"

Indeed, the sea had clearly darkened. The night was still many hours away, but the sun had gone behind a wall of yellow-gray haze that had risen over the western horizon. The light of day shone through this smoke, a dirty yellowish glow, strange and mysterious.

"A storm is upon us, too," said the helmsman.

"Let it come quickly!" Melicles almost shouted.

"It's coming," Kalias repeated. "But will it come in time?"

He glanced again at the strange boat and at the overcast horizon. The sky grew rapidly darker. A sudden wind rose, giving their boat speed.

"O, Poseidon!" Kalias cried, raising his hands towards heaven. "O, thou all-powerful lord of the seas! O, brother of the highest, save us, your children! Is it possible that you would allow us to be taken back to Carthage, to be despoiled by the hideous Phoenicians who mock you? Have they ever offered you a single heifer? Not one, I am sure! O, Poseidon, consider this!"

A distant thunder answered him. This made a suitable impression, but the thunder was very far away. Kalias shook his head.

"It's all for nothing," he said. "The storm will be here in an hour, and they'll be here in half an hour. Or sooner."

Indeed, the strange ship was now close enough for them to make out individual faces of armed men on its deck. Her sails hung helplessly, but the evil tentacles of her oars moved rhythmically, driving her on. She looked like an evil beetle rushing towards them on the water.

"Rogues! Robbers! Bandits!" Kalias shouted. "Look how they rush!"

He began to tear at his beard again. Then he knelt down and pulled two old, rusty swords from the bottom of the boat. Their pursuers were now no farther than a few thousand steps.

"We are done for," he moaned. "We are lost, o, Zeus!"

"No. We are saved," answered the helmsman suddenly, leaning into the rudder.

Everyone looked at him in amazement. The boat turned around and came to a full stop.

"What are you doing, fool?!" Kalias roared.

The helmsman did not answer, only pointed to the north and then began to untie hurriedly the straps of the sail.

The sea to the north of them, still calm and smooth, suddenly became covered with a multitude of small, white wrinkles approaching them quickly. One minute more and a great gust of wind blasted the sail, the mast creaked with a violent heave, and the boat, like a horse smacked by a whip, jumped forward. But the strange ship, not prepared for the unexpected gust of wind, suddenly tilted to one side and swung around, coming to a full stop. Screams and shouts from the ship came to the ears of the Greeks through the roar of the gathering wind. But only for a moment because another powerful gust of wind suddenly put a lot of sea between them.

And now, all pursuit would be futile. The wind increased again. The sky turned even darker. Rain broke. A veil of downpour covered the horizon. Gray, dirty clouds rushed forward in front of a navy-blue curtain of the storm. Waves rose suddenly, became huge mountains, and began to toss the little boat. Everything – the whole world – suddenly started into a mad, unstoppable dash. The mast creaked under the pressure of the wind. The prow began to hammer the waves, and the waves began to break over the sides.

Kalias and Melicles dropped the sail halfway and loosened its ropes; their boat ran forward like a racing hound. Then a torrential downpour hit them, and the whole world disappeared behind the wall of rain. Now, they could only see the waves running right in front of them, blown by the wind, roaring, heaving, splashing, foaming, crashing. Suddenly, it was totally dark, and a flash of lightning tore the sky. One, two, three thunderbolts. A terrible northwestern storm was upon them.

The rain and the wind turned icy cold, and the sailors' hands holding onto the boat became numb. The helmsman leaned into the rudder with all his strength, Melicles and the third member of the crew – a Libyan boy – furiously bailed water, now ankle-deep and splashing again and again over the sides as the boat rocked and pitched. They clung to the boards and ropes in the dark to not fall overboard. To fall overboard now into the black boiling, raging sea would have meant certain death.

But Melicles knew this storm, the crazy dance of the deck. He gritted his teeth, fell, scrambled up, fell again, was up again, and again, and again, but did not stop bailing. *Whoosh*, a new wave washed overboard, *whoosh*, the boat was full again; they bailed and bailed – the water would not stop coming, but they would not stop bailing.

There was a wild exhilaration in the struggle with the terrible element. O, sea! O, wind! We will not give up!

The old man tried to help but stumbled almost immediately, fell, and nearly tumbled overboard into the darkness. Melicles gave him a rope to tie himself to the bench at the bow of the ship, and the old man gave up on further attempts to cooperate.

Hours passed. The storm kept on raging. Kalias took over the rudder from the exhausted helmsman and handed the care of the sail to Melicles. At first, he watched anxiously to see if the boy could handle it, but after a while, he relaxed. Despite his young age, Melicles was an experienced sailor. His hand was sure, his arm strong, his eye watchful.

My son will grow up like this, thought Kalias.

Around midnight, the storm stopped at last and the wind eased. Kalias corrected their course for Sicily and watched Melicles reset the sail.

"Definitely worth the sixty drachmas," he muttered to himself.

The danger was over.

When the day broke, there was no trace of the strange ship, no sailing ship of any kind anywhere in sight. Nothing around but the sea, still restless, heaving, here and there scarred by a foaming crest, but no longer dangerous, and gradually growing calmer. A strong, even westerly wind now carried them straight to their destination, north, towards the shores of Sicily.

"The first thing we do when we arrive in Syracuse will be to offer a white heifer to Poseidon. He saved us today," said Kalias. "He answered my prayer. He sent the storm to save us from pirates."

He fell silent and thought for a moment. After which, because he regretted the cost of the heifer, he turned to the old man:

"You, too, sir, should contribute to the purchase of this heifer. You, too, were saved by the mighty brother of Zeus."

But Nehurabhed shook his head.

"I am a worshiper of only one god, great and good," he replied slowly, "who defends the noble and the brave and who abhors sacrifices."

"What is this god called, my lord?" Melicles asked.

"Men call him Ahura-Mazda. It means The Just One," replied the old man.

Chapter Three
# My Special Friend

On the same day, at the same hour, in the guardian's palace in the city of Carthage, a council was held. In attendance were Asarhan, the high priest of the temple of Moloch; Hiram, member of the Great Phoenician Council and head of the city guard; and Barcas, one of the richest merchants of the city. They sat in silence. Finally, Hiram shifted impatiently.

"Where's this dog?" he asked Barcas.

"He'll be here soon."

"Is he Greek?"

"Greek."

"And you trust him?"

"We pay him well, and he is smart enough to know on which side his barley cake is oiled."

Hiram nodded.

"Better make this worth his while."

The old merchant's face lengthened.

"And what is all this for, Asarhan? You had him in your hand, that Persian."

"He isn't Persian; he's a Mede."

"Same difference! The plague on all Medes and all Persians. It will now cost us a fortune to recapture him. And you had him in your hand."

"So I did! But the council said not to hold him by force!"

"But they did tell you to be careful, yes?"

"My guards had orders not to let him out of the gate."

Barcas shrugged.

"So, he jumped over the wall. How hard was that to foresee? What? Old age, Asarhan, old age. It does not sharpen the acuity of the mind, does it?"

Agitated, Asarhan rose sharply.

"Hiram, do not allow Phoenician dignitaries to be offended in your house."

"And what if this dignitary acted like a baby?"

"Barcas!" Asarhan slammed the table with his palm. "Hiram, I'm saying this to you because this dog, although my relative, is not worth human speech. I was told to treat this Mede like an honored guest and not hurt him. What was I supposed to do? And now, everyone is after me for letting him get away – both the prince and the highest council. Everyone on poor little me. But they made him an honored guest, yes?"

"They said that because he is an envoy and a priest."

"High priest, actually, but not an envoy."

"Well, if he isn't an envoy, then why take so much trouble with him? If he had fallen somewhere – down some convenient stairs – and hurt his neck, who would have complained?"

"Hiram, now you speak like a child. If anything happened to him here, would you then go to Media?"

"Why would I go there? I have no business there."

"You don't, but our brothers, the Phoenicians of Tyre, Cyprus, and Sidon, do."

"Well, if he had just... disappeared... who would have known why?"

"And if our men then started disappearing in Media, no one would know why either, yes?"

"All right. But we could have detained him by force."

"Yes, by Moloch, and we should have done just that. But the supreme council did not order him imprisoned, and there is little point arguing about it now."

"But why imprison him?"

"Because he knows too much. He's been everywhere, sniffing."

"Why was he here, this Persian?"

"Not a Persian. A Mede."

"Whatever. That priest."

"Not a priest. A high priest."

"Same thing!" said Barcas with exasperation.

"It is not the same thing at all." Asarhan was offended. "There is actually a big difference between a priest and a high priest. You have never heard of high priests, Barcas? As in: 'Chaldean[16] high priests'?"

"Oh, yeah. Clever fellows, they say."

"Clever? Too clever for you. And have you heard about Median Mages?"

"Say what?"

"O, gods! He has not heard of the Mages! Do you know? They are even smarter than the Chaldeans! They know more than the sages of Egypt! They know such arts that the head swells to hear about them. It's scary just to think about these guys. Okay, Barcas?"

"All right, all right. I did not know that in other countries, er, high priests were so wise."

"Barcas!"

Hiram broke into the conversation quickly:

"You have not yet told me why this Persian was hanging around here."

"This Mede?"

---

[16] *Chaldean*: an old name for the people of ancient Babylon

"Yes, this Mede."

"Hiram, no one should know that."

"Okay. But I'm not no one, and if you know, I'll know."

"What I say must fall as a rock falls into the deep sea, Hiram."

"Fine."

"So, he, that Mede, came here to make peace between Phoenicians and Greeks in Egypt."

"Huh? What does he care?"

"He wants Egypt to be strong."

"I don't get why this matters to us. But what's that to him? Is he an Egyptian?"

"No, but Egypt is an ally of Media. This is – how should I put it? – level-five power politics. Okay?"

"No, I don't get it. Those are very distant countries. What do we care if he wants to make peace in Egypt?"

Asarhan and Barcas looked at each other with exasperation.

"What do you mean, what do we care? Don't you understand this, Hiram? Don't you understand that the Greeks must be done away with, once and for all? It's either them or us!

"By Moloch, by the terrible Astarte, either them or us. Who's taking all trade from us? Greeks. Who establishes colonies, trading posts, settlements everywhere right under our noses? Greeks. Who turns up now in places where we have been left alone to do our business for centuries? Who breeds like rabbits? Who builds more ships than we do? Who takes away our cargoes and our earnings?"

"Carthage is rich."

"Yes! And how much richer she would be if not for these ~~damned~~ Greeks! They were already all over the north fifty years ago, but, thankfully, they left us alone here in Africa at least. And now? Ask Barcas how much he loses every year since that lousy Greek settlement in Cyrene went up. A pox upon Cyrene! Half the ships from the east no longer come straight to us but transship in Cyrene. Or in Barca – that's another poxy Greek town in Africa, if you must know. And ask our partners in Egypt how they are faring. Same story! Who formerly ruled in Egypt?"

"Egyptians?"

"Gods! You are a child, Hiram! Egyptians, indeed! Maybe in the past, a thousand years ago. But now it's our bankers, our treasurers, our advisers to his holiness, the pharaoh. Bankers and consultants, you know. Even when Assyrians ruled there for a while, Egypt wasn't a bad place for us.

"And now? Yikes! There are already more Greeks there than Phoenicians, and they keep pushing in from all sides. And most of all, into the army. Into the army. So, who gets all the new offices, palaces, and honors? ██████ Greeks is who: for their officers, for their chiefs, for their mangy dogs, everything for the Greeks. Asarhan is right – we can't wait any longer. The longer we wait, the harder the future fight will be. So, let's do it now. It's either them or us, and now, we have a good chance."

Hiram shuddered.

"War," he whispered.

"Yes. We have to end with them once and for all, in Egypt and Cyrene and all over Africa."

Hiram groaned.

"War is a terrible thing."

"Hiram, you are the commander of the guard, and you fear war?"

"And who is to be afraid of war if not me? You? You will stay at home, with your musicians and your slave girls. And so will Asarhan. It's me who will have to go out and get killed, yes?"

"Oh, don't be so scared, Hiram. Nobody's pushing you to attack the Greeks. We aren't here to fight – we'll let others do it."

"Who?"

"Egypt."

Hiram nodded. His face lit up.

"Ah, well, that's different. That's Phoenician. That is prudent and rational. Etruscans fight for us in the north, the pirates prey on the Greeks at sea, and now let's have Egyptians fight for us in Libya. I like that. But what does this have to do with this Persian?"

"This Mede?"

"This Mede."

"I've already told you, Hiram – he wants to make peace between us and the Greeks in Egypt! And we want war because now is the best time for it. If this Mede goes to Egypt, he'll break everything we have fixed and fix everything we have broken. He knows the pharaoh, the nomarchs[17]. He knows a lot. Too much. He is completely unnecessary there. And now, thanks to the supreme vigilance of our city guard, he is free to go there."

"That's bad."

"Very bad."

"So... you shouldn't have let him go. It would have been better to kill him."

"But why? We only had to hold him here long enough for the ball to start rolling in Egypt. Then let him go wherever. It's never a good idea to kill a priest."

"A high priest."

"Right. A high priest. Big whoop," said Barcas.

"Barcas, you are stupider than a young dog. You don't know what these high priests can do. Have you heard what happened to one of our princes in Cyprus? He received such a wise man as a guest. For an extended visit. A Chaldean. You know, one of those Babylonian fellows. And he wanted to get rid of him. So, he gave him a roast of fattened dog for dinner every day."

"So what? Dog is very good meat."

"Yeah, but Chaldeans don't eat it! Maybe they can't. Maybe they don't like it – I don't know. Maybe their god says no dog and no hanky-panky."

"I get it. Go on."

"Well, so this priest would not eat it. Anyway, he was polite and said nothing on the first day. Nothing on the second day, either. But on the fifth day, he had had enough and left. Only on departure, he said to this prince: 'I see, worthy prince, that you like dog meat very much. From now on, everything you eat will remind you of this

---

[17] *Nomarch*: a governor of an Egyptian province

37

delicacy.' And he left. And you know what, Barcas? Many years have passed since then, and he, this prince, every time he eats something, it all tastes like dog fat. At first, he kept changing cooks. Now, he gave up. The poor man lost weight. He's ruined. I saw him. He said that even when he eats grapes, they reek of dog fat."

Barcas shook his head.

"That's a swinish revenge," he said. "I didn't know they could do stuff like this."

"Well, never mind that. Now, let's talk about this Mede. How do we stop him? He isn't here anymore."

"No, he's not, indeed," Asarhan confirmed, "because your guards keep real good watch over the port."

"Asarhan," said Hiram sadly, "you got your tongue lashing from the Supreme Council. So did I. And what have I done? Yesterday, before daybreak, I sent a signal to our post on the eastern cape. They saw a boat and sent the fastest galley in pursuit, but the storm got in the way. Too late to do anything about that now. Better we ask Barcas what to do now. Okay?"

"And that is?"

"Ha!" said Barcas. "This is where my special friend comes in. My Greek friend. He'll fix all of this. Never worry – he's going to set out today. He will take with him your servant, the one who knows this Mede and can identify him. They will go by fast ship straight to Syracuse."

"Why there?"

"The Supreme Council thinks the Mede must have gone there."

"Okay. Then what?"

"Well! In Syracuse, your man will recognize this Mede and point him out to my man."

"And then?"

"And then my man will take care of business."

"What do you mean, take care of business?"

"I mean, he will do something to prevent this dog from reaching Egypt."

"Pray, not kill him?"

"No, no. Better not. The high council said better not to do this, maybe as a last resort."

"So, how is he going to stop him?"

"That's his business. He says it can be done. He is cunning and has his own friends in various Greek ports."

"Greek friends?"

"Greek friends. But you know how the Greeks are: they don't stick together worth squat. In fact, when we're not around, they're at each other's throats like mad dogs. Every little town does what it wants."

At that moment, Hiram's servant entered the chamber.

"My lord," he said, "a Greek man has come to see you and is waiting in the vestibule."

"All right, let him in."

Asarhan rose from his seat.

"I'm going out," he said. "It is not fitting for my dignified office to come in contact with impure animals. You two already know everything there is to know. I'll send my servant here immediately – that fellow who saw the Mede and who will go to Syracuse to identify him."

"Fine. Just tell me one thing, Asarhan: what is this Persian's name?"

"This Mede's?"

"This Mede's."

"His name is... well, it doesn't matter because he can change names like sandals. But his mother called him Nehurabhed."

Chapter Four
# If I Say So Myself

In those days, the city of Syracuse consisted of two parts. One, located on the small island of Ortygia, was the original old town and had by then already existed for several hundred years, remembering perhaps the days of Odysseus[18]. A narrow channel cut off this island from a much larger peninsula, where the newer and more modern part of the city lay.

Old Ortygia was crowded, with two- and three-story houses piled one on top of the other and narrow, winding passages between them. There were few places in these streets where two carts could pass each other, and most were only accessible by foot. There were no gardens or greenery, and the traditional, open-air courtyards of Greek homes were tiny here. Most of the residents were working poor and slaves. Even the square in front of the old town hall, the Bouleuterion,

---

[18] *Odysseus*: king of Ithaca, hero of Homer's *Odyssey*

was extremely small, not at all corresponding in size to the importance of this great city.

Everything here was subordinated to one goal: to fit as many houses and people into the tiny space of the island as possible. Only one patch of land near the spring of Arethusa[19] was surrounded by a small wreath of greenery: palms, rhododendrons, and quince trees.

People crowded here because the island's position offered protection: Ortygia could be attacked only from the sea. This position determined the development of the city. From its very beginnings and for centuries, Syracuse had striven to become and remain above all a sea power. Centuries of investment paid off: Syracuse was by now one of the three largest commercial and naval ports in the entire Mediterranean, and she commanded the third largest naval fleet in the world.

Twice in her history was she to cross swords with the greatest maritime powers of her time: once with Carthage, several decades after the events described here, and the second time with Athens, several dozen years after that. Both wars were to end in the defeat of her enemies, and the dates of those victories were to become the major turning points in the history of the entire Greek world.

As the city grew, tiny Ortygia could no longer accommodate all of its inhabitants, and therefore, the second part of the city was established on the mainland. This new part extended more widely and more freely and soon exceeded the home island in size and splendor. The houses there were more spacious and richer. Behind their white walls, single-story villas stood in delightful gardens, and clumps of palm trees, fig trees, and olive trees swayed overhead in gentle sea breezes. Massive defensive fortifications protected the new city. A large sea wall was also built to protect the entrance to the Ortygia channel between the island and the peninsula. South of this dam, between the shores of two cities, was the port, full of countless boats, ships, barges, and great war galleys.

---

[19] *Arethusa*: a nymph turned by Demeter into a spring

And into this port, on the third day, came the little boat of the runaways from Carthage.

Kalias's house was in the newer, western part of Syracuse, near the sea and the great defensive walls enclosing the city from the land side. But it was not possible to moor the boat here because the shore was a steep cliff, and the sea was full of treacherous rocks. And so, they left the boat at a considerable distance from the house, where the shore descended gently towards the sea, allowing it to be hauled out on dry land.

They arrived at dawn and almost immediately went to Kalias's house for a well-deserved rest. Everyone slept the whole day through. But in the evening, as was customary, all the neighbors and friends of Kalias, and friends of these friends, and all his relatives and relatives of these relatives gathered in a great throng to listen to the stories of the returning traveler.

There came so many of them that the house and its courtyard could not accommodate them all, so they sat down on the waterfront in front of the house. They brought wine, wheat and barley cakes, olives, and cheese and began to feast and make merry, laughing and joking, surrounded by a crowd of playing children.

Kalias, the most important person of the moment, sat down in the middle of the crowd on a large boulder and talked long and colorfully about all his recent adventures, embroidering richly. Greeks loved such stories, enjoyed them like children, not really caring whether everything in them was entirely true. Only one thing was shameful in a storyteller, and that was when he was boring, unable to frighten or delight his audience.

Of this, however, there was no fear. Even when nothing remarkable happened to him, Kalias could talk about it in fascinating and entertaining ways, even more so now, when he really did have something to tell.

The word of their adventure had spread somehow even as the runaways were sleeping, so the crowd turned up in large numbers, expecting a good tale. They plied Kalias copiously with wine, clapped hands, cheered, asked questions. And Kalias, excited by the party, warmed by wine, looking at the enraptured faces of the listeners, talked, added, twisted, and told it all: what had been and what could have been and what had not been at all.

And thus, according to him, as they were leaving Carthage, several guard galleys had spotted them at the entrance to the port and chased them for several hours, and only thanks to Kalias's agility and to the darkness of the night had they managed to get away safely. He described the details of the chase so poignantly – about how they had heard the voices and saw the lights of the galleys surrounding them – that not only all the Syracusans but even Melicles himself trembled with excitement and suspense.

Kalias then went on to relate their encounter with the pirate boat.

"The robbers," he said, "were so close now that they began pelting us with arrows. We, of course, were not idle, and I myself (you know how good I am with the bow and arrows) am pleased to tell you that I shot one of these scoundrels right in the face. He got it so good that he didn't even manage a yelp – he just keeled over the side and – *whoop!* – plunged into the sea. That served him right! By Hermes, I tell you, it was a ▮▮▮▮ good shot, comrades!"

The horror of the story and the audience's excitement came to a crescendo when Kalias showed his *khiton*[20] pierced through by an arrow. (In fact, it was torn already in Syracuse as they pulled the boat ashore). Everyone was moved. Nehurabhed, who appeared at the door of the house and listened to the story, only shook his head in admiration.

Kalias spoke primarily of himself, of course, but he did not spare words of praise for the others: for the helmsman who had seen the

---

[20] *Khiton*: traditional man's outfit, consisting of two pieces of cloth held together by pins at the shoulders

coming of the wind just in time and who, by turning the boat around, probably saved them from sinking; and for Melicles, who had grabbed a sword, ready to defend himself and later helped pilot the boat in the storm, and for the foreigner who had stood ready to fight hand to hand alongside them, despite his – er – advanced decrepitude.

When Kalias finished, there was shouting and applause. Everyone took him in their arms and hugged him, inquiring about the minutest details.

"We have not heard such a good story in a long time," they all said unanimously.

Then Melicles, in turn, had to tell his own story: how pirates had attacked his uncle's boat between Massilia and Parthenope. How he fought; how he was wounded; how he worked and suffered in his inhuman captivity; how he tried to escape, was recaptured and condemned to a cruel death; and how, at the last minute, Kalias and the mysterious foreigner turned up to rescue him. He didn't speak, it must be understood, as well as Kalias, but truth shone in his story, and the audience did not spare him words of sympathy and appreciation.

Then the conversation turned to other topics.

Some old Greek described a recent battle against the Etruscans, whom he had been obliged to fight when a storm forced him on the Etruscan shore during a journey from Massalia to Cumae. Someone else described how, in a similar battle against the Etruscans two years ago, he had been captured and then escaped to take refuge among the Ramans. He spoke of the great city of these Ramans called Rama, or Roma[21], and which was almost as beautiful as Syracuse, except it lay inland, far away from the shore.

Most of the listeners already knew these stories but listened to them willingly again because nothing could be more pleasing to a Greek than to experience travel in this way, learning about foreign peoples, countries, cities, their mysteries, monsters, and dangers. Night fell, the moon rose over the bay, distant hills disappeared in the black night, and they still chatted, remembering old times, mocking a little

---

[21] *Roma*: Rome

and making fun of each other and themselves. Only the chill of midnight – as it was already late autumn – drove them home at last.

Then, busy days began for Melicles – busy but calm and measured, full of steady work on the boat, replacing worn-out planks, sewing a new sail, repairing damaged nets, twisting and coiling ropes, hewing new oars – these activities filled his whole day. There was a lot of work, and Kalias was both demanding and quick-tempered, but Melicles felt joyful and happy. He knew this work well. The son of a sailor and a fisherman, the nephew of a ship's carpenter, familiar from childhood with such life, he performed well, and Kalias found him useful.

This did not save him from the Syracusan's anger on several occasions because Kalias could not live without such outbursts, but they were never too dangerous. Whenever the boy took these displays of displeasure too much to heart, Kalias became a little abashed, smiled kindly, joked and, patting him on the shoulder, repeated:

"Come on, boy. When you stay longer with me, with Kalias, you will learn it all perfectly."

But he treated the boy better every day.

"Indeed, it is a good thing that we saved this kid," nearly escaped his lips one evening as he spoke to Nehurabhed.

The mysterious stranger remained a guest in Kalias's house throughout his stay in Syracuse. The Greek was clearly pleased with this – first because the hospitality was not free, but also and above all because the man's presence added weight and splendor to his house. He told everyone about Nehurabhed, explained that he must be a very important person, probably an ambassador, maybe even a prince or great priest or fortune teller, and most likely all of the above. He treated Nehurabhed with great deference, especially in the presence of others, so that everyone might see what kind of an exalted guest he, Kalias, had in his house.

As always, Nehurabhed took it silently and indifferently, which only increased the mystery. The Greek did not know much more about him now than he had known before, but he soon learned that the old man had been to the town hall and the council's palace, and to Praxilaos himself, the deputy of the absent tyrant[22] of Syracuse.

Nehurabhed was an important person, it seemed, whoever he was.

Melicles rarely saw Nehurabhed now since he spent whole days working on the boat and even slept by it every other night, unrolling his mat on the wide bench at the stern. However, whenever they met, the distinguished guest always asked him in detail how his work went, how he liked it, and how long he had committed to working as a laborer for Kalias. The boy looked at him with the same respect and awe as before, but these feelings were now connected in a strange way with a growing, blind, almost childish trust. He also sincerely regretted that the old man was leaving Syracuse in a few days on his way to Greece or Egypt, and he thought with sadness about the upcoming goodbye.

And then, an accident happened, which again turned his life upside down.

---

[22] *Tyrant*: an absolute ruler of a Greek city

Chapter Five

# Mind Your Own Business

It happened on the sixth or seventh day after their arrival in Syracuse. The hour was approaching evening, his favorite time of day. By then, Melicles had finished all his work and only needed to keep an eye on the boat, sails, and the barrels on the deck – until the Libyan turned up. That day, it was the Libyan's turn to sleep on a boat.

At this hour of the evening, Melicles usually climbed higher on the bank, not too far, just a few dozen paces so as not to lose sight of the boat. He sat there on a rocky ledge from which he could admire the pretty view: the port on one side and a small square on the other.

This square was now the most important place in Syracuse for him. All his thoughts and dreams ran tirelessly towards it. Every evening, boys such as himself or just a little older whom people called *epheboi*[23] came after work to this square. They formed a circle. Two

---

[23] *Ephebe* (plural: *ephebes or epheboi*): teenage youths

would shed their clothes and wrestle. Others watched them, offering advice, praise, and applause.

Older, gray-haired fishermen and sailors who happened to pass by also stopped there for a while to look at the games. These street games, called *agon*[24], had trained many great wrestlers of the times, wrestlers whose names then went on to resound with glory far abroad, even as far as the sacred groves of Olympia. All those onlookers – both young and old – knew the sport well, knew the rules, which grips were allowed and which were not: they didn't need any referees. In these games, competitors were not allowed to hurt their opponents, kick, bite, or scratch them, or twist a limb or break a joint. One fought not through harm and pain but through strength and dexterity.

Of course, sometimes, in the heat of the fight, the participants lost control of themselves, and the friendly competition became a real fight without any rules and without restraint. Such outbursts, however, happened rarely because the boys' dream was, of course, that everything should be like at the real games. And they all realized that losing control over one's emotions at such games was the greatest possible disgrace to a player.

Melicles remembered the same spectacles from the gardens of Miletus and the squares of Parthenope. His eyes were burning with the desire to take part. And soon, the Syracusan boys noticed him too and began to challenge him to a fight.

This was terrible.

He trembled with the overwhelming desire to go down and accept the challenge, but he could not go because he had to guard the boat and not lose sight of it. Among the boys, there were a few who had heard his story, and they began to taunt him: he was such a hero and killed two pirates, and now he was too chicken to show what he was made of. "Strong mouth," they called him.

Melicles trembled at these insults. He clenched his fists, threw jeering insults back at them, and swore to himself repeatedly that he would take revenge one day. But for now, all he could do was remain

---

[24] *Agon*: in ancient Greek: struggle, contest

where he was. If only this blasted Libyan turned up a little earlier, then he might still have time to go down and wrestle! Then he would show them what he could do.

Meanwhile, an interesting fight ensued in the square, and all attention turned away from him. The war of words flying in the air died down. Melicles turned impatiently in the direction of Kalias's house from where the Libyan was supposed to come.

Then, suddenly, he started. The hateful sound of Phoenician speech struck his ears while two people pushed through the circle surrounding the wrestlers and walked past Melicles, just within earshot. One of them had obvious sharp Phoenician features. The other was probably Greek.

"He is old, gray, tall, has a large white beard, and looks like a high priest," said the Phoenician. "He's easy to spot."

"You better cover your face, or he could recognize you," replied his companion.

They passed by.

Melicles froze.

He had learned enough Phoenician in Carthage to understand the meaning of the overheard words – or so he thought. He could not be sure. But it occurred to him that the two were talking about his protector, the old man, Nehurabhed.

After a moment's reflection, he decided to follow them.

The two strangers walked towards the coastal gate – in the direction of Kalias's house. A little while later, a third man joined them. He was a large, broad-shouldered peasant, poorly dressed, looking like a common vagabond: half beggar, half-thief, the sort one could meet by the dozen in the port district. The three men stopped and spoke in an undertone.

Melicles drew near to them. They noticed him and looked at him quizzically. Then they moved on. The boy stopped to think. In fact – where did he get the idea that this was somehow about Nehurabhed? Perhaps he had just imagined it.

Anyhow, he had been ordered to guard the boat, so he could not go anywhere. He returned to it and sat at its side. He suddenly lost all interest in the *agon* games. He felt anxious. That hateful Phoenician speech! And why did that Phoenician have to cover his face? Why was he afraid of being recognized? This whole thing made him feel uneasy.

It was already dusk when the Libyan finally arrived. Melicles was free and could now do whatever he wanted. He went ashore. The games were over, and the *epheboi* had all scattered away. But Melicles paid no attention to it. He was walking hurriedly along the shore to the house of Kalias when suddenly, right in front of him, he saw the three walking towards him: the Phoenician, the Greek, and the third, the thug.

He saw them, and he heard the Phoenician's words:

"Yes, it's him!"

Again, Melicles couldn't help feeling that they were talking about Nehurabhed. This time, he did not stop to think but turned to follow them. If he could only overhear what they were saying or see where they were going!

It was already dusk and getting darker every minute, but there were still many people milling in the street so he was able to hide in the crowd without being noticed and yet keep an eye on the three.

The strangers reached the great sea wall connecting the new city with Ortygia, walked past it, and then continued along the coast to the north. Melicles stopped next to the dam. He hesitated. Until now, it had seemed to him that he could not be noticed. But now, it was suddenly much more difficult to hide because here there were almost no people, the coast was rocky and steep, and was practically empty. It grew darker and darker. One could not see beyond a few hundred paces.

*What am I doing? I should turn back,* thought Melicles, but curiosity got the better of him. "All right, I'll go just a little farther," he told himself. "Maybe I'll see where they turn."

But he did not advance more than a few hundred steps when he had to slow down. The three strangers walking in front of him had come to a stop, huddled as if they were consulting each other; then, one of them drifted away from the others and turned back in the direction of the sea wall while the others continued on.

Melicles hesitated; he looked closely at the approaching man. Yes – it was that tattered tramp he had already passed twice. He was sure he would pass him by this time, too. But suddenly, the thug changed direction and walked straight towards him. Amazed, Melicles stepped back, wanting to jump back, but at that moment, a powerful punch in the face knocked him off his feet. He fell flat on his back just a few feet from the edge of the seawall.

"Next time, midget, you will be less curious," he heard a voice.

Melicles struggled to his feet, his head ringing. There was blood on his cheek and some trickling from his ear. He felt searing pain, but terrible anger rose in him much stronger than the pain. Would he, Melicles, allow himself to be beaten like a dog? Without thinking, he rushed with his fists after the stranger. The stranger stopped.

"Wasn't that enough for you, dwarf?" he asked.

They leaped at each other. The thug was a big, broad-shouldered, strong peasant. Melicles was smaller, lighter, skinny from years of hunger and stooped from carrying heavy loads in captivity. But he had a lot of strength, much more than other boys his age. Years of hard work and fighting had hardened his lithe body like the best Etruscan sword, and his muscles were flexible like those of a lynx. The tramp had been wrong to think that he would have an easy job of this pipsqueak.

The thug wrestled with the boy for a while, gasping and cursing with rage, and finally reached for his knife. But at that moment, he stumbled and fell – or rather, they both fell, rolling on the stone pier like biting dogs. The thug, however, fell on top, crushing the boy and pinning him down. He put an iron hold on the boy's neck, choking him, pressed his head into the stone, and began to punch him with his other hand.

Melicles felt himself fainting and, out of desperation, in one desperate lunge, he pushed back. He managed to get to his knees, shoving and punching furiously, unseeing, mad. Suddenly, a terrible scream escaped from both their mouths. The ground at their feet gave away: one cannot fight blindly for long on the very brink of a precipice.

Melicles let go of his enemy, trying to grab the edge of the wall, but his fingers slipped on the smooth, wet surface, and the two of them fell like a rock.

His heart now in his throat, Melicles felt the sharp slap of the surface of the water and a moment later another blunter thud against the bottom. He became dazed for a moment, but breathlessness brought him to. He shot up for the surface, half-blind with terror. With one hand, he grabbed hold of a barnacle-studded rock. His other arm was useless and burning like fire. He shook the water from his head. He was alive. He was conscious.

There was no sign of the thug.

He looked up. Above him loomed the steep wall: several men high, smooth as glass, overgrown with slippery seaweed. Behind him was the sea. The water was barely up to his shoulders, but it swayed, undulated, splashed between the rocks. His feet kept slipping on the rocks at the bottom. The pain in his arm became terrible. He realized that he wouldn't last like this for long.

He looked desperately in both directions along the wall. There, to the right, several dozen steps away, where the wall ended and connected to the living rock, the rock was not so steep. It descended more gently towards the sea. There, yes – that was his only hope. Without waiting or thinking, he threw himself onto the water, on his back, and swam with his legs alone. He was a child of the sea. He swam like a fish, even when he could not use his arms.

His legs and knees burned in the saltwater, where the rocks had gored them during his fall.

He gritted his teeth. In a few minutes, he reached the saving shore. With the last of his strength, he reached for the rocks with his one good arm, tried to heave himself up – and realized that he could not possibly climb the shore, even here. He was spent. Finished. Dead.

But then, suddenly, strong hands reached out to him, grasped his forearms and hair, pulled him up. Two boys had clambered down the rock and were now scrambling up it, hauling him along. Melicles looked at them with eyes half-conscious from pain and fatigue: the same boys had challenged him to a fight in the square earlier that evening, then taunted him and mocked him. Later, they had spotted him in the street and followed him because they wanted to catch him and finally corner him into a wrestling match. This was how they saw him fight with the thug – a real fight, a fight for life and death.

"When we realized that he had a knife, we decided to jump on him to save you, but we were too late! You guys just took and went over the ledge. By Heracles[25]! What a splash!"

"What happened to him?"

"No idea. He went over the ledge with you, went underwater, and – never came out."

"You sure gave him a royal duking, Milesian! You're a hero! What did he want from you, that louse?"

But Melicles no longer heard these words.

"Guys... take me to Kalias, to Kalias's house," he whispers with effort. "I already... I don't know anything anymore. I know nothing, I can't..."

Darkness covered his eyes. He clung to the shoulders of his companions, slumped limp at their feet.

He only regained consciousness in the yard of Kalias's house. The Greek stood over him, both amazed and terrified at the same time. A few moments later, Nehurabhed showed up.

"What happened to you? Who was it? How did it start?" both asked.

"I don't know. I saw a Phoenician. He seemed familiar to me; I followed him along the sea wall, then I was attacked by some drunk tramp, heavy, strong as a bear, I fought and... and... we both fell into the sea."

"What happened to him?"

---

[25] *Heracles*: Greek mythical hero, famous for having performed twelve great works

"I don't know... He – never surfaced."

Kalias shook his head. There was no more questioning because Nehurabhed saw the boy's condition, and he stopped the interview. He immediately started examining his bruised arms and legs. As he reset his dislocated arm, Melicles fainted again, and by the time he came to again, he was lying on his bed in his alcove. He felt clearer and more alert now, the pain in his shoulder going from sharp to pulsating dull.

Nehurabhed sat by his side.

"I think you'll be fine," he said sternly. "You haven't broken anything; your bones are untouched. Are you feeling better?"

Melicles nodded.

"Much better. It doesn't hurt anymore."

"Yes. Well, in ten days, you'll be as good as new. You made it, but in the future, don't try such tricks again. Next time, you may not get off so easily. Kalias is furious with you, and he is right – you nearly lost your life in a stupid, drunken brawl!"

Melicles winced.

"That, my lord, was not quite what happened."

"What do you mean?"

Melicles recounted everything, starting with the conversation he had overheard, his trailing of the men, and the unexpected attack by the thug. Nehurabhed sat, motionless. Not a single muscle moved in his face.

"Why didn't you tell Kalias about it?"

"I'm not sure... I had the feeling that maybe you, lord, wouldn't have liked me telling him. I preferred to save this story for you."

Nehurabhed looked at him searchingly.

"Yes, I understand," he said slowly. "I don't know if your suspicions are justified, and I cannot be sure whether you really did me a favor, but clearly, you wanted to look after me, and that counts."

He narrowed his eyes and, after a while, continued:

"And it's a good thing you didn't say anything to Kalias. Our friend talks a lot – an amazing lot, even for a Greek."

He fell silent, rested his head on his hand, and sat for a long time, lost in thought.

"How long did you commit to working for Kalias?" he finally asked.

"One and a half years."

"Wow... That's a long time. Would you like to see your mother sooner?"

Melicles folded his hands in prayer.

"Oh, my lord!" he whispered.

The old man nodded.

"If you were to come with me on my journey," he said at last, "well, it might not be completely safe... Though, maybe not. It seems that a boy like you can find danger even on the straight and narrow here in Syracuse.

"Besides, the family of that thug is probably somewhere in Syracuse... and they might well realize one day that he is missing, and then they might wish to find you. So, it may be safer for you to move on. Now, if you were to leave with me... I am going to Egypt first, but from there... It's hard to foresee what will happen exactly, but, in any case, in six months at the latest, I will be in Asia Minor, in Ionia. From there, you could easily find your way to Miletus. And on the way, well, you could be useful to me. I think I might have use for a young man like you. Would you like that?"

Melicles set up on the bed. He was trembling with excitement.

"How would that be possible, my lord? After all, Kalias paid for my freedom, I have promised him..."

Nehurabhed stood.

"Well, I don't know anything yet, my boy, I don't know. I need to think about it first, then talk to Kalias. Give me a day or two. Meanwhile, lie still and rest. You must get well soon."

Chapter Six

# The Heart of a Spartan Woman

Sometime later, Melicles was woken by the sound of voices coming from the other side of the curtain of his alcove. He must have slept long and soundly because he felt refreshed. A sliver of golden light shone through an opening in the curtain: the light of olive oil lamps.

It was evening. The hubbub of so many voices confused and surprised him. Only after a while did he remember that today was the day of a feast and that guests had been invited to come and dine together, drink wine, and chat.

Now, Melicles distinguished individual voices clearly.

Someone talked long and movingly about Delphi[26], the greatest and most revered of all temples of Apollo[27], now being rebuilt with

---

[26] *Delphi*: one of the most important religious centers in Greece, dedicated to Apollo

[27] *Apollo*: Greek god of art, healing, and prophecy

great splendor with the contributions of many Greek states. There was talk of treasures flowing in from all corners of the earth to celebrate the city of the true god. Solon's[28] generosity was praised – he was the lawgiver of Athens. People were also astonished by the rich gifts of Croesus – the young king of Lydia, who, although not Greek himself, was also a worshiper of Apollo.

Then, the conversation turned to Solon again, to his great work and the changes he was introducing in Athens.

"What has Athens been until recently?" asked a poignant voice. "A city like many, probably lesser than Miletus, hardly much bigger than Corinth, or your Syracuse, or Taranto in Greater Greece. And today? It teems with people! Streets widen, new public buildings go up, the city is growing, as is the port of Piraeus, and the wealth of its citizens is rising. And why? Because the cruel, ruthless exploitation of the nation by a handful of rent-seeking landlords was abolished. Tens of thousands of peasants who had groaned under the burden of massive debt had their debts extinguished and the threat of debt slavery lifted from their shoulders. They have been allowed to live like men again, make their own way and keep the profits of their labor.

"Ah, Solon. Yes – there is a true hero. There is a wise man indeed. His reform of Athenian education alone will make his name famous for all succeeding ages."

"Someone tells me that in Athens, they are now writing down the sacred songs of Homer[29]," said another voice.

Several voices gasped. The great poem about the destruction of Troy, which professional bards had until now memorized and performed orally from one generation to the next, was now to be written down by priests.

And then, after a little silence, Melicles heard a voice chanting the verses familiar to all Greeks: the immortal history of Priam's city and of the anger of Achilles.

Melicles sat up on his cushion and pulled back the curtain.

---

[28] *Solon*: Athenian political reformer
[29] *Homer*: the greatest poet of ancient Greece, author of *Iliad* and *Odyssey*

In the megaron[30] of the modest house of Kalias, lit with numerous oil lamps, a dozen or so guests sat on low benches running the length of all walls. In the center, an old man sat on a tripod chair, chanting rhythmically and reciting the poem in a strong, singsong voice.

Melicles looked at the faces of the guests. He saw Kalias and Nehurabhed, who – although a foreigner – was a distinguished guest and had been invited to the feast. But in the place of honor, on the bench facing the entrance, there sat another man whose form, monstrous and terrifying, was striking in its uniqueness.

The huge, bald head was sunk deep between upraised pointed shoulders, and a large hump protruded from his back. His unnaturally long arms, with fingers like predator's claws, twitched nervously. His black eyes stared menacingly from under his bushy eyebrows. It was a visitor from far-away Greece, Arkesilaos from Corinth: a great master potter, painter, and artist.

All eyes turned to him. Whenever he spoke, they all fell silent. Kalias served him before all the others, proud of the honor the man's presence bestowed on his house. When the singing of the poem ended, the praise of Solon's work began again.

"Athens will soon be the shining light of all Greek cities," said Arkesilaos. "Just as the Olympic games are today the soul of Greece, so will soon Athens be."

They fell to arguing which city in the whole Greek world was the most important. Some were for Athens. Some praised the rich Miletus, making Melicles's heart leap with pride. A few young men praised Sparta, which won the most trophies in every games and was invincible in war.

Arkesilaos frowned at this, remained silent for a while, and finally said:

"Who among you has ever been to Sparta?"

No one answered him.

---

[30] *Megaron*: the central room of the oldest Greek houses, with an open fire in the center and an opening in the ceiling

Arkesilaos smiled contemptuously. He bit his lips as if to hold back words welling up. Then he burst out with sudden, unrestrained passion:

"Sparta is a disgrace to Greece! Where are her cities, her temples? Where are her statues, her pottery, her textiles? What makes her famous? What great men has she brought to the world?"

There was silence again.

"Lycurgus[31]," someone said.

"Lycurgus was a criminal!" replied the old man impetuously.

A murmur went through the crowd.

Lycurgus, the lawgiver of Sparta, was worshiped as a holy man sent by the gods, like the mythical Theseus[32] or Heracles.

Seeing the impression caused by his blasphemous words, the old man threw back his gigantic head proudly, his fiery eyes gazed at the revelers, one by one, and slowly and clearly, he announced:

"I am a Spartan, Syracusans! I am a Spartan!"

And when no one responded, he continued:

"Yes, my friends, I was born in Sparta, in Sparta itself. I come from an outstanding military family, one of the most honored and powerful.

"Yes! I grew up in Sparta, a happy child! I played with a group of my peers. How healthy, strong, ruddy, and simple we all were! I was just over four years old – I was like your youngest son, good Kalias, just like that – when misfortune struck. A dead tree fell on me, and a branch broke my back.

"They brought me home, barely alive. Many, many months, I lay motionless, first unconscious, then unable to move because of terrible pain. My mother watched over me, not sleeping, not eating. Until slowly, very slowly, I began to regain my strength – but not my former health. No, not to my former health. My broken body began to form on my back this monstrous hump, yes, this awful thing you see here.

---

[31] *Lycurgus*: mythical law giver of Sparta

[32] *Theseus*: mythical hero of Athens, killer of the Minotaur

"My mother looked at it with animal fear. I did not understand why but her fear terrified the little child I was. For years, my mother wouldn't let me leave the house. She hid me from others. I was only a child. I didn't understand anything. You see, I didn't know that in Sparta... I had no right to live.

"I was a cripple. And no cripples are suffered in Sparta. Such is Spartan law, o, Syracusans, the law of the divine Lycurgus, the gods' equal. Yes! You've all heard about that rock from which infirm children are thrown, the crippled, the retarded, all those who could be a burden to them, to the great, glorious, oh so glorious Spartans.

"This was supposed to be my future.

"I didn't know about it, of course, and I played as innocently as before. But my mother – my mother cried all day, and at night she slept right next to me, her arms tight around me. Whenever I woke, I saw her eyes staring at me, black, motionless, terrible. At such times, I was afraid of my mother.

"One day, she learned that they were coming to get me. O, Kalias! O, Syracusans! Think about it: when the tiny, lovely hands of your children reach out to you with trust and faith, when their pink lips smile at you with their trusting smile, think! I was the same – to my mother!"

Arkesilaos paused, took a deep breath and, with a trembling hand, raised his wine goblet to his wide mouth and drained it. After a while, he continued:

"The night before they came to take me, my mother slipped out of the house, carrying me in her arms. Yes – at night. Secretly. Alone. She did not take a maid with her or a slave. She confided in no one, not even her husband. How could she? Someone was liable to turn her in, to report a woman daring to break the sacred laws of the state. Think about it: a mere woman daring to go against the dictates of the divine Lycurgus, the gods' equal! Such audacity, such disobedience! It was unthinkable!

"O, my mother! She left the house where she had grown up. She left her husband. She gave up all her other children: she knew she would never see them again. O, Syracusans, think, think! She gave up her own children – forever. But these children were safe and healthy. They were not in danger. And I...

"She walked blindly on, straight ahead, out into the world. We wandered long days and nights. When I tired, she took me in her arms and walked, walked, always forward, always ahead.

"She was strong like a heifer and persistent like a lioness. Oh, my mother, yes! She was a true Spartan indeed! We didn't go into any village, to any people. We spent the nights in the forest, in trees, in caves. How we survived, avoided falling prey to wild animals, avoided capture by animals worse than animals – slave hunters – I don't know."

He paused.

There was a silence.

"At last, we came to Corinth, but my mother's misfortune did not end there. She had to work hard. She – a general's daughter and a general's wife – became a port laborer. She cooked food for slaves, washed their rags, scrubbed the decks of the sailing ships. Indeed, no human misery was alien to her. No one understood her there. No one knew her fate. No one offered a helping hand. People suspected that we were runaway slaves and refused as much as to look at us.

"She was all alone. All alone, all by herself. Her only reward was in the evening, when she returned home, exhausted from her work, and she could embrace a small, poor, broken body: me, her crippled son. Indeed, we were both poor, abused by fate and people.

"And in this way, many years have passed. O, Syracusans, many years! We survived somehow. When I was ten years old, I started working for Lysias the potter. From then on, slowly, everything began to change. Over time, I became my master's favorite apprentice. He sent me to Etruria – to Volscii, to Veii – to study. I learned the art of the Etruscans. I learned their secrets."

He smiled, nodded his great head, and continued:

"And now you have learned something new, my friends. Now you know what no one else knows: that whatever my name means in Corinth, or Athens, or here, in your venerable and splendid city, and whatever these decorative cups of mine, these *amphoras*[33], these *kraters*[34] are worth to collectors, we do not owe them to me, the unworthy me, but to my mother! To my mother without whose courage and persistence my unworthy misshapen bones would long since have shattered at the bottom of a cliff in the unparalleled, divine, sacred Spartan soil!"

He finished, but no one dared break the silence.

"Yes," answered a voice after a long moment. "It's true that the laws of Sparta are harsh, yet it must be admitted that her people are heroic and brave."

Arkesilaos shrugged.

"Yes," he replied. "But the wolf is brave, and the lion and the panther. Why! Even pirates, those who attack your ships, are said to be brave. Do we worship them? No! We exterminate them like vermin. Sparta is a disease, an ulcer on the beautiful body of Greece. There, I said it, and I won't take it back. None of you knows Sparta as I know her. Ten times, a hundred times, my mother told me about my distant homeland.

"Spartans are brave, you say. Yes! Well! Do you know, friends, how they acquire their valor? When a Spartan is a boy of fourteen or fifteen, he is sent alone into the mountains and forests to hunt runaway slaves. He can shoot them with a bow or cut them down with a sword as he likes. At first, he does it awkwardly. Well, too bad his little hands aren't yet strong enough.

"But every good blow is applauded by the elders!

"Mercy? Pity? Those words do not exist in the Spartan language. To beg for mercy in Sparta? This is a school of valor, right? A beautiful school indeed. Perhaps you would like to teach your children this, too?

"And think of something else – look, I see you have here, Kalias, and of course, while you are well off, yet you are not fabulously rich like others, here you have on your table a beautiful Etruscan *krater*, strangely noble in lines and exquisitely painted. And there I see a

---

[33] *Amphora*: a very large Greek vessel for storing and transporting oil and wine
[34] *Krater*: a large bowl used for mixing wine

beautiful curtain. It is old and a bit faded, but so deliciously colorful and beautifully embroidered – it is a wonderful work from distant Syria, is it not? But in Sparta, in Great Sparta, you would not be allowed, o noble Kalias, to have any of these things. Oh, no! Luxury is forbidden by law! And rightly so, yes? Do you say? Why would a warrior need a beautiful *krater* or cloth or anything that pleases the eye? Why? Such things could only distract you, Kalias, were you a Spartan, from the one and only important thing in life – which is to kill and to rule.

"And you, Epictetus, who so defends Sparta... People say that you have a beautiful vineyard and a garden full of flowers and in that garden a fountain beautifully carved in rare marble and that you spend all your free time in that garden of yours, enjoying it, being happy. But in Sparta, my friend, you couldn't have any of these things. They would be forbidden. Why? Because while strolling in such a beautiful garden, you just might too easily forget about the only thing worthy of a warrior, the only true and great purpose of your life – which is to kill and to rule.

"And it is said about you Syracusans that you love your beautiful temples, public statues in city parks, beautifully decorated grottoes built around sacred springs... That you like to gather in the shade of beautiful porticoes to talk about truth and beauty and immortal gods and to recite poetry.

"You would look in vain for any of these things in brave Sparta. What purpose could they possibly serve there? A person could relax among them, reflect, dream about great and distant things – and perhaps come to doubt the one and only important thing which is, yes, you already know – to kill and to rule."

Arkesilaos laughed a short, evil laugh.

Suddenly he stood up and threw his head back, his shapeless hands stretched out in front of him.

"Blessed be my mother!" he exclaimed. "Blessed be my hump and the misery of my childhood and my hunger and my disability! What would I be without them? A soulless soldier in war, a slavecatcher in peace. I would be a Spartan, my friends, a Spartan!

What a misery! How sorry I am for my unknown brothers and my father. Nothing worthy of man is known to them!"

He fell silent and closed his eyes; his face slowly brightened.

"Do you know?" he was saying now in a changed, soft voice. "Do you know what has been my greatest worry in all the waking hours of my long life? It was this. Because the Spartans preach that it is fit and proper to destroy all cripples and hunchbacks like me; because they say the immortal gods themselves cannot look at perversions like me without disgust; therefore, I have been worried, my friends, that all these vases, jugs, and craters which have left my hands, these vessels on which I painted most often the deeds of my beloved god, Apollo – well, I trembled that maybe he, the radiant Apollo, god of the sun, despised me and my ugliness and all the work of my hands. Yes, my friends, I did ask myself that every day!

"And now know this: we were just a while ago talking about Delphi. Well, now, the priests of Apollo of Delphi have commissioned me, a cripple and an outcast, to make for them the complete set of ritual vessels in which they will offer sacred sacrifices to my god. My hands will now shape and decorate every little object to be used in the worship, sacrifice, and prayer to Apollo!

"So, Syracusans! So, now you see, it turns out that the radiant god did not despise my work after all! I must have earned his acceptance for my ugly, crippled body with all the thousands of shapes and paintings that came out of my over-big hands.

"My god, Apollo, has been pleased by my work!"

He spoke ever quieter, staring far ahead with unseeing eyes.

"Or maybe," he whispered, his voice barely audible, "maybe... who knows? Who does really know what the immortal gods see, what they feel? Maybe... Maybe he was pleased above all else by my mother's heart?"

### Chapter Seven

# In Taranto

Two weeks later, Melicles departed with Nehurabhed aboard a Tarantine ship for Taranto, in Southern Italy, which Greeks in those days called Greater Greece. He was fully recovered and excited to be at sea again.

A meaningful change had occurred in his life. He was no longer a laborer for Kalias. Instead, he became a servant, student, and travel companion to Nehurabhed. Seeing how much the boy missed his people, the old man decided to take him along and, at the same time, take advantage of his service in the hardships of the long journey ahead.

After a short negotiation, Nehurabhed struck a mutually beneficial agreement with Kalias. He did not pay Kalias all the money the Syracusan had paid for Melicles because Kalias, with rare generosity, waived a part of the ransom. The clever Greek sincerely felt for Melicles because he liked him and learned to value him as a good sailor and a dedicated worker. He understood, however, that the old man had the same rights to the boy's services as he did himself, and he wanted to oblige Nehurabhed. Plus, he was afraid that, sooner or later, the cause of the mysterious thug's disappearance would come to light, and he preferred that Melicles not be found in his house when that happened.

And so, the whole negotiation went smoothly. All were satisfied with the concluded contract, most of all Melicles. He positively trembled with excitement and expectation. Such an extraordinary journey, with such a great lord for guide and companion, and the goal – his mother and Miletus – getting closer! By Zeus, what more could one want?

On the day of departure, Kalias accompanied them to their ship. He was excited and talkative above his usual measure. He talked and laughed so much that everyone turned their heads to look at him. He had a good reason to be happy: he had been appointed second-in-command on one of the great sailing ships carrying goods between Sicily and Egypt. It was a mark of recognition for his sailing ability and trading prowess.

Kalias had sought the position for a long time because, while there was much more work on a large ship and much more responsibility, there was also a lot more profit, even if it had to be shared among the ship's owners and its commanders. Finally, traveling on such a great ship was much safer than trying to sneak past pirates' nests in a small shell with barely any crew and no defenses. During his last adventure, Kalias had learned to appreciate the safety of a large ship, with a crew of several dozen people, sailors, and rowers, who were all armed and ready to repel any attack.

"Any pirate will think a dozen times before he takes on a ship that size," he said.

He was scheduled to travel on his first journey to Egypt within a few weeks. Excited by the new prospects now opening up before him, he tried to persuade Nehurabhed to delay his departure and travel with him. And he swelled with pride as he spoke about it. He praised himself and "his," as he said, ship, which was (of course) the best ship in all of Syracuse. He knew that the old man was heading for Egypt, and here was the opportunity to go on Kalias's ship, under his excellent care and consummate command. Why wouldn't he?

But Nehurabhed did not want to wait those two extra weeks. Winter was coming and with it the season of difficult and slow sailing. In response to the flowery flow of the Greek's words, he only shook his head, said goodbye to him, and expressed the wish that they might meet again in Egypt or elsewhere.

They said goodbye, and the Tarantine ship left the shore.

And thus, Melicles was back on the high seas again, heard again the sound of waves lapping the sides of a ship, the splash of oars, the flapping of the sail. He looked around the beautiful ship with the practiced eye of an expert sailor, studying the passengers and crew.

And then, suddenly, something tugged at his mind. One of the passengers – that fellow over there – was he not the strange Greek who walked side-by-side with the Phoenician two weeks ago? Melicles studied him for a long time but couldn't be sure. No, he wasn't sure. People could look so similar to each other. That was two weeks ago, in semi-darkness. So much had happened since then. The fellow seemed occupied with his business, paying them no attention. Maybe it was not the same man, after all.

They sailed along the eastern shores of Sicily, stopping along the way in all major Greek cities. Trading ships often traveled like this, dropping off and picking up cargo and passengers along the way and usually staying within sight of the shore.

Traveling in this way, one got to know all the cities, towns, and villages along the way and all parts of the mainland. And the land along which they sailed was truly worthy of learning. On the second day after leaving Syracuse, they saw on the horizon, far inland and high in the sky, the enormous mountain range of Mount Etna. Its steep slopes, grayish-blue in the distant mist, here and there streaked with snow, ran down to the sea, covered in their lower ranges with a skirt of dark green forests and light green meadows. The mountain's peak was covered with snow and shone bright and cold in the blazing sun. A soft spray of dark smoke, barely visible in the distance, rose from the top – the smoke from Hephaestus' forge.

Melicles had seen a similar mountain in Neapolis on the Campanian shore before, but he was always spellbound by the mysterious phenomenon and watched it with admiration and superstition. This was the home of the god Hephaestus, the lord of fire, the terrible son of Zeus – indeed a house worthy of a great god.

"Could there be anything grander, more dangerous, more proud?" he whispered reverently, staring at the peak which shone before him like a polished shield. Nehurabhed also gazed at the marvelous sight; a shadow seemed to flit across his face.

"There are mountains much higher and much more dangerous," he said slowly. "Not singles ones like this but standing in massive chains, whole ranges stretching for hundreds of miles."

"Can any mountains be higher than this?"

"Oh, yes, Melicles – clouds cannot even reach their peaks because they become entangled in the black forests at their feet. And above that point, there are only naked rocks, inaccessible to humans – only eagles dare penetrate that stone desert world. Great freezing winds blow at those heights, and on a clear day, you can see snow blowing off their peaks in great gales."

"It must be terrible there, my lord!"

The old man shook his head but said nothing. Only after a long silence, he whispered in a barely audible voice:

"My home is there."

On the third day of their journey, they reached Messenia, a colony recently founded by Messenians who had been expelled from their country by their neighbor, Sparta. Here, Melicles saw the familiar Italian shores and the world-famous strait, always turbulent and angry. According to old stories, two monsters once hid among these rocks, lying in wait for sailors going through to swallow them up: the terrible Scylla and Charybdis[35]. Their route, however, did not lead through this strait. Instead, they turned east-north-east and followed the shore of Greater Greece. Then, two days later, they arrived in Taranto.

Immediately upon arrival, they began looking in the bustling harbor for a boat heading east: for the Peloponnese, or Crete, or Egypt. Here, however, they came upon an unexpected difficulty: sailors arriving from Greece brought the sinister news that a plague had broken out in Athens, Corinth, and other eastern cities. This terrible disease appeared every dozen years or so, almost always in winter. There was no defense against it and no cure for it, and wherever it struck, hundreds of people died and thousands bore monstrous traces of disfigurement for the rest of their lives. There had already been a few cases of it in Taranto, sailors whispered with a trembling heart.

People told the usual exaggerated stories about the extent of the disease in Greece, which deterred sailors from sailing east. In these circumstances, it was only after a long search that they managed – with the help of the commander of the ship which had brought them from Syracuse – to find a boat going east to Greece and then farther south.

These sailors were wealthy merchants and owners of the ship: Sosias – a Tarantine; and Philolaos – a Spartan. Their ship was one of the largest in the port, and it was a galley – in addition to sails, it had two rows of oars pulled by a complement of slaves. The crew was partly Tarantine and partly Spartan. Spartan sailors were a rare sight in those days: unlike all other Greeks, Spartans did not take to sailing, were reluctant to go to sea, and rarely left their homeland.

They also founded only one overseas colony outside of Greece, and this colony was – Taranto. Thus, it was only here, between Taranto and Gythion, the port of Sparta, that one ever found boats with either partial or entirely Spartan crews.

The galley of Sosias and Philolaos was leaving with a consignment of Italian wine intended for Egypt, but it was taking it

---

[35] *Scylla and Charybdis*: legendary monsters lying in wait to devour sailors trying to pass through the Messenian Strait between Sicily and the Italian Peninsula

only as far as Heraklion in Crete, where it would be reloaded onto an Egyptian ship. Still, the two merchants assured Nehurabhed that the Egyptian ship would certainly agree to take him along on his journey farther south.

This pleased Nehurabhed – this, and the fact that their departure was scheduled for the following morning, at first light. The old man was in a hurry, and each day saved on the journey was important to him. Thus, they quickly struck a deal. It was only after its conclusion that Nehurabhed realized that the crew was mostly Spartan. This information brought a frown to his forehead, but he said nothing and did not change his mind.

There was a lot of time until evening, so the two travelers went ashore, intending to stroll around town. But as they set out on their walk, Melicles learned that the day happened to be the last day of a five-day holiday in honor of Demeter[36] – the earth goddess. On that day, great ceremonial games were held in her honor at the temple complex just outside the city walls. A dancing procession and choral singing would then follow the games.

This holiday was celebrated each year during the time of winter solstice. Because at this wintery hour, the earth froze and everything green, fresh, and young died, dried up, and decayed, the holiday was somber and gloomy in character.

The myth of Demeter's daughter, the divine Kora, carried off by the god of the underworld, was presented in sad and mournful hymns. But the end of the celebration was different in tone, bright and joyous: after all, starting tomorrow, days would start growing longer, the life-giving rays of sunlight would return, spring would come, and with it the hope of rebirth and resurrection of all nature. In time, all would return to life, greenery would cover fields and forests again, vegetation would burst into flower, seeds into crops, and Kora, the kidnapped girl, would return to her mother, and the two goddesses would stay together until the following winter.

---

[36] *Demeter*: Greek goddess of earth and harvest; her daughter, Kora (or Persephone), was kidnapped by Hades, king of the underground land of the dead

The feast was celebrated all over Greece at that time, but the most festive celebrations were held here in Taranto, which, like Syracuse, based its power on agriculture and drew her great wealth from her fertile hinterland. And so, Demeter was worshiped here before all other gods.

The city was now deserted – everyone had gone to the games. Melicles quickly found out where the games were held and rushed there, having said goodbye to Nehurabhed, who did not want to or could not follow him. Yet, for all his haste, Melicles did not make it to the games in time. By the time he arrived at the spot and pushed his way through the gathered crowd, the games were already over, and the holy procession was forming, heading for the temple of Demeter.

The procession was led by priests and priestesses in white woolen robes, with gold wreaths on their heads. They were followed by flute players whining on reed pipes slow, sad, monotonous melodies. Then came the competitors, the winners of today's games. Here, whispers and murmurs resounded in the crowd. People pointed out the best players, named their names, and applauded their favorites.

The competitors walked on, their heads held high with a rhythmic, ceremonial step, oak wreaths of victory on their foreheads. Others followed: players who had failed to win prizes but who, by merely participating, had honored the goddess; they, too, deserved a distinguished place in the procession. Then, a group of veteran sportsmen walked farther behind, winners of previous games, and then young boys, sixteen- or eighteen-year-old *epheboi* hoping to take part in next year's games. Behind them, a group of musicians – flute players and *khitarists*[37] – followed, and behind them, young girls in rows holding hands. The girls wore flowing robes, their shoulders bare and their heads uncovered.

It was one of the very few public holidays in Greece in which women were allowed to take part publicly. It was, after all, the feast of the mother-goddess – a celebration in which women were the equals of men. They were allowed to dance, sing, and compete to honor her.

---

[37] *Khitara*: Greek stringed instrument, ancestor of the guitar

And now they walked in a slow dancing procession, half walking, half flowing, bending their lithe, youthful figures to the melody of the flutes. Their faces were solemn, though often still childish, curious, and amused.

Young girls who, like all women in Greece, were not allowed to walk in the street alone with their faces uncovered, could show their faces in public without shame on that one day of the year. They smiled with pride as they walked, singing a song in an undertone, confident in their beauty and status on this solemn day. They were the daughters of Demeter, her heiresses, the future mothers of the future world.

Melicles stared at the scene before him. And when they passed, when the crowd dispersed and the people started going home in small groups of three or four and when the swift winter evening was already falling over the city, Melicles slowly returned to the port, lost in thought. Before his eyes, he still saw these images: he could see the slender figure of the leading dancer, the profound and serious eyes of another, and the amused, almost childish gaze of another yet, which had briefly met his own.

"This holiday in honor of Demeter is incomparable!" he told Nehurabhed with excitement. "What a magnificent procession, how inspiring the proud winners of the games, and how beautiful, how wonderfully beautiful the dancing girls of Taranto!"

"Yes, yes!" he repeated with deep conviction. "Everything was so gorgeous, so strangely beautiful! How wonderful is life!"

Nehurabhed looked at him and smiled.

Chapter Eight
# That Man Again

It was night. Melicles and Nehurabhed slept aboard the ship because its departure was expected at first light. They slept on deck, under a roof of sailcloth spread out overhead, shielding them from both the wind and the fine drizzle, which had started at nightfall.

Melicles woke in the middle of the night and couldn't get back to sleep. He lay awake. He felt overwhelmed by strange anxiety. It was an incomprehensible feeling – it had come from nowhere.

He stared distrustfully into the darkness surrounding him. There were snoring sounds all around – the breathing of the sleeping crew. Some distance away, a lamp burned on the mast with a dim, flickering light. Far away, in the port, one could hear the calls of the night watch. Everything was as usual aboard a ship at night. And yet, the boy couldn't understand the reason for this feeling of strange dread.

And then recognition struck him: he realized with a start that the ship reminded him of the pirate ship that had captured him many years ago, on the way back from Massalia. That ship had been much bigger than this but just as black, shabby, and old. Melicles, the son of a sailor and nephew of a ship's carpenter, knew all kinds of ships, larger and smaller boats. He often compared a beautiful but gentle little boat to a small girl; a strong, gorgeous sailing ship to a tall man, bold and strong; a loaded, heavy galley to a plodding harbor porter laden with goods. But this ship was like none of those. Instead, it was like a great old witch – black, somber, and menacing.

Yes, that was it: it wasn't a boat he could trust.

And the commanders of the ship were the same. The Spartan Philolaos – thin, long, stooped, forward-leaning, sharp-faced, with a nose like a hawk's beak with a high, balding forehead and a small goatee, with the penetrating the eyes of a predator – stood on deck in the lamplight, wrapped in a spacious cloak. He gave the impression of a hungry vulture waiting for his prey.

And the other one, Sosias – old, half-gray, half-bald, his hair combed from above one ear over his pate, with restless, flying eyes – reminded Melicles at times of the hideous Phoenician merchants of Carthage.

Melicles shuddered. He vainly tried to persuade himself that Philolaos and Sosias were well-regarded merchants and sailors and that the commander of the ship on which they had come from Syracuse had spoken of them highly. Still, the anxiety persisted.

Suddenly, in the middle of the ship, someone moved with a torch in his hand. The boards creaked. A man boarded the ship. Philolaos, the commander of the barge, must have been expecting him and approached him briskly. The light of the torch sizzled and danced in the damp mist, but Melicles saw the stranger's face clearly. He shuddered. The man who now climbed onto the deck and spoke so intimately with Philolaos was that same man again! That mysterious Greek who had accompanied them on the way from Syracuse to Taranto and who, some days before that, had spoken in Phoenician in the port of Syracuse!

Yes, Melicles was sure this time: this was the same man! But what was he doing here? Would he travel with them again? And what were he and Philolaos discussing so fervently now? He strained his ears, but they kept their voices low. Were they talking about them, about Nehurabhed?

Melicles rose. He crawled out from under the canvas on all fours as silently as possible. He slipped behind a row of barrels, close to one side of the ship, and advanced towards the light inch by inch, closer, closer. He could now hear their voices but not yet make out the words. Just a little closer! He held his breath. He couldn't go any farther now – the barrels ended, there was no more cover, and Philolaos's torch cast a circle of light on the deck. He froze and listened. The torch hissed in the fine rain, flickered, smoked, barely smoldering.

"He must not reach Egypt," said the newcomer. "He's a spy. He escaped from Carthage, and the Phoenicians are looking for him. My friends have five hundred drachmas saying he will not reach Egypt."

"What to do with him, then?" Philolaos asked.

"Don't take him to Heraklion. Instead, take him to the Phoenician settlement of Aphoria and turn him over to the local guard. That's all."

"What's their business in this?"

"By Hermes! What business is that of ours? The Phoenicians will detain him and reward us all well: you, Philolaos, Sosias, and me. I have no clue what they want or why – it seems he is an enemy of both Carthage and all the other Phoenicians, but don't ask me more. I neither know nor care."

Philolaos shook his head.

"Well and good, but what will Sparta say to it? And my partners in Gythion?"

"You needn't tell them anything! Why would you? Besides, even if they do find out, they won't care. Sparta is now doing good business with the Phoenicians and wants to stay friends with them. I know this for sure. So, what does Sparta care about some stupid foreigner?"

"I don't know whether Sparta cares. But I trade with Egyptians. And if this man is on his way to Egypt, and is expected there, and is on my ship and then somehow disappears, I may be in for a row."

"A row? With whom?"

"With the Egyptians!"

"Oh, come on, Philolaos! What on earth are you talking about? The Egyptians will know only as much as the Phoenicians tell them, and why would the Phoenicians tell them anything?"

"But what if he's some kind of very important person? He looks important. By Hades, he looks like a priest."

"Oh, come on, he's not a very important person! Since when do very important people book passage on your boat? Ha, ha. Besides, it's not like you are doing him any harm. He wants to go to Crete; well, you take him there. You aim for Heraklion, but it's winter and bad weather, and by accident, you arrive in Aphoria. It's not like you are going to harm him. So, you arrive in Aphoria, and the Phoenicians there force you to give him up. You're innocent. Yes? What they will do with him, that's their business."

Philolaos, undecided, shook his head.

"I don't like to do business I don't understand."

"But you understand three hundred drachmas?"

"No."

"How about four hundred drachmas?"

Philolaos looked thoughtful.

"I understand that four hundred drachmas is very little," he said at last.

The sum, however, made an impression on him.

"So, how about four hundred and fifty? Look, I want to make something in this, too, you know."

"I will have to add two days from Knossos to Aphoria."

"Oh, come on, you are making two hundred and twenty-five drachmas for each day lost. On Hermes! May you never do better business in your life!"

The vulture face of Philolaos sharpened even more; his eyes flashed, then narrowed.

"So, what's your profit in this?"

They began to haggle over the division of the prize. They argued fiercely in low whispers; their argument sounded like the growling of angry dogs.

Melicles leaned a little closer. Suddenly, the torch, touched by a gust of wind, sent out a puff of sparks; the deck grew lighter for a moment. The boy tried to shrink back, but it was too late – they had seen his shadow. The conversation broke off. Philolaos stood up from the crate on which he had been sitting.

Melicles slipped back between the barrels as quickly as he could. He crawled, disregarding the noise he was making, to his bed, lay down beside Nehurabhed, and threw his woolen blanket on his head. At that moment, Philolaos entered, torch in hand. He stared long at Nehurabhed. The old man slept the calm sleep of the innocent, snoring heavily. Philolaos looked at Melicles huddled under his cloak, shook his head, and walked away.

Melicles lay still for a long time, numb with fear. Then he began to yank Nehurabhed's sleeve – once, twice, three times. The old man woke at last and sat straight up, immediately wide awake. The boy put his mouth to the old man's ear and, his voice choked with emotion, began to tell him everything he had just heard. The old man listened carefully and was silent for a moment.

"Very well," he said finally. "We must leave the ship immediately."

He pulled himself up from the mat. They started picking up their things in a hurry, feeling for them in the dark.

The crew was already waking up. First commands for departure sounded. Down below deck where the unfortunate galley slaves were kept, the voices of the slave drivers were heard, shouting and cursing. The boards creaked. A couple of flickering lights shone in the dark. When Melicles and Nehurabhed came out from under their canvas, they saw a narrow pencil line of light over the horizon to the east. The day was breaking.

Suddenly, the tall figure of Philolaos emerged before them. Behind him stood Sosias and the mysterious stranger, the friend of the Phoenicians. Nehurabhed made his way towards the gangway connecting the boat to the shore without a word. But Philolaos barred his way.

"Where are you going, my lord?" he asked.

"Before I leave, I must consult with the commander who brought me here from Syracuse," replied Nehurabhed.

"There is no time for that," Philolaos said. "We're leaving right now."

"You may, my lord, send your servant to the other ship," said Sosias. "He'll run there and return in time."

Nehurabhed shook his head.

"No, I have to go there myself."

There was a moment of silence. The three Greeks glanced at each other.

"We can't wait a moment longer," Philolaos said finally.

"Then I can't go with you; I'll take another ship," said Nehurabhed sharply.

Melicles moved closer.

Instead of answering, Philolaos barked an order to his crew: "Lift the gangplank! Cast off!"

Nehurabhed put his hand into the folds of his robe on his breast; his face twitched strangely, lips pressed together. Several of the sailors loomed around them. The gangplank was hauled aboard, the lines were untied, and the coils of ropes were thrown onto the deck. The ship shuddered. Oars struck water. The black gap between the ship's side and the shore began to widen.

Nehurabhed stood still for a moment.

Slowly, his face grew expressionless as if carved in stone.

"Am I your prisoner?" he asked.

Philolaos bowed his head low in front of him.

"Oh, no! Worthy lord!" he said with humble subservience. "You, a prisoner? Gods almighty forbid! You are the most valuable passenger I have ever had the honor to host on my ship. You are such a distinguished guest that I don't want to lose you! I don't want to allow some other competitor the honor of taking you to Crete."

He bowed again.

"All that my poor boat can serve is at your command."

Nehurabhed remained silent. Then he shrugged and turned away. He stood at the far side and stared towards the shore.

Swathed in morning mist, still dark gray in the lazily rising day, the banks of Taranto receded into the distance.

### Chapter Nine
# Smallpox

Nehurabhed and Melicles sat at the ship's bow as it flew over the waters, powered by the force of forty oars.

"That was foolish, my boy," said the old man, "foolish. That is just the kind of thing that happens when you act quickly, without thinking."

He shook his head sadly.

"If I had only pretended that I had no clue what they were up to, I might now be able to go ashore at the next port of call, looking all carefree and innocent and – disappear. But now, they won't let me leave the boat until we reach Aphoria."

"What do we do?" Melicles asked.

"First of all, we think," replied the old man.

After a while, Melicles asked again:

"Who are you, my lord, and is it true what that scoundrel said to Philolaos?"

Nehurabhed looked around. At first, he did not answer; he just listened. The sailors nearby, busy sewing sails, were talking loudly. They spoke about what troubled everyone: the plague. One of them repeated a story he had heard about how this monstrous disease was spreading, especially in the crowded port of Corinth. And another about how a Tarantine ship had recently arrived from there, having had to abandon two travelers along the way because they showed early symptoms of the disease. The two were left, as was the custom, at the mercy of fate somewhere on the nearest shore. Other sailors complained that they were now heading in the direction of the plague. They cursed their fate but consoled themselves that they did not have to stop at any larger ports along the way.

"Perhaps good Zeus will save us from this misfortune," they repeated glumly.

Seeing that none of the crew was paying attention to them, the old man turned to Melicles and said:

"Listen, my boy. I should have told you this a long time ago. I have always known that you wouldn't betray me. But I hadn't realized that traveling with me could be this dangerous. Well, in truth, I don't think that you yourself are in any danger yet. I don't think anyone would try to stop you from leaving the ship at the next port of call."

The old man thought for a moment.

"So, hear what I tell you," he said. "And remember that you need not risk your own life for my sake."

Melicles jumped as if stung by those words.

"I will not abandon you, my lord. I will not abandon you now or ever, and please do not talk to me this way again," he said impetuously. "You saved my life there, in Carthage, and you didn't even know who I was. But I know you now. And I will not abandon you. I can't."

Nehurabhed looked at him for a long time.

"Well then, sit down and hear this," he said.

He looked around again. Then he began to speak slowly and thoughtfully:

"I am not a spy, but I am an envoy. I am an envoy of a mighty king – my king, the ruler of Medes and Persians, Astyages, son of Cyaxares, may his name be praised. I have been on this mission for almost a year now. I have been to Phoenicia; I visited the great Solon in Athens and Aeaces in Samos, and I was in Carthage and Syracuse. And next, I must go to Egypt, where I must speak to the worthy high priests, the advisers of his holiness, the pharaoh Apries.

"There, in Egypt, another envoy of my king is awaiting me. He was supposed to set out on his mission right after me and proceed as an official ambassador of my king, with rich gifts, straight to Egypt. I believe he is already there."

The old man paused for a moment. Melicles moved away from him fearfully, amazed by the importance of his master.

Here is a man who speaks with the greatest princes of this world, he thought.

He was speechless, unable to get a word out of his throat. He watched Nehurabhed as if he were seeing him for the first time.

"And with such a man, I shared a blanket last night! Gods! What shameless presumption on my part!" he thought.

After a while, the old man continued:

"I am telling you all this so that you know that traveling with me is not likely to be simple and easy and that you should not think it is free of risk. You have learned this on your own skin twice already. Therefore, it would be best for your own good if you got off this boat at the next port of call and never returned."

Melicles made no reply to that. Only after a long moment did he dare to ask:

"My lord... envoys... envoys and heralds cannot be imprisoned or killed."

Nehurabhed shrugged and said:

"I don't think the Phoenicians will kill me. I don't suppose they will dare. As you say, one does not kill heralds. Though it is true that I am not traveling on an official mission, surrounded by retinue and with my king's insignia, the Phoenicians know well who I am. Neither does one kill priests, and I am a priest. So, I'm not in danger of being killed. Or I don't think I am. They can try to detain me for a month, or six months, perhaps even a year, or release me only when my king asks for my release. Or not release me at all – such things have happened. But kill me? Probably not."

He nodded his head.

There was silence for a long time.

"What do we do now?" Melicles asked again.

"I already told you, my boy – we have to think carefully," he replied calmly. "We have a lot of time to think."

The youth did not like this advice. He wanted to act, do something immediately. He considered bold plans to run away, to break out, sword in hand, or to jump overboard at night and swim for the shore. That last idea he had to abandon quickly: Nehurabhed could not swim.

The boy wandered all over the ship; he approached the rudders – the two gigantic oars slicing through the water in the back of the ship, oars as wide as whale fins, connected with a single crossbeam held firmly by the hands of the helmsman. He glared with hatred at the Spartan and Tarantine sailors climbing the ropes onto the mast. But they paid him no attention.

Everything on the ship continued normally, as on any other cruise. Nehurabhed was treated kindly, indeed respectfully, and he kept to himself, away from everyone, maintaining a proud and contemptuous silence. And so, the hours passed.

Towards evening, a gloomy event interrupted the uniformity of the lazy day: one of the galley slaves was flogged for some offense. The screams of the unfortunate man made Melicles shudder with horror. The memory of his recent past flashed before his eyes. A wave of sympathy and anger flooded him, and his hands squeezed themselves tightly into fists at the thought of the defenselessness of the tortured.

He was with him now, with all his soul; he knew what the other felt and thought, felt the pain of the cut skin as if it were his own.

He went down below deck, into the long, low, monstrously stinking room where they sat chained to their benches, up to their ankles in excrement and vomit: the half-naked galley slaves, in two rows, their heads almost touching the low ceiling. One of them struggled and twisted under the blows of a heavy rod but did not plead. There was no point: no one who could hear him would or could come to his aid.

Melicles, struggling to restrain his innate terror, stepped into the narrow passage between the rowers and dared to speak up in the slave's defense. They all looked at him with surprise, but no one answered him. Then, suddenly, the punishment ended because the prisoner passed out.

Melicles stood with his head bowed, then slowly returned to the deck. On the way, he noticed one of the galley slaves, stooped, thin, with a great head of matted, shaggy hair. The man spoke to him rapidly in a whisper; said something in broken Greek, something about a locked box or a chest, a plea for help. Melicles wanted to stop and hear him out, but one of the two slave drivers pushed him impatiently towards the exit and struck the galley slave full on the mouth.

The steersman at the rudder shouted an order. The slave driver gave the rowers tempo: one, two, one, two, one, two. The oars stirred, sweaty, grimy backs arched, heads tipped back, the bearings of the oars groaned, seawater splashed; the ship began to move again.

Melicles lay at night with clenched teeth. He thought about what he had seen under the deck, about the dozens of human heads and backs moving rhythmically. And so hours, days, months, years, forever in the same motion. Eternally at the same oar, eternally the same boards enclosing the world, eternally the same chain. Forever. Hopeless, until death. No hope of liberation, no hope of escape. When the ship went down, the galley slaves would go down with it – and that was the best fate they could hope for. It was far worse to boil in the stuffy, stinking, hot room; to faint with thirst; to groan under the blows of the rod; to gradually wear out your body among the foul odors of human sweat and excrement; and to wait – wait, wait, wait – for the only deliverance to the shameful, hateful life: death.

This might well have been his own destiny. There was once talk of selling him for a galley slave, given how muscular he was. But he was too small to be a rowing machine, and that saved him then.

The boy shuddered with horror. He cursed the moment he had set his foot on this blasted ship. He remembered the unhappy face of the prisoner who had turned to him with his plea, the flash of his bloodshot eyes. If only he could help him! If only he could reach him! But it was impossible now: there were now two or three Spartans always keeping an eye on the two of them. True, they did not care about Melicles all that much, but he would not be allowed below deck again.

The boy understood that, out of consideration for his master's safety, he must not irritate the Spartans anymore. Indeed, now they had to think above all about their own rescue, regardless of what happened under their feet, under the planks of the deck.

He did not think for a moment about leaving the old man. After all, he owed him his life and more than that, his freedom. He remembered the care the old man had given him when he was recovering from his fight in Syracuse. He was proud to have won the trust and friendship of such a great person. He wouldn't give it up for anything. He thought with fear and sadness of what might happen to him in Phoenician captivity. He was also worried that the old man looked completely resigned, like someone who had come to terms with his fate and had no more will to fight it. Nehurabhed ate as usual, slept as usual, gazed serenely at the shores past which they now sailed. He was as calm as ever, motionless, silent.

The next day, Melicles, trembling with impatience, asked Nehurabhed again what he intended to do – had he figured something out? Did he have a plan? The old man stroked his beautiful beard for a long time.

"Maybe I do," he said finally.

The boy was on fire with curiosity.

Nehurabhed watched the approaching shore.

They were on their way to Saios, the last Greek town in Italy; then, they would leave the shore and strike out clear across the Adriatic Sea towards Greece. They were to stop at this port for a few hours, refresh their water supply, give the crew a short break.

Nehurabhed was lost in thought.

"There's no other way," he whispered to himself.

Then he turned to Melicles.

"Listen, my boy," he said, "I accept your friendship. Do not leave me just yet. You can still do me one more favor before we leave Italy."

"Everything you say, my lord," the boy said eagerly.

"Very well then. When we come to port, they'll let you go; they're watching you only because of me – you don't matter to them."

"Yes, my lord," said Melicles.

"So, when we land in Saios, you will go ashore, to the market, and find prawns for me. Buy them and bring them to me."

"Prawns? Shrimp?" Melicles asked, amazed.

"Yes, prawns. They are these little sea creatures with lots of legs," explained the old man.

"I know what shrimp are!" the boy replied impatiently. "But why? Why do you need shrimp?"

Now the old man looked at him with surprise.

"What do you mean, why? To eat them, of course," he explained calmly.

Melicles was struck dumb with irritation.

"But what must I do to save you, my lord?" he exploded.

Nehurabhed shrugged.

They were already reaching the shore.

"Well, if you love me, go buy me these prawns," he repeated emphatically.

"I'll get them for you," the boy replied with resignation.

As they expected, Melicles was allowed to go ashore without any difficulty. He bought the prawns and brought them to the ship, curious to see what would happen next. He still nursed a secret hope that Nehurabhed required the prawns for some magical spell to make some miraculous concoction with which he would intoxicate and stun the guards or turn the two of them invisible.

But the old man told him to simply cook the shrimp for his supper – and then he ate them. He ate them slowly, carefully, with a show of appetite that was rare in him, and then he went to sleep. This was how the shrimp ended up: as soup! This was how their last opportunity in port was used before they left for Greece!

They cast off at dawn.

Melicles was inconsolable about the missed chance to do something in Saios. He stood at the ship's bow for a long time, gazing at the land disappearing in the distance.

His distress was magnified by the fact that his old master was not feeling well. From early morning, he complained about headaches and chills; at midday, he refused to eat; and again refused to eat at dinnertime. He remained sprawled on his mat and only asked for water from time to time. He was irritable and impatient. He complained about the rocking of the ship, of the hardship of the journey. This was quite a change because the old man had, until now, endured his fate with exceptional calm and dignity, and the journey was proceeding as uneventfully now as it had so far.

The sea was calm, the boat rocked slightly, and though the weather was gray and drizzly, it was not too annoying. But everything seemed wrong to Nehurabhed. By nightfall, he developed a fever, his face became flushed, his eyes were glazed, and he began to breathe laboriously. His difficulty breathing kept him awake at night. He kept waking the boy to fetch him water or wine to drink and ordered him to make cold compresses. He was short-tempered, irritated, grumbling.

Soon, the whole crew learned about his illness and carefully avoided their end of the boat. Melicles sat by his companion's side, ready to serve him, watching him with increasing concern. After falling asleep at last, the old man woke seemingly refreshed, but he now began to complain of itchy skin and scratched his arms, chest, and face. The itching did not go away. By noon, red, swollen patches began to appear on his hands, his forehead, and his cheeks. Melicles looked at them in horror. The old man, too, became morose. He forbade the boy to approach him. He looked at his hands for a long time and shook his head, sighing heavily. Melicles had tears in his eyes.

"What is it, my lord? What is this disease?" he asked with trembling in his voice.

Nehurabhed did not answer for a long time; he closed his eyes.

At last, he said softly: "Smallpox."

"The pox!" Melicles cried out.

"Yes, there is no doubt," replied the old man in a broken voice. "I am afraid there can be no question about it."

He groaned hollowly and rolled over on his side.

"My boy," he continued after a moment, "do not come close to me now and do not touch me. You are young and have much to live for. You have your family; you have your mother. Do not allow yourself to be infected. Smallpox is a terrible disease."

He spoke slowly, in a broken voice. Melicles had tears in his eyes. The man looked at him with tenderness.

"Get me a jug of water now, set it by my mat so that I can easily reach it, and go away. Tonight, you must make your bed elsewhere."

Melicles did as he was told but sat down not too far off, ready to serve his master. Nehurabhed dozed off, waking up several times complaining of chills and itchy skin, moaning quietly. Hours passed like this.

Now, the entire ship knew about Nehurabhed's illness. One of the crew came along, stopped some distance away, and looked glumly at the old man lying on his mat. The red blotches on his hands and face were visible from far away. Philolaos came too, looked for a long time with an angry, concerned expression, then shook his head anxiously and walked away.

He returned sometime later and called for Melicles.

"It's smallpox," he said, pointing to the sick man.

Instead of answering, Melicles looked despairingly at the sky and nodded. Philolaos left without a word.

A meeting was held on the ship that afternoon. The entire crew gathered at the other end of the deck. They spoke in undertones, but Melicles guessed from the individual words that they were talking about Nehurabhed. The ship was now approaching the shores of Greece. Mountainous, forest-covered shores of wild Epirus emerged clearly on the port side.

Philolaos ordered the boat to approach the shore.

He walked over to Nehurabhed, stopping a few steps away, and said firmly:

"You must leave the ship immediately."

Nehurabhed looked up at him, eyes shining with fever.

"How is that?" he asked in a trembling voice.

"You must leave the ship immediately," the Spartan repeated. "Get off. Now. We are already close to the shore."

Nehurabhed struggled to get up, breathing heavily.

"I don't know if I can leave. I'm weak," the old man complained.

Philolaos stamped his foot.

"Get out now, old man, and damn the day you boarded my ship! And take that poxy servant of yours with you!"

"Lord," Melicles turned to Philolaos with an earnest plea. "Let us stay overnight, at least. You see how sick he is. Perhaps he will get better by tomorrow. And look at the shore; it's completely wild and empty, there is no place to hide, no one to help us here, and the night is falling."

But Philolaos was inexorable.

"I don't care where he goes; he can go to hell. He cannot stay here," he growled.

Nehurabhed got up, swaying on his feet. Melicles wanted to hold him up, but the old man pushed him away angrily, frowned, and said in a changed voice:

"Melicles! I already told you, don't touch me – get away from me, stay here on the ship! Beware of the plague, my boy, beware of the plague! You cannot help me anymore, and if you go ashore with me in this wild place, you, too, will be lost!"

His voice cracked. Melicles sobbed but did not want to hear about leaving the old man at such a moment. He was following close behind, his head lowered glumly.

The sailors stepped aside to make passage.

The ship scraped against the gravel of the shore, and the plank was lowered. Swaying and panting heavily, Nehurabhed left the boat and walked into the shallow water. Melicles followed him. As soon as they came ashore, the plank was drawn up, and the ship pulled away.

The two clambered out of the water and onto the beach. Nehurabhed sat down heavily on a rock, staring glumly as the ship disappeared in the falling dusk.

But as soon as the ship was gone, the old man stood, opened his arms wide to embrace Melicles and, in a surprisingly strong voice, exclaimed:

"Melicles, my dear boy, let me embrace you!"

Melicles embraced the old man, deeply touched. He trembled both with emotion and with the ordinary human fear that he would now surely become infected with pox. He was both surprised and sad that the old man had become so confused in his fever that he had forgotten all his former caution.

But Nehurabhed held him for a long time in his strong embrace, and at last, he said:

"You are very dear, very brave, my boy – the best and the bravest boy I know. Yes, yes, Melicles. And don't be afraid of me. You should know that if you ever do catch this terrible disease, from which terrible fate may the Good Lord protect you, you will not catch it from me. Not from me, not now."

Melicles moved away from him.

"How is it, my lord? Is this not smallpox?" he asked.

The old man shook his head.

"And the blotches on your hands and face?" asked Melicles.

"These blotches," replied Nehurabhed, looking at his hands. "It's nothing. It's the prawns."

"Prawns?"

"Well, yes. You see, whenever I've eaten prawns in the past, I have always been a little sick afterward. I got a slight fever and such blotches on my skin. But this will pass quickly!"

"Why then, my lord, did you order me to cook these prawns?" Melicles exclaimed in surprise.

The old man looked at him searchingly.

"Ah, Melicles! You act quickly, but you think slowly! That's exactly why I ate the prawns: to get the fever and these blotches! I wanted these blotches so as to make Philolaos think that I had contracted smallpox. So that he would feel forced to maroon me onshore."

Melicles looked up at Nehurabhed, opened-mouthed, and stood there for a long while, petrified.

"Oh, lord," he stammered at last. "But why didn't you tell me?"

Nehurabhed shook his head.

"I couldn't, my boy. I couldn't tell you. Had I told you, would you have been so sincerely worried about my health? Would you have despaired so fervently, so poignantly? I felt sorry for your grief, but I couldn't tell you. Your eyes are so clear; they are such open, sincere eyes. You cannot hide anything! Your honest eyes would have betrayed us immediately."

He nodded with a smile.

"That is all well, my Melicles. This is why I like you so much," he added after a moment.

Chapter Ten

# The Wolves of Epirus

But this was no time to rejoice in their newly found freedom. The position of the castaways was serious and now possibly even more dangerous. They were utterly alone, without food or any means to defend themselves, abandoned at the mercy of their fate in a wild, nearly uninhabited part of northern Greece.

Dusk was falling. Melicles looked apprehensively around the unfamiliar coast. A jagged rocky cliff rose above them like a great fortress. In a few places where the cliff had collapsed, landslides came down to the sea, blocking the beach with piles of debris. Higher up, over the cliff's edge, rose a thick spruce forest, looming, black, and threatening. A dense tangle of branches and bushes, it presented an impenetrable wall through which not only man but not even a ray of sunlight could squeeze. There was total and absolute darkness at the bottom of that forest, all day and all night.

Melicles felt dread exuding from this hostile world.

There was silence all around. The sea stirred lazily behind them. The only other sound was the murmur of rainwater dripping down the rocks.

It was getting dark now. Snow began to fall: wet, sticky, mixed with rain. Melicles and Nehurabhed walked along the shore, looking for a place to overnight. But after only a few hundred paces, the old man became completely exhausted; he could go no farther. He was not as seriously ill as he had pretended on the ship, but he was weak from the fever he had passed, and he needed rest.

At one point, they came upon a stretch of the forest that reached through a gap in the cliff all the way down to the beach. Here, the old man slumped without strength against a tree. Melicles started gathering branches and building a fire. Soaked with rain, the wood refused to catch fire. It dimmed, smoked, went out, then flared up again. The boy's hands were already stiff with cold, and he felt breathless from constantly blowing onto the embers, but in the end, his stubbornness paid off. The firewood burst into flame, and the life-giving fire lit up the darkness around them. The old man curled up in the fire's warmth and fell asleep like a rock.

Melicles remained awake for a while yet, adding branches to the fire to ensure it did not go out, but finally, he, too, became overwhelmed with sleep. He tried to fight it off, but the warmth and the silence calmed him down. He huddled at the old man's feet, rested his head on his knees, and fell asleep – he didn't even realize when and how.

He woke with a start, feeling a strange sense of dread. He sat up abruptly and listened. The fire had died down: only a few half-burnt branches hissed and smoked. Darkness and silence reigned all around. The sea, much higher now, steadily struck lazy waves against the rocky shores, splashing and gurgling among the scattered boulders. The shadows of these boulders, barely visible in the light of the fire, appeared like hulking, menacing giants. Somewhere deep in the woods, he heard the hooting of the great owl.

Suddenly, the boy felt a shudder of horror rush over him. He had an inexplicable sensation that something terrible and hateful was slowly creeping up on them, under the veil of the night, that it was near, right there, within a hand's reach. He couldn't bear the tension any longer; he woke Nehurabhed while, at the same time, blowing with all his might into the embers of the fire. But his efforts were in vain: a couple of twigs caught faint flames, but the rest only smoked and hissed in darkness.

And then they heard it: the howl of a wolf, right behind them, no more than a few dozen steps away. Nehurabhed and Melicles jumped up. From the depths of the forest came the reply of other wolves, here and there, closer and farther, on all sides. It wasn't so much howling as cackling – as if choking with uncontrollable, sinister laughter. This terrible conversation went on without interruption; then the cackling turned to barking then to impatient, fierce snarling.

Nehurabhed and Melicles stood still, helplessly trying to see through the surrounding darkness. At one point, they thought they saw the eyes of a wolf, reflecting the pale flame of their dying fire. There were other flashes of other eyes farther back.

Melicles felt his hair stand on end, and a scream escaped from his chest. Death, terrible death, stood over them. They were both screaming now, trying to scare the wolves away. Melicles leaned once more over the fire, trying in vain to blow the barely smoldering ashes back to life.

At that moment, the black hulk of a giant wolfhound emerged from the darkness and jumped at the boy. Melicles grabbed a handful of smoking ash with his bare hand and threw it in the wolf's snout. A cluster of sparks flashed in the night, and the wolf jumped back. The fire hissed one last time, sent out a column of acrid smoke, and went out. And now it was completely dark.

Melicles grabbed the old man by the arm and pulled him towards the sea.

"What are you doing?!" cried the old man.

But Melicles knew what he was doing. He held onto the old man's arm and, pulling him, reached the sea in a few strides, strode into the water, plunged into it up to his ankles, to his knees, and waded on, disregarding everything else. The water was icy cold, but the boy paid

94

it no heed: fear lit up their bodies with great fire; they felt hot, not cold. Stumbling over underwater stones, waist-deep in water, Melicles reached one of the offshore boulders, and once there, he first helped the old man climb up, then pulled himself up onto the slippery rock. He slipped again and again, cutting his hands on the rock, but the terror of his position gave him strength. Finally, he found support with his back to the rock. His one hand propped up Nehurabhed, the other clutched a protruding edge.

Ahead of them, on the beach, a dozen or so steps away, the shadows of the wolves slunk about in the dark. The wolves tried to follow their escaping prey into the water, but as soon as they lost ground with their feet, they turned back to land, grunting and scowling in rage. A wolf can swim, but he cannot fight in water.

Finally, the wolves gave up and sat down in a semi-circle on the beach, now and then giving a blood-chilling yelp from their hungry maws. And so they faced each other in the darkness, the two men and the dozen wolves for long minutes, then hours.

The boy, soaked through, frozen with cold, felt as if his skin was gripped by an icy armor right down to his belly. His teeth chattered, but he stood still, aware that he might slip and fall into the sea at the slightest twitch. Now and then, a stronger wave washed his feet with icy cold, but the boy no longer felt it. His skin was numb; his bones felt twisted, stiff; cold bit ever deeper into his flesh.

Melicles felt overwhelmed with despair and fury. At times, the blind desire to rush ashore and kill the wolves with his bare hands rose within him. Whenever that happened, he only managed to hold back from that crazy step with a supreme effort of will. The horror of their situation was magnified by the fact that Nehurabhed now weakened completely. He did not complain or ask for help, but he barely hung, half-fainted, on the top of the boulder. He did not slide down into the sea only thanks to the helping hand of Melicles.

Snow continued to fall. There was silence in the air. The wolves stopped scowling and lay down on the beach, waiting. The silence was broken from time to time by the groan of the great owl or some animal's cry of agony. The usual, nightly drama of life and death was unfolding in the forest above them. All the monsters of the wilderness were out on the prowl to feed; all helpless and weak creatures clung to their hiding places, trembling.

At one point, it seemed to Melicles that the shadows of the wolves had faded away, but he couldn't be sure. The snow mixed with rain drizzled thicker and thicker. He could hardly distinguish the shoreline in the darkness – a darkness blacker than the night. In his eyes shimmered imaginary shadows of wolves, coastal boulders, splashes of foam, the undulating sea, everything mixed and confused together. He could no longer distinguish anything. He became overwhelmed with supreme fatigue, faintness, drowsiness.

Whenever that happened, he would dig his fingers in the rock until they hurt, until the skin cracked, so as not to fall asleep, lose balance, and fall into the sea.

It was a terrible night.

After many long hours that seemed like centuries, gray, dirty dawn began to lift the darkness. It was no longer snowing. The coast was empty. The wolves disappeared somewhere; perhaps they found some other prey. The day was rising.

Melicles climbed into the water with difficulty. Movement restored strength to his numb limbs. Half dragging and half carrying the old man, he transported him ashore. Then he sprinted along the beach, turned back and sprinted again, pounded himself with fists, pinched, and slapped at his skin until he warmed up. He then began to rub Nehurabhed's hands and feet hard until his blood circulated more vigorously in him. The old man then rose and leaned on the boy's shoulder, and they started forward again.

They walked on along the beach, ahead, ahead, to leave this terrible place as quickly and as far behind as possible. The old man stopped to catch his breath every few hundred paces, then walked on in despair but with fierce persistence.

Walking warmed them up and restored them to life. And then the rising sun, finding an opening in the clouds, shone upon them and strengthened them with hope, dried their soaked garments, warmed them with its warming rays.

They rested every few hundred steps. When the old man sat resting, Melicles scrambled up to the top of the cliff, looking around, checking for smoke, any sign of human habitation, or any sign of a boat. All in vain. Their monstrous fatigue and cold were now joined by hunger. They had had nothing to eat since noon of the preceding day. Melicles found a pair of ancient oaks at the edge of the forest and collected a few handfuls of acorns. He shared them with the old man, deceiving their hunger with the miserable fare.

And so, they walked on, or rather dragged on patiently, for most of the day.

Only towards the evening, when they were already resigning themselves to the idea of sleeping rough on the beach again, did Melicles notice human footprints and a path leading up the cliff. He followed the trail, leaving the weary old man on the coast.

The path took him into the forest, and after a while, he reached a small clearing. At its edge stood a poor wooden hut. It was a very simple affair, built of untreated logs, insulated with moss, and covered with a roof of grass, black and sooted with smoke. A giant emerged from under its roof: an immensely tall creature, overgrown like his hut. Thick, shaggy covered his entire face in which only his eyes shone like little black pieces of coal.

Melicles froze, thinking that evil fate had thrown him, as it once did Odysseus, prey to some cyclops, satyr, or some other evil forest deity. But the giant, as much surprised by the meeting as Melicles was himself, did not show evil intentions. He had difficulty communicating with Melicles because he spoke in a strange language, half barbaric, interweaving Greek words with foreign ones and oddly distorting them all. He was a highlander from the wild, semi-barbarian tribe of Epirots – mountaineers, shepherds, and hunters – dwelling in this wilderness and, like their land, remote, inaccessible, and dangerous.

Having learned that the old man on the beach was a priest, the giant proved eager to assist them. The fame of nearby Delphi was great, and the general respect for the priestly cast was well established.

Without a word of opposition and even with a certain humble zeal, the wild highlander set off with the boy to fetch Nehurabhed.

It was already nightfall when they returned to the hut, half-carrying the old man. An hour later, the two travelers, drunk full of hot milk and fed with cheese, buried themselves up to their heads in bear- and wolf-skins and fell sound asleep.

Three days later, they walked on again, heading south along the shore. They were both refreshed and healthy. The iron health of the young boy endured all the hardships unscathed, and the old man was used to winters a hundred times colder than this. The fever caused by food poisoning passed away, leaving no trace on his face or hands. Everything was fine again. They had survived.

Though seemingly wild and formidable, the highlander had treated Nehurabhed with submissive humility and accompanied them part of the way to the nearest settlement. Gradually they came into flatlands, and the terrain became less wild. They now walked past meadows with grazing animals, fields plowed over and sewn with winter grain, and the air was not so cold anymore: winter – never too harsh in these parts, relaxed her biting breath.

"And so, we survive to live another day," Nehurabhed said to Melicles as they rested on a grassy bank of a stream. "It is good that you cared for me in my illness, my boy. It is good that Philolaos threw us off his boat, but it is even better that you didn't leave me then. Because if it weren't for you, I would have died not once, but ten times, both from exhaustion and cold, and perhaps devoured by the wolves," he said softly, nodding his gray, dignified head, as was his custom.

"Yes, yes, my boy, it is all good, all good. And only one thing went wrong. You see, Melicles, sometime sooner or later, here in Greece, or in Egypt, or in Asia Minor, we will have to part ways. That time will come. Well, it's life, I suppose, and each of us must make his own way. But then, just then, well, Melicles, when the time comes..." The old man stuttered. "Then, you see... it will be a very sad moment."

Chapter Eleven
# That Ship Again

They reached the first town in this sparsely inhabited country a few days later. It was a poor little harbor town: no more than a dozen houses and a dozen boats in the port. They were now in Acarnania. Ships from Greater Greece sometimes stopped here – ships from Taranto, Croton, and Brundisium. Nehurabhed had little hope of finding a long-distance boat in such a small port, a boat going all the way to Egypt or Crete, but he hoped to get on any boat to any bigger, busier city where they might then find such a ship.

But the opportunity came sooner, and it was far better than they could have expected.

On the second day after their arrival, a large galley with two dozen crew came into the bay. It was a magnificent ship. It had a raised prow carved into the shape of a large fish and forty oars on each side. The settlement became animated, and the shore swarmed instantly with vendors running out to meet the boat. Everyone was in a hurry because the ship was stopping only for a few hours.

Nehurabhed and Melicles also rushed ashore, asking about the ship along the way.

"It's a ship from Syracuse, going all the way to Egypt," someone told them

They came on board, asking to see the commander of the boat, and their jaws dropped open with amazement when he came out to see them, parting his sailors with an imperious gesture: it was none other than their good friend, Kalias.

Kalias had changed a little, now bearing himself with the dignity appropriate for his high office of second-in-command of a large merchant ship. He was astonished to see Nehurabhed and Melicles and welcomed them joyfully. Nehurabhed explained in a few words that he had argued with the crew of the Spartan ship and disembarked, not wishing to go any farther with that crew. He did not mention his imprisonment, illness, and removal from the ship. Instead, he asked the Greek to take them to Egypt. Kalias agreed without hesitation and cleared the decision with Sotion, the commander. And so, they were on their way to Egypt again.

They sailed along the wooded banks of Acarnania, passing on the starboard the land of Ithaca, barely visible far away in the low-lying mist – the native island of divine Odysseus. Then, on the port side, they saw the narrow mouth of the Gulf of Corinth, teeming with all sizes of sailing ships. And then, as they now sailed along the shores of the Peloponnese, they passed the small port of Elis, situated near the mouth of the river Alpheios.

There, out of sight, beyond Alpheios and beyond a range of low hills barely visible on the horizon, lay the sacred grove of Olympia, beloved of the gods, a revered corner of Greece. The world-famous

Olympic games were held there every four years in honor of the great god Zeus.

Every four years, all who would gain fame for their cities – Greeks from Miletus and the Hellespont[38] and the Black Sea – gathered there to compete in honor of the gods. There they met their fellow Greek competitors from Croton, Neapolis, and Syracuse, and, with surprise and joy, they rediscovered the fraternal similarity of customs, traditions, and beliefs. During the breaks between competitions, there were ceremonies, parades, processions, singing, and dancing, so that the whole time spent near the sacred groves turned into one magical pageant.

Everyone who had ever attended the Olympic Games, and there were a few among the numerous crew of the ship, remembered those solemn moments with reverence and profound emotion. They looked with nostalgia towards the distant site. They recalled the beautiful temple of Rheia – the mother of Hera[39] – and, above all, the gigantic statue of Zeus, the father and king of all gods, and the great ancient trees of the sacred grove dedicated to him.

Many years ago, Kalias himself, while still a young man, was dispatched by his Syracusan family to participate in the games. So now, of course, he talked loudest – about the near victories he allegedly won, describing his consummate skill in jumping and discus throwing. Sailors gathered around him and listened to him with the rapt attention due to their commander.

However, they did not enter any of the ports from which the road to Olympia led. Indeed, they avoided all major ports because, like the Spartans, they feared the plague of which the news still circulated widely.

They traveled slowly: the ship was heavy with goods, and Kalias did not want to exhaust his rowers ahead of the arduous sea crossing awaiting them beyond Crete. Days passed slowly, varied only with storytelling and sometimes a quarrel among the crew.

---

[38] *Hellespont*: Greek name of the straits of Dardanelles
[39] *Hera*: Greek goddess, wife of Zeus

Kalias blossomed in his new position in the center of attention of a crowd of subordinates. He was in his element: he commanded, shouted, boasted, bragged, mocked, galled, derided, and cursed. There was plenty of him everywhere, whether he was needed there or not. At the drop of a hat, he would explode with anger, stamp his feet, his face red; it seemed that he would rush with his fists at his poor victim. But in fact, he never hurt anyone, he didn't deal out any punishments, and everything always ended in just that: a great torrent of loud tongue-lashing.

The crew obeyed him, even if they sometimes mocked him in private. They found his volatile personality entertaining, with its quarrels and boastful tales lavishly laced with inspired curses. It all served to break up the monotony of the long journey.

And the journey was long indeed.

On the seventh day, they left the Greek mainland behind and set off for the open sea, and on the ninth, before evening, they came to the legendary land of Crete, famous for its many wonders.

They landed at Heraklion, a port in the vicinity of Knossos – the same Knossos which, in heroic times, had been the capital of a powerful state, perhaps the greatest sea power of ancient times. There had once been magnificent palaces here, swarming with courtiers, but now they had all turned to ruin. Delightful gardens had once descended in manicured terraces to the sea, but now they had turned into an unruly jungle. A few centuries ago, an invasion of peoples from the north demolished the great state, smashed its palaces and temples, and ravaged the land. An island blossoming with wealth and power became a desert, and only legends of its former glory circulated among the inhabitants of mainland Greece.

Colorful myths were told about treasures hidden under the palace ruins and about the underground labyrinth, guarded by the monster Minotaur. Storytellers derived genealogies of their greatest heroes from legendary Cretan ancestors, thus borrowing a little of the glory of ancient Crete.

The island never really recovered from its fall. It gradually repopulated with new settlers from Phoenicia, the Greek mainland,

and the Ionian islands in the centuries since its despoliation. But there were now at most a few dozen villages here, perhaps a score of settlements in all, and only a few towns. All this was merely a pale shadow of its former glory.

These days, Heraklion, where their ship now came to dock, was a meager Greek town with a small port at the mouth of the river. There were only a few sailing ships here, some fishing boats, and one great galley distinguished by its mighty size and the gray, gloomy color of its sails.

Melicles recognized this galley instantly: it was none other than the hateful Spartan ship. Nehurabhed recognized it, too, but showed no reaction. He had always guessed that such a meeting was possible and now, just in case, decided not to disembark during what he expected would only be a short visit.

But things turned out differently.

The Syracusan ship had suffered some minor damages during its journey. Although they were slight, Sotion and Kalias decided that it was better to make the repairs now before they set off on the sea leg to Egypt, across the vast expanse of empty water. This small and peaceful harbor seemed an excellent place to break for a few days.

They moored to the shore a few hundred steps from the Spartan galley and planned to remain there for several days.

Melicles was initially worried about it, but seeing that Nehurabhed didn't seem to take the matter to heart, stopped paying it any heed. They were now in completely different circumstances, no longer among the hateful Spartans but in the care and under the protection of the Syracusans. Nothing could threaten them.

And so, carefree and at peace with the world, the boy set out with a few young sailors ashore to explore the city one morning. Having found nothing remarkable among the few cramped clay hovels of the town, they decided to explore the former palace courtyards. They wandered among the old ruins for a long time, climbed the crumbling castle wall, and prowled among the broken fragments of gates and fallen columns.

Small lizards, basking in the sun on cracked stone stairs, bolted away, frightened by the sailors' laughter. Grazing goats stared at them mindlessly, nibbling clumps of grass where centuries ago, the great kings of land and sea received heroes and ambassadors in sumptuously decorated halls. Great trees now grew on the ruins, splitting the masonry with their powerful roots. Sometimes, from small scraps of tattered and blackened plaster, strange paintings of unknown people or deities looked down on Melicles. This was a melancholy, deserted, bone-dried world, slowly disintegrating into rubble and dust.

But Melicles was far from sad. He enjoyed the green grass of spring shooting up among the rubble and gazed with delight at the marvelous sight looming above the ruins. Behold! Down there, among the rocky hills, lay the town, the bay, and the port – and, in the port, their ship! Sun shone on the surface of the water, and beyond that lay the sea, the blue, glorious sea. And above it rose the great blue sky, bluer yet than the sea. And there, on the slopes of the hill, grew a magnificent green forest. And what a delicious forest! Lush, subtropical vegetation: palm and fig trees, acacia and rhododendron, giant cedars and plane trees, bushes of rose and mimosa – all growing together, in a crazy riot, fresh, fragrant, and juicy.

In Epirus and Acarnania, in the north of Greece, where they had just been, it was still freezing winter, but here, in this country, there was eternal warmth, winter was no more than early spring, a mere short rest in fruit-bearing, alternately bathed in streams of rain and sun. And now the sun was high in the sky, golden and delicious like an orange, and hot.

Melicles and his companions ran through the forest, yelling and shouting. They parted the rich, moist greenery with their hands. They rushed blindly through the thicket until they emerged into the sun again at the bottom of the slope, at the mouth of the river flowing into the bay. Here, they tore off their clothes and plunged into the water, swam, and splashed, dove, and swam underwater, not emerging until they reached the other side.

Melicles challenged his companions to a swimming contest. They took him on, thinking they could easily beat him, the little kid. But Melicles laughed at them in the secrecy of his heart. In Neapolis, two years ago, when he had really been no more than a child, he used to beat the city's best swimmers by two full-lengths, and now he was incomparably stronger, bigger, and firmer.

He'd already recovered from the injury he'd received in Syracuse, and he looked with joy at the resilient muscles flexing under his smooth skin. Blood pulsed in his veins in a strong, joyful rhythm. He felt power, health, life brimming inside him.

And, of course, he won the swimming race and then won it again and again until the irritated Syracusans began to pelt him with lumps of wet sand and splash him with water. They shoved and pushed like children, their body heat blazing because the water had been so cold. Then they headed back to their ship, singing, half-walking, half-running along the bay.

And then Melicles froze: they were now walking past the Spartan galley. Out of the galley, over the plank in a long procession, slowly wobbled heavily loaded slaves one after the other. They walked down onto the shore and then up to a warehouse in town. They walked with difficulty on their emaciated legs, lugging on their backs sacks and crates and jars. They walked, panting, exhausted. They deposited their burdens in the warehouse then returned to fetch new loads. Several Spartans with flogging rods in their hands stood watch over the work.

The gloomy procession passed before Melicles's eyes. The boy shuddered and took a step back because, suddenly, his eyes met those of one of the slaves. It was that same oarsman, that fellow with a great shaggy head who had turned to him there, below the deck of the ship, at the fifth window, with his urgent plea.

The other recognized him, too. For a moment, the eyes of the unfortunate flashed a brief hint of despair – or perhaps a plea. He paused for a blink of an eye. His lips moved as if to say something, but he said nothing and silently walked on, hunched even lower.

Melicles stood motionless for a long time, and then, with a slow, heavy step, he started on his way. His companions, the Syracusan sailors, ran past him and jeered him from afar. But the boy didn't answer; he paid them no heed. He walked slowly, with his head bowed, biting his quivering lips.

Chapter Twelve
# Swimming At Night

Late at night, when the whole world fell into sleep and silence, Melicles crawled out on the deck. He took off his clothes, hid them behind a coil of ropes, and slipped over the side and down into the water. Then, slowly, carefully, so as not to make the slightest murmur, he swam towards the Spartan ship.

The black shadow of the enormous galley loomed clearly in front of him against the starry sky. The boy came right up to the ship, then rounded the bow. He remembered clearly at which oar the unfortunate galley slave had sat. Now, he swam to that spot and stopped, resting his hand on the side of the ship.

There was a lamp up on the deck, but here, overboard and just below the ship, there was complete darkness.

Melicles waited until his eyes adjusted to it. He listened; there was complete silence all around. He looked up and saw the oar openings. He counted them: first, second, third, fourth, fifth – yes, this was it. He heaved himself slowly out of the water, caught the edge of the opening with his strong fingers, raised himself up, and scratched very gently on the side of the boat. Once. Then again. His heart pounded in his chest like a hammer. He heard a barely audible whisper.

Melicles pulled himself up with both hands and pressed his face against the opening. Now, he heard and understood, heard and was heard. Yes, it was the same prisoner, the same voice twitching with pain, though now subdued, muffled. Melicles whispered into the opening, and they talked this way for a long time, not so much whispering as breathing at each other.

After some time, the boy slipped into the sea and swam back towards his ship.

The keenest eye would not have spotted his head in the darkness, and the keenest ear would not have caught the slightest murmur of the water parted by his arms. Unnoticed by anyone, he climbed back into the Syracusan ship. He sneaked back onto his mat and lay down next to Nehurabhed.

But he hardly slept a wink that night. He was cold and, at the same time, feverish. He pondered ten times, a hundred times, everything he had learned. He considered dozens of escape and rescue plans.

The slave he had spoken to was not Greek; he was Tyrrhenian. That was what the Greeks called Etruscans, a people from central Italy. The man had fallen into Greek captivity seven years ago. For seven years now, he had served as a rowing machine, constantly chained to the oars of the Spartan ship. For seven years now, he had lived the most horrible life of a galley slave – a life that evoked pity and terror even among other slaves.

At first, the unfortunate man deluded himself, hoping that his family might find a way to ransom him. Twice in the first couple of years, he thought he had succeeded in sending a message to his hometown; even now, he wanted to send a message home through Melicles. But, in fact, he no longer had much hope that this would be successful. Melicles, who knew only too well the customary usage of the human market, knew that ransom, if it came, then it always came in the first two years of captivity – or it did not come at all.

Besides, the Tyrrhenian did not have a wealthy family. And more importantly, his family, judging from his story, had either perished in the tragic war in which he was taken or they, too, went into captivity. No rescue from that direction could be expected, and Melicles could only deprive the man of all remaining illusions.

But then, the Tyrrhenian turned to him with a different request:

He had lived this awful life for seven years now. He did not want to and could not live this life any longer. He wanted to try to run away or at least die trying. He realized that escape was not really possible and that, therefore, he would probably die. So much the better. Let all this misery stop now. This week, during these few days on land, when they would be unshackled to carry cargo, he must attempt his escape.

The Spartans would catch him and either crucify him or flog him to death, objected Melicles. But the Tyrrhenian would not listen. The Spartans would catch with him, yes; they would hunt him down like a dog, yes; but they would not take him alive. Not this time. Never again. That was why he must have a sword, one, simple, sharp sword to kill as many of the scoundrels as he could and then perish with a weapon in hand, like a soldier. Sword in hand. It was all he asked, his last request, his only request. He begged for it with tears in his voice. Put this sword on the deck, right between the cargo crates. When he went out in the morning to take a load, he would find it. And then everything would be decided very quickly. And one way or another, he would be free. Free.

Melicles advised him against this desperate step, but he himself did not know what to do. How terribly well he understood the prisoner's plea! To die taking revenge, fighting to his last breath – how many times he himself had dreamed that dream! How many times he prayed for just that kind of death, reaching out his manacled hands to Zeus. He did not refuse the Tyrrhenian, but he made him no promises, either. He only promised that he would return the next night. Then they would decide something.

But now, he lay there in the dark and could not come up with anything. The Tyrrhenian had told him that all the galley slaves were ready for any madness, any desperate step only to end their vile life. And so Melicles thought that maybe, if they could all break out and run at the same time, and if they scattered in all directions, it would be easier for a few of them to slip away in such a confusion, hide somewhere and remain free. The first thing to do was to examine the entire area, examine the lay of the land.

From early morning the next day, Melicles went out scouting. He walked all around the port, the entire nearby coast, and carefully examined the forest grove where they had swum the day before. He went out to the surrounding hills and asked shepherds about mountain paths. And he returned despairing, without a single good idea.

The only larger forest nearby, which could offer, at best, only temporary shelter, was this one remnant of the former royal park. Beyond this forest and all around, there were only rocky hills covered with tufted juniper and stunted cypress, where even goats could not hide. Besides, to get to the forest, a man would have to run the whole length of the port, where there were always crowds of fishermen and local sailors. And every one of them would gladly take part in the chase, if only for the expected prize money.

And these people knew all the roads and paths, all the thickets and hiding places, incomparably better than Melicles could ever learn them in the next few days. And they had watchful dogs and horses and donkeys at their disposal. Any attempt to escape under these circumstances would have to fail, thought Melicles.

But did he have the right to deny hope to the slaves?

Out of this place of despair, he decided to confide in Nehurabhed. Meanwhile, at the ship's plank, he met Kalias returning from the city, redder than usual, more agitated than usual, wheezing loud with barely contained fury.

There, in town, he had just met Philolaos, who dared to demand from him – from him, Kalias! – that he give up Nehurabhed, a suspected spy. That Spartan dog must have learned somehow that

Nehurabhed was present on the Syracusan ship. He then told Kalias that he had orders from Sparta to capture and imprison Nehurabhed and, seeing that that argument did not carry much weight, offered him money in exchange for the old man. Kalias was incensed by this proposal and replied that perhaps it was the custom in Sparta to betray one's house guests in return for money, but this was not the custom in Syracuse.

"A traveler on my ship is a guest in my house," he said proudly. And the commands of the Spartan government, thanks be to Zeus, did not yet extend to Syracuse.

They exchanged hard words, and Philolaos, flying into passion, pointed out to Kalias that he had taken onto his ship a pox-ridden foreigner, an infected dog, spreading hideous disease among righteous Greeks. These last words really hit home. Kalias was not just furious because of the brazen demand of the Spartans but also mad at Nehurabhed that he had dared to mount his ship immediately after such a terrible illness and sleep and eat among his men.

Melicles, seeing that the whole thing had already come to light, told Kalias the whole story: how Nehurabhed successfully feigned disease with the help of innocent prawns, how they fooled the Spartans, and how they were marooned in Epirus. Kalias did not want to listen at first, but then he stared at him in disbelief, then with amazement, and, finally, when he understood the whole truth, he was struck speechless and stood there silent for a while.

Then his belly began to shake, his hands began to slap his thighs, he turned beet-red and snorted in an unstoppable, broad, thunderous laughter. He choked until tears fell from his eyes; he ran up the gangplank and, finding Nehurabhed, gave him a hearty hug. Nehurabhed took this sudden outburst of tenderness with utmost amazement, but Kalias turned right around and rushed ashore. He then practically flew to the tavern where sailors and port workers took their afternoon drinks. There he found Philolaos with his companions and a group of his own crew. And then he began to make fun of the Spartan. He made fun of his boundless naivety, teased and taunted, mocked and jeered until all were bursting with laughter.

"They had him in their hand!" he shouted. "They had him in their hand, and they told him to leave. No! They ordered him to leave! Gentle lambs! Good gods! They ordered him to hasten! O, gracious ones! O, charitable souls!"

Philolaos was furious. The Spartans wanted to pounce on Kalias with their fists, but there were more Syracusans than Spartans, and more Syracusans were coming, drawn by the loud perorations of their leader. The Spartans left unrepentant, slamming the door and cursing and swearing – and that was the end of that brawl: the brawl that wasn't.

But both crews now watched each other with hate, and small quarrels started to break out between them.

Nehurabhed, the involuntary cause of the whole incident, was not too pleased with his unexpected fame. Also, Sotion, the actual commander who, being indisposed, did not move from the ship, was angry that the matter had gone so far. He admitted that Philolaos's demand was brazen, but he preferred to avoid quarreling with Spartans.

But Kalias was in seventh heaven. He reckoned that the crews of the two ships were more or less of equal size, but in the event of any dispute, his rowers, who were free men and old friends from Syracuse, would stand behind him; while the Spartans, of course, could not possibly call on their own rowers to fight. He was, therefore, of good cheer and regretted nothing.

Melicles, seeing Kalias's anger at Philolaos, thought this might be a good opportunity to tell Kalias about his plan. But first, it was necessary to speak to Nehurabhed. Having heard him out, the old man began to advise him against as much as talking to the slaves.

"You don't know, my boy, what you are exposing yourself to. You don't know how terribly the law punishes people for helping slaves escape."

He asked the boy to give up these childish ideas, and his voice trembled with anxiety and emotion. But the boy's stubborn resolution grew even stronger, though for now, he only gritted his teeth in powerless silence. Nehurabhed, sensing the boy's intransigence, added a further precaution:

"Do not think, Melicles, that I will always be able to save you."

"But you, my lord, you saved me then! Why don't you let me save these slaves now?"

"I saved you according to the law, in a way that no one could possibly hold against me."

Melicles lowered his head. After a while, the old man spoke very seriously:

"What are you trying to do, my dear boy? Free slaves? One or two, or many? Or all? You will not free every slave in the world! If you at least knew these unfortunates! But you don't! They are total strangers to you!"

"But I know slavery," the boy whispered.

The old man put his hands on his shoulders and looked in his face for a long time.

"You cannot live like this, Melicles," he said emphatically. "You cannot live like this. Do you hear?"

But Melicles did not answer him. He repeated in dull despair:

"I can't abandon them. I can't!"

Hoping to get through to the boy and break through his stubbornness, Nehurabhed advised him to talk to Kalias. He was sure that the clever Greek would object. And he was right.

First of all, Kalias did not understand what the point was: that someone should care about other people's slaves – and not even Greeks! – was beyond him. He did understand that Melicles wanted to play a terrible prank on the Spartans, and he liked that thought well enough. But he thought the idea was impossible and might put the boy in terrible danger. In a few words, he spelled out the utter impossibility of escape.

"Look, the slaves are not taken out to work all at once. Only some of them are, while the rest remain on the ship," he said. "At most half, maybe twenty to twenty-five men. Only three or four slave drivers watch over them, that's true, but the entire crew is always nearby, ready to jump at the first signal. Most importantly, however – and this is absolutely decisive – these galley slaves can't run. Have you seen how they walk, Melicles?"

Indeed, Melicles did notice the wobbling, uncertain gait of the unfortunates. Most of them had not done any walking in years. Onshore, they were awkward, heavy, clumsy, like ducks wobbling on the sand.

"They can't even walk properly, let alone run!" Kalias repeated. "For years, the only exercise they ever had was rowing. They do nothing else. Nothing. A lifetime of nothing, nothing else at all, just pulling and pushing the oars. On the water – well, perhaps on the water, no one in the world would catch up with them, but even a ten-year-old would catch them on land. Yes?"

Melicles understood that well; he also understood that his whole plan was falling apart. But then a thought occurred to him:

"So... What if they... Escaped by water?" he asked.

"What do you mean?"

"What if they took over the ship and escaped on it?"

Kalias shrugged.

"That might make more sense," he said after a moment of reflection. "But they would have to kill the slave drivers first, then jump back on the ship and cast off before the crew could catch up with them. Well, it is not impossible. But difficult and risky. That's a tough call."

"If only you would let me have five or six swords, my lord," the boy then said with timid stubbornness.

But Kalias was indignant:

"A nice thing it would be for an honest merchant and ship commander to engage in conspiracies with slaves!"

"But no one would know about it," the boy argued.

But Kalias forbade him even to mention it. He also announced sternly that it was time to stop talking nonsense once and for all.

And that was where that conversation ended.

But the thought of escaping by sea had lodged itself in the boy's head and would not go away. And when night fell, he swam back to the Spartan galley and talked a long time with the Tyrrhenian.

This time, however, he did not return unnoticed. Nehurabhed was awake and waiting for him, pacing back and forth on the deck. When Melicles returned, he only said reproachfully:

"You are losing your soul, my boy, remember!"

But he no longer counseled him against it.

Chapter Thirteen

# Run, Slave, Run!

The next day was very eventful.

First, in the morning, four Syracusan sailors brought a piece of shiny green stone to the beach, which they had found on the grounds of the ruined palace. The stone was polished smooth and looked like it had once been part of a large column, the rest of which probably remained buried in the rubble. Nehurabhed identified it as a piece of malachite, a semi-precious stone and probably quite valuable when in one large piece like this. Since the value of the whole column – if that was what it was – could be quite substantial, a dozen Syracusans immediately set out with shovels, crowbars, and pickaxes to the place of discovery.

However, Philolaos and the Spartans also showed up within a short time. They brought with them a peasant from Heraklion, the owner of the piece of land on which the stone had been found. Citing the peasant's property rights, they forbade the Syracusans to dig on the site.

Gods only knew how the Spartans learned of this – though, perhaps, Nehurabhed was no stranger to the matter because he had spent the entire morning sitting by the side of the ship, telling every passer-by about the discovery the Syracusans had made with effusive garrulity quite unusual in him.

Anyway, an argument broke out. Syracusans had no intention to back down. Temporarily outnumbered by the Spartans, they called for reinforcements from the ship. Kalias himself ran there with a group of rowers who had been busy with some repairs. The screams and shouting rose so high that they could be heard in the port below, even though the excavated pillar lay at the far end of town. Hearing this, Melicles also jumped, sword in hand, certain that he would now find a way to use it in battle.

So far, however, there was no battle. Both sides kept a prudent distance, threatening each other with fists, swords, and shovels – anything to hand, but none of it too close. But there sure was a lot of shouting and abuse.

It was a beautiful verbal fight. And, of course, it turned out that, in a verbal fight, no one could match Kalias. His booming voice towered over the uproar. An unstoppable stream of curses, abuse, and mockery flowed from his open mouth.

The extraordinary talent of their leader enchanted the Syracusans. Here was the master of masters! Here was a man who could curse for a whole hour without once repeating himself! Every now and then, when a particularly apt remark from Kalias aroused general delight, loud laughter erupted and screams rose up to the heavens.

Admittedly, Philolaos also called Kalias "a stuffed hog," which enraged the Syracusan. Still, it was clear to everyone that in a terrible duel of tongues, it was he, Kalias, who won all laurels.

The Spartans, a martial race, could not countenance taking such a devastating defeat lying down and, having no better verbal response, started throwing rocks at the speaker. One of the stones hit Kalias in the belly, and this abruptly arrested the fluent flow of his invective. Holding his stomach with both hands, Kalias retreated from the front ranks.

The Spartans then announced that they would smash the head of anyone who even came close to the excavated column. Or shoot him with arrows. Or stab him with swords. The Syracusans promised the Spartans the same thing. And so the two sides made two camps, and halfway between them lay the malachite pillar.

Hours passed like this. Eventually, both sides became impatient and returned to their ships, leaving only a few sentries to guard access to the column. The sentries were to stay there overnight.

Kalias returned to the ship, extremely irritated. The name of "stuffed hog" smarted, the bruised belly hurt, his blood boiled inside him. The intention to wreak hellish revenge bloomed in his brain like a beautiful tropical flower. He paced along the deck for a long time, then finally summoned Melicles. He led him to a lonely corner of the ship, looked around to see if anyone was listening and, breathing out sharply, said:

"Melicles, I'll give you those six swords. Let Hades swallow Philolaos, Sosias, and all the Spartans! I'll give you those six swords."

Then he corrected himself.

"That is, I will not give them to you. But if you wanted to take them – you know, steal them, without my knowledge or permission, the swords can be found in a green crate below the deck, at the bow of the ship."

Kalias suddenly felt great, dazzling, and brilliant. He discovered in himself the abilities of a born general, a *strategos*[40] of Agamemnon[41] and Odysseus simultaneously. His eyes flashed with fire; in a few words, he introduced the boy to his plan to crush the wretched Philolaos.

---

[40] *Strategos* (Greek): commanding general

[41] *Agamemnon*: commander of Greek armies in the Trojan war, described in Homer's *Iliad*.

"Let the slaves take these weapons," he said. "Let them seize the boat, then cast away and then row like mad wherever they want to go. But don't let them do that crazy thing when all the Spartan crew are around. No. That would be stupid. They must wait for a fight to break out upon the hill by that cursed column. Only when they see that the Spartan crew has run there, then let them begin. Start by killing the slave drivers.

"So. We do this. We attack simultaneously on two sides. A two-pronged attack. A pincer movement. You understand, Melicles? We go for the column; your slaves go for the boat. Yes? Hmm?"

Melicles understood, and his eyes shone like those of a hungry wolf. Kalias continued:

"Anyway, Philolaos will get the whipping he deserves, and that's all there is to it. Oh, grant it, great Zeus, protector of the righteous, and I will offer you a heifer and adore you as long as I live! Just remember, Melicles," he suddenly turned severe again. "Remember that I don't know anything about any slaves, any missing swords, nothing at all. If they catch you, or if your slaves betray you, I will deny everything. I will renounce you. I will sacrifice you without hesitation. I will let them kill you, crucify you, impale you on a stake – I don't care."

At this point, he reflected that, most likely, he could not keep up this terrible oath, so he added angrily:

"All right, whether I hand you over or not is my business. But you must act as if you were sure I would."

Melicles nodded.

"Now, be silent, go away, and don't come near me," ended Kalias and walked away.

And so, the die had been cast.

Melicles swam out to the Spartan galley twice that night. He had to be even more careful than in the past because the Spartans put up sentries. They feared that Kalias would try to take possession of the precious column at night, and they wanted to be at the ready. The sentries, however, stood on the shore, listening for a cry from their fellows by the column. But at least one slave driver was always awake, guarding the galley slaves under deck.

There was no one on the deck itself, though.

The night was rainy, calm, extremely dark. Under these conditions, Melicles managed without great difficulty, lifting himself over the side, to slip a valuable load of weapons between the crates – a place agreed with the Tyrrhenian.

Having done his job, he hurried back to his ship.

Kalias met him aboard but didn't speak to him. They merely nodded to each other.

Then the big day came.

Everyone understood that a decision was imminent. Repairs had been completed; the ship was ready. Sotion, sick and eager to get to Egypt, urged the crew to hurry. Therefore, the departure was to take place that day, the next morning at the latest. And this meant that the malachite column had to be taken that day or left to the Spartans.

The eyes of the entire crew were on Kalias, but Kalias remained calm and cold-blooded. Like a great general before battle, he showed no emotion. Only when he saw that normal activity began on the Spartan galley and the slaves started with the work of unloading their ship did he decide that the time had come to strike.

Softly and quietly, he summoned a dozen of the crew to the beach behind the ship, checked their weapons, took command, and led them by a roundabout path, sneaking behind warehouses and privies towards the malachite column on the hill. Behind him, he left a dozen or so rowers and sailors on the ship. They had been given swords in the event that they had to defend it from attack.

Kalias had forgotten nothing.

Melicles remained on board to see the coming action. His heart pounded like a hammer; blood pulsed in his temples. For a long time, nothing happened. Finally, Melicles heard distant screams, and then immediately, in an instant, as if on command, a swarm of Spartan sailors ran out from among the coastal buildings. Evidently, they had waited at the ready because they ran out immediately, and all were armed.

They rushed out of town and in the direction of the broken column.

Then there was apparent silence again. Everyone breathed in softly, listening for distant sounds at the far end of the bay. Melicles kept looking at the Spartan boat.

Now! Now! he thought. Now they should begin! What are they waiting for? Gods, gods!

The slaves continued to carry burdens, driven by the flogging rods of the slave drivers, humble, hunched over as always.

And there it was: the noise of battle coming from the direction of the malachite column.

Melicles wrung his hands in despair.

Suddenly, a close, terrible scream split the air. A man pushed off the deck of the Spartan galley and tumbled head down into the sea. At the same time, a great tumult arose on shore; the slaves threw their loads down and hurried back onto the galley. A battle raged on the plank, swords flashed, someone fell into the water again, someone groaned, called for help, someone jumped off into the sea and swam ashore. The slaves pushed their way towards the ship, crowding, shoving. They were up there in a moment; everyone was on board now, pulling up the plank and cutting off the lines.

The Syracusans looked at everything with utmost amazement. One of the Spartan slave drivers ran, screaming, towards the city.

Melicles's fingers tightened on the railing of the ship. Sweat dripped from his face.

"Zeus, Zeus, when will they push off?" he whispered through clenched teeth.

There was hectic activity on the Spartan galley, people were running to and fro, oars began to emerge from beneath the deck. But they were still at the shore. The boy trembled as if in a fever. Suddenly, he saw the Spartan sailors running down the slope, from the site of the column, down into the city. They ran head over heel just to reach the ship on time to catch and crush the rebels. And yet the galley was standing still!

*They can't see them!* thought the boy. He wanted to scream and bit his fingers with impotent rage. Nehurabhed put a hand on his shoulder, clenching his arm until it hurt. The Spartans were now emerging on the beach, running pell-mell towards the ship. But just then, the oars bit into the water, and the ship jerked suddenly, swayed, and pushed away from the shore. Now the oars were working. One, two, one, two. The distance from the land began to increase. Twenty paces, thirty paces, fifty.

The boy breathed a heavy sigh of relief.

Philolaos and his companions ran helplessly up and down the shore, yelling and cursing. Someone began to throw stones at the galley, but it was already several hundred paces away from shore. Frantic, a few Spartans began to push one of the small sailing boats lying on the beach into the water, hoping to chase the galley, but it was useless: the galley was by now in the middle of the bay and heading out to sea at full speed. Trying to give chase in a small sailing boat, equipped with two or three pairs of oars at most, on a calm, windless day like today was hopeless.

The galley was now speeding away, her oars beating the sea in wonderful harmony. She headed away from land, as straight as an arrow, north, north, chased by the impotent cries and curses of her erstwhile masters.

Their anger now turned against the Syracusans, whom they accused of collusion with the rebels. It reached a crescendo when they saw a horde of Syracusans returning from beyond the city, carrying their malachite loot, Kalias at their head. Kalias had excavated only part of the column and found that the rest of it was broken into tiny pieces. So, he picked up only the larger fragments and set off with them and the entire crew back towards his ship.

He and his men arrived just in time, for the Spartans were livid with anger. It was absolute havoc now. Several Spartans had been killed or wounded in the fight with the slaves; a few had set sail for the sea trying to catch the galley; the rest, led by Philolaos, did not equal even half the Syracusans in number. For all their famed valor, the Spartans would have paid dearly for the outburst of violence had it not been for Sotion. He had had enough of the whole business. He was surprised and furious to hear that he had been accused of conspiring with galley slaves, and, rising from his sickbed, he ran ashore. He was not afraid of the Spartans, but he was afraid of being accused of conspiracy: he was afraid that this whole business might end up besmirching his reputation and banishing him from the profitable Taranto trade.

So, he ran between the already-fighting sailors and broke up the fight. And old Sosias, too, seeing that any confrontation with the Syracusans must now go against his men, did his best to hold back Philolaos. And thus, the historical Battle of Heraklion between Spartans and Syracusans... never took place.

Sotion, wishing to avert the suspicion that he deliberately incited the slave rebellion so that he might seize the malachite column, ordered further excavations to stop immediately and his men to return to the ship. After a short argument with his superior, Kalias had to give in. His thirst for revenge was fully satiated, and the value of the shattered column was far less than anyone had expected.

A few hours later, the Syracusan ship cast off from the shores of the peaceful and sleepy port of Heraklion.

Nehurabhed and Melicles stood by the ship's bow, looking out towards the sea. The old man stole a curious glance at the boy every now and again. And he, Melicles, stood erect, somehow taller than his usual medium height, and looked straight ahead – out to sea, towards the horizon. He was looking to the north, where the galley had disappeared in the distance, powered by her rebellious slaves.

What would happen to them now? Where would they go? Where would their fate carry them? Would they scatter along foreign shores? Would they reach their cities and families? What would tomorrow bring?

No one could know. But one thing was certain: today, they had regained control of their lives. With the rudder of their life in their hands again, they could now face the world, work, and fight to shape their fate. They were no longer a mere shameful bundle of muscles, driven by someone else's whip. Today, they became men again.

And who is man but he who fights to shape his own fate?

And not only his own. Yes, Melicles?

# PART TWO

Chapter Fourteen
# Temple Secrets

Memphis: the immemorial capital of Egypt. The holy city of gods –
and of its kings, gods' equals. A city as ancient as the Nile and as the
desert sand, and as ancient as the never-ending struggle between the
life-giving river and the death-dealing wasteland.

In the first days of his stay in Memphis, Melicles was stunned by its
enormous size and uniqueness. He had known big cities in his short
life: Miletus, Carthage, Syracuse, Taranto. They were all crowded and
noisy, their streets full of people and traffic and commerce. Here,
however, everything was not only huge but also completely different.

The vast river, the extremely long harbor quay; the straight,
narrow, very long streets, some stretching for miles, tightly crowded
on both sides with three-story houses; the houses all looking like each
other, once covered with brightly colored plaster now faded and

shabby and peeling, all equally gray and drab. Some, uninhabited for years, unused, were slowly crumbling into rubble, staring at passers-by with the empty sockets of broken windows, like skulls. Rubble of broken bricks and desiccated clay spilled out of their bellies onto the street.

These skeletons of ancient human dwellings, not found in any other city Melicles had seen, made a depressing sight. The city itself, however, had not died. There were many people in the streets. But there was none of the usual hustle and bustle, common in great ports. And if you heard any loud voices, shouts, or quarrels – those voices seemed always to belong to Phoenicians or Greeks or Syrians. The Egyptians themselves were distinguished not only by the copper color of their skin but, most of all, by their external calm. They did not laugh but at most smiled; they did not run but only quickened their pace; they didn't shout, just spoke more slowly and clearly. There was in their eyes a kind of weariness as if nothing in the world mattered.

The people were poor, humble, emaciated, and listless. It was rare to come across aimless strollers, but one often came across workers marching in units under the command of a man with a stick. Some of them carried goods; others led pack animals; others pushed loaded carts. Melicles at first thought they were all slaves. But he was wrong. It was the ordinary urban population employed in port works, in unloading ships, repairing canals, and shoring up the banks. Their lives, it seemed, were not significantly different from those of slaves. Over the millennia, all their energy, free time, and resources had been confiscated by the omnipotent state in constant pursuit of its own monumental goals.

It seemed almost as if slowly, over these millennia, the people had been taught by their all-powerful priests to demand nothing for themselves or their families. Obedient, retiring, they never seemed to rebel against their priests and royal officials; they took their beatings which were their everyday bread; paid their astronomical rents and taxes; and worked, worked, worked. Only their eyes grew gloomier, and sometimes it seemed that one detected a dull indifference in their faces. Overworked and underfed, the population was shrinking. Egypt was dying.

A century ago, its weakness had reached a breaking point and its greatest enemy, Assyria, conquered the country. Egypt eventually liberated itself after several dozen years of devastating warfare. It regained its freedom with foreign aid and largely with the hands of foreign mercenaries, mostly Greeks. Egypt was independent again, but there was no return to its former glory.

Outwardly, everything seemed to follow the old, eternal mode. Priests and high-ranking state dignitaries lived in plenty. They had beautiful palaces and gardens, armies of servants, magnificent litters, and exquisitely gilt boats. The army was quite numerous and well-equipped but consisted largely of foreign mercenaries – Greeks, Ethiopians, and Libyans.

The ports were crowded, full of ships, but all these ships, all warehouses, and all workshops belonged to enterprising foreigners. These foreigners also owned or leased some of the richest agricultural estates throughout the land and exploited them mercilessly, giving nothing in return. Melicles was astonished to see the crushing majorities of foreigners in Egypt's coastal cities: Greeks, Phoenicians, Libyans, Ethiopians, Syrians, Lydians, Arabs, Jews. Here, in ancient Memphis, these foreigners were fewer, but even here, entire districts had been taken over by them. The Egyptian population of the city, poor and exhausted, looked enviously at these busy visitors with their disorientingly different customs, costumes, speech, and religion.

And the foreigners quarreled among themselves: the Phoenician with the Greeks in particular; disputes and disagreements broke out daily, there were frequent fights, every few years a riot. The priests and officials of the great king did the best they could to keep these animosities from spilling over.

Melicles stood in the vestibule of the great temple of Ptah[42], the oldest and the most venerable temple in Memphis. It was like standing in the vestibule of a gigantic stone city because the temple consisted of a dozen or so large buildings connected by colonnades, stairs, terraces both high and low, and surrounded by monstrously thick walls with massive towers.

The boy was waiting for his master, companion, and lord, Nehurabhed, who had gone in to confer with the saintly priests of Ptah. While he waited, he looked around with superstitious fear. There loomed over him two rows of columns – heavy stone pillars. These columns seemed to fill the entire space, overwhelming the visitor with their immense, stony presence. The scant light falling from the open door and a few openings in the ceiling did little to dispel the darkness. It was murky, gloomy, quiet, and empty.

Two soldiers in temple service stood motionless at the entrance. An enormous gate at the far end of the vestibule was hung from top to bottom with a vast curtain. It shimmered with purple reflections in the uncertain light. That gate led to the first or lower temple. Melicles stepped closer, pulled back the heavy curtain, and peered behind.

It was even darker inside. The only light came from three oil lamps set on monumental tripods, glowing with reddish flames. The pale light from these lamps crawled over the reddish stone columns, the reddish stone floor, and the steps of a high dais on which a great statue stood.

The statue, made of black granite, depicted an unknown deity, seated upright, with hands folded in its lap. Out of the face of this deity, half-lost in the enveloping darkness, stared great white stone eyes, straight ahead, with an expression of all-knowing calm and perfect indifference. From the figure exuded a sense of immense

---

[42] *Ptah*: Egyptian god of wisdom and writing

power, so otherworldly, alien, and inhuman that Melicles felt a sudden shudder of horror.

Next to his own gods who were just a kind of older brethren of men, gods with human feelings, passions, anger, pride, jealousy, sometimes angry, sometimes joyful, gods who sometimes took revenge and sometimes forgave like any commoner – next to those gods – how different was this god, how alien, how strange and how incomprehensible, how utterly otherworldly. Melicles suddenly felt weak, puny, insignificant before the mysterious, indifferent power emanating from this silent statue.

He lowered the curtain and stepped back.

At that moment, a hand touched his shoulder. Near him stood an Egyptian priest, bare-chested except for a panther skin draped across his shoulder. He silently signaled to the boy to follow him. Melicles obeyed, thinking that perhaps Nehurabhed was calling him. The priest led him out of the hall, into the bright sunlight, and then through a narrow passage into a small yard enclosed by tall windowless walls on all sides.

A muffled sound of voices came through a kind of narrow lattice running in one wall, just above the ground. They were not so much voices as groans. Groans and wails of pain. Melicles shuddered. The priest touched his shoulder again.

"These are the voices of those who tried to learn the secret of our temples," he said in Greek.

And then he left.

Melicles returned to the vestibule, but he did not go in this time. He hovered as close to the exit as possible, trembling with anxiety.

Waiting for his master and companion, he whiled his time away studying the wonderful team of horses that was also waiting in the square by the gate. Four extraordinarily beautiful white horses with crowns of colored feathers pawed the ground and shook their heads. They were harnessed to a chariot positively blazing with the glow of shiny bronze finials, stars, and studs that decorated its four posts. Between the posts stretched a brilliant canopy, screening from the sun a magnificent seat upholstered in red velvet. Two drivers waited by the chariot, chatting in an incomprehensible language.

The wait was long, and finally, tired of standing, Melicles sat down on the temple steps. At that moment, a commotion began within. Four completely black, half-naked men, barely visible in the gloomy depths, pulled apart the heavy curtain – and out from behind it stepped out two Nehurabheds.

They wore equally long, flowing robes, and sported equally long, white, curly beards. They walked with equally majestic steps, holding their noble faces equally proudly upraised under their equally bushy eyebrows. Only when they passed halfway through the vestibule did Melicles notice, his mouth still agape in amazement, that while his master wore a mantle of dark blue and a bronze armband above the elbow and, on his forehead, a leather headband with bronze studs, the other master was in a dark purple robe, wore numerous gold bracelets on the wrists of both hands, and his headband was of white textile embroidered with gold thread.

They passed him slowly, descending the wide steps hot from the burning sun. The boy heard them speaking in a foreign tongue. He now realized that the stranger – the other Nehurabhed – was the second envoy of the king of the Medes, who had come to Egypt with an official mission and whom Nehurabhed had expected to meet in Memphis.

Having reached the chariot, the two men talked to each other for some time, then said goodbye, exchanging deep bows. The purple-and-gold dignitary climbed up into his carriage and drove away; the blue-and-silver one nodded at Melicles, and they walked home. Despite the seriousness and calmness of both men, the boy had sensed that they were troubled, so he kept silent as they walked.

After a long silence, Nehurabhed spoke as if to himself:

"Egypt is mysterious and dangerous. Very dangerous."

Only then did Melicles dare tell him about his adventure in the temple. The old man, having listened carefully, decided that Melicles would never again accompany him on his visits to Egyptian temples.

"The walls here are hopelessly thick and hide various dangerous secrets. My distinguished friend, whom you have just seen and who is returning to our homeland today, did not succeed in getting anywhere, in learning anything, in convincing anyone, despite four long months of work. Maybe I can. I am... grayer," the old man ended by muttering to himself.

And when they got home, he said to Melicles:

"Beware, my boy! Remember that in Egypt, it is always better to have one eye closed and not to be too curious about anything." And then he added, while stroking his beard, "Unless you absolutely must..."

Chapter Fifteen
# Anythe

Melicles was not the least upset about his master's prohibition to visit any more temples and spent most days in the company of Kalias. He often visited him on the ship, helping the crew with the loading and unloading of goods. But he was happiest when he could accompany him and old Sotion to the Greek merchant Philemon, with whom the two ship commanders were staying.

Philemon was a wealthy merchant and an old acquaintance of Sotion. He owned a large wholesale warehouse of wines and dried fruit, right next to the port. The warehouse was located in an old, dilapidated, three-story house. The entire ground floor and the tiny yard were full of crates, wine jars, and fruit baskets. There was always a wagon at the ready and a small stable with a few mules. On the second floor was the merchant's apartment, where the family lived, and a couple of rooms where visitors sometimes stayed. On the third floor were the attics and sleeping quarters of the servants. The whole house was full of people and buzzing with activity from dawn to dusk.

Melicles assisted with the bottling of wine and sorting of fruit. Kalias was surprised by the boy's sudden interest in merchant work. He even wondered whether Melicles intended to launch himself in the trading profession and hoped to apprentice with Philemon.

However, there was a different reason for the boy's sudden interest in wholesale trade: Philemon had a large family, a few small children of his own, and an older adolescent niece named Anythe.

Anythe was fourteen and lovely. Her hair was light-golden, wheat-straw-colored, falling in soft curls about her cheeks, which were often flushed with a pink blush. The playfulness of a child often struggled in her face with the seriousness of an adult, which she tried to impose on herself.

When Melicles saw her for the first time and heard her voice, high and resonant, clear as crystal, he was so confused that he could not speak. That was especially embarrassing because, just at that moment, Kalias was praising him to Philemon as a smart, exceptionally brave, and very eloquent boy.

And from that moment on, all the boy's thoughts and efforts were directed towards one purpose: to see Anythe again or at least to hear her voice. He would work several hours in the courtyard pouring wine from jars into bottles, just to catch the sight of her descending the outer steps of the house, in her white peplos[43], her uncovered head held up. He then tended to lose his breath, confuse his hands, and spill out streams of wine on the ground, just as he struggled to display exceptional dexterity.

Once, invited with Kalias to supper at Philemon's, he related to the merchant his adventures with Nehurabhed; he spoke boldly and vividly when Anythe entered, a *krater* in hand, to refill wine for the guests. At that moment, Melicles stuttered, became confused, lost the plot of his story, and clammed up until Kalias nudged him and reminded him what he had been saying.

---

[43] *Peplos*: traditional dress of Greek women

During that supper, Anythe's father, Diomenes, unexpectedly showed up. He was an officer in a Greek unit in the service of his holiness, the pharaoh: he was a *lochagos*[44] – that is, a commander of a few hundred men. He was an older man, with a severe, furrowed face and eyes staring piercingly from under bushy gray eyebrows. He had lived in Egypt for several decades. Here, he had risen from simple soldier to the rank of *lochagos*. Here he married a Greek woman who had come from Asia. Here, after losing his wife, he raised his children all alone. Here, too, he had helped raise his younger brother Philemon and set him up in business.

But Diomenes had spent his childhood in Ephesus, on the Ionian shore, and for a short time attended school in Miletus. Now, learning that Melicles hailed from there, he was kind to the boy, remembering the days of his own youth.

Diomenes now lived with his son, whom he trained to be a soldier in the military settlement near Sais, a large city in Lower Egypt where the pharaoh now resided. But he had given his daughter, Anythe, to his sister-in-law for upbringing, seeing that the girl needed a woman's hand. And now he came to Memphis to fetch her, his little Anythe – to take her back to Sais for a few months. The old soldier guessed from certain unmistakable signs that a war was brewing, and he wanted to enjoy time with his family before the coming separation. Melicles, learning that Anythe was leaving in a few days, frowned and returned to Nehurabhed's rooms severely depressed.

But then, an unexpected turn of events forced him to forget Anythe, forget Diomenes, and deal with something completely different.

---

[44] *Lochagos*: a commander of a *lochos* (between 100 and 600 men)

Chapter Sixteen
# Meet the Crocodile God

It started with Kalias drinking too much. One day, he had been sitting in a big Phoenician inn, surrounded by his sailor retinue. He had just struck a really good shipping deal and was in an excellent mood.

His theme that day was to mock the foolishness of the Egyptians, who knew nothing about trade or goods; who, in fact, were complete morons and knew nothing at all, and were bamboozled by the Greeks and Phoenicians at every turn; and, no less, by their own cunning priests who told them to worship and offer sacrifices to stupid things like bulls and rams and crocodiles. Kalias, red, sweating, spoke so loud that he could be heard all over the inn and out in the street. A few of his more sober companions tried to restrain him in vain. The man was in his element. He was talking.

In the inn, apart from the Phoenicians, there were a few Egyptian soldiers who, if they did not understand everything, certainly understood enough to catch his drift. And it wasn't like Kalias was going to leave anything to the imagination. He gestured wildly, posed, mimicked, put hands to his head to act like a bull, and bleated like a ram.

Now, Kalias had recently seen a procession in which a dozen or so priests solemnly led the holy bull Apis[45] down one of the main thoroughfares of Memphis. The stately bull walked with great solemnity, his horns painted red, his neck hung with garlands of flowers, surrounded by a crowd of the pious. At one point, however, he dropped onto the street the irrefutable proof that he was fed properly and had a healthy stomach.

The recollection of the incident delighted Kalias. Staggering uncertainly from his seat, he walked up to the Egyptian soldiers and asked them what the reverend priests commanded them to do with the sacred dung of the sacred bull. The Egyptians were embarrassed by the questioning and pretended not to understand, but Kalias proceeded to explain the matter so bluntly that the onlookers roared with delight.

The innkeeper himself finally fell on the carousing Greek and dragged him back to his seat. Kalias, however, with drunken stubbornness, advanced immediately on a new issue, to wit, of whether the sacred crocodile had the right to eat the sacred bull and what would happen in the case of such a confrontation.

The Egyptians did not wait for Kalias to continue. Red with indignation, they left the inn. Shortly thereafter, the Greek sobered up and forgot about the whole business.

But the Egyptians did not.

A couple of days later, Kalias and Melicles were walking through the city. Kalias was exuberant. All business had gone swimmingly, and he was due to set off back to Syracuse in a few days. He was now strolling in the streets, looking for gifts to take back to his wife and children. At one point, as they passed by the great temple of Sobek[46],

---

[45] *Apis*: sacred bull worshipped in Memphis

[46] *Sobek*: Egyptian god of military prowess, represented as having a human body and the head of a crocodile

half a dozen temple guards suddenly ran out of the gate. One of them rammed a sack over Kalias's head. Two grabbed his hands, two grabbed his legs, and the other two tackled Melicles to the ground. They then carried Kalias off through a small side door in the masonry. It all happened so quickly that before Melicles regained his presence of mind and flung himself to help, the heavy door slammed in his face. Only the soft groans of Kalias, muffled by the sack, could be heard through the door.

Melicles tried to open the door – in vain.

Furious, blinded with anger, he kicked the door and pounded it with fists. Silence answered him. Desperate, he began to call for help and turned to passers-by, swearing and pleading. But they ignored him, as if they had not noticed anything or as if what had just happened was the most ordinary thing in the world.

Suddenly, Melicles saw the door give way slightly. He strode up and pulled it open – and this time, it gave no resistance. Without thinking, he rushed inside.

He found himself in a long, narrow dark corridor. He stopped. He looked around. He took a few steps. Nothing. Silence. A strange feeling of terrible danger overcame him and rooted him in place. He listened. Suddenly, not so much in front of him as under him, he heard a soft hiss. He looked down: two enormous cobras were slithering along the floor towards him. One was already brushing his foot. The boy screamed in an inhuman voice and, with one leap, jumped out into the street.

He thought he had been nicked on the leg, and, looking down, he saw a few drops of blood on his shin. But there was no puncture mark. Perhaps he had torn his skin on the iron-clad door when he kicked it? But what if it was a bite of the cobra?

The boy started to run blindly, unconscious with fear. Out of breath, he burst into the little cottage where he lived with Nehurabhed. The old man was at home, and upon learning what had happened, he froze with terror. But after inspecting the nick on Melicles's shin, he calmed down considerably.

"It doesn't look like a snake bite," he said firmly.

Just in case, he opened up the wound with a knife until it began to bleed profusely. Then he studied the blood for a long time and breathed a sigh of relief. After, he fixed the boy a tincture – a glass of transparent liquid.

"This may not help, but at least it won't hurt," he said.

Melicles drained his drink in one gulp. The fluid felt cold in his mouth, but once it went down, it began to burn his insides with great heat. A scalding fire burned his throat, his head buzzed unbearably, the whole room danced before his eyes.

"O, my lord, I must be dying," whispered the boy.

Nehurabhed waved his hand dismissively. He was now quite sure the boy was in good health. He ordered him to relate the story of Kalias in detail. When he heard about the incident at the inn, he became somber, rested his head in his hands, and sat for a long time in silence.

"What to do, my lord?" whispered Melicles.

Nehurabhed shrugged.

"The man is lost," he said. "And I don't know whether anyone can help him."

"But you, my lord, know many priests. Maybe someone can intercede for Kalias? After all, Kalias was drunk! He didn't know what he was saying!"

The old man nodded.

"Oh, yes," he said. "I know well the high priest of the temple of Sobek! I know him well enough to have no doubt that he will do whatever he can to upset me. No! The worthy Mekhroes should not even guess that Kalias is an acquaintance of mine. It would only make matters worse, and they are very bad as it is. Mekhroes, the high priest of the temple of Sobek, is one of the most stubborn people I have ever known. And as those things usually go together, he is also stupid and vengeful. Kalias has fallen into terrible hands."

Melicles clenched his fists.

"But it can't be... can't be that there is no hope!" he cried from despair. "There must be some way. Some way!"

Nehurabhed was silent for a moment, then spoke with an unexpectedly stern voice:

"Kalias is an irresponsible drunk and trouble-maker. He truly deserves a proper whipping in the marketplace. If it were up to me, I would have him whipped so hard it would be a month before he could sit on his behind again. But I am afraid this is not the kind of punishment the reverend Mekhroes has in mind. I think that Kalias is in mortal danger."

He reflected for a while longer and then said.

"I will try to learn – not myself, but through some Syrian priests I know – where Kalias is now held, with what crime he is charged, and what penalty awaits him. You will now go to Philemon and Sotion and tell them the whole story, and you will beg them to do nothing until I have some information. Please explain to them that tomorrow, as soon as I know something, you will bring them the news and a plan of action. Make triple sure they tell absolutely no one that I know this good-for-nothing."

The next morning, Nehurabhed went to Philemon to explain the situation to the Greeks. A general meeting was held in Philemon's apartment: besides the host himself, there was his brother, the *lochagos* Diomenes, Sotion, Nehurabhed, and Melicles. Nehurabhed presented in a few words the horror of the situation.

"Things are very bad," he said. "Kalias has been accused of insulting a god and ridiculing sacred religion. The death penalty awaits him. If times were different, or if Kalias weren't Greek, it might have been possible to soothe inflamed passions and somehow solve the problem, and the matter might have ended in a public flogging. But as things stand now..."

Diomenes interrupted him:

"If Kalias weren't Greek? Why would that matter? Why would the reverend priests be especially bitter against Greeks?"

Nehurabhed looked at the old soldier.

"Because you Greeks," he stressed his words, "are today the least welcome of all the foreigners teeming within the land of Egypt."

Diomenes bridled at that.

"It seems strange to me, worthy foreigner, that you should say that," he said. "I have lived in Egypt most of my life. I have been here the longest of all of you, and this makes me feel justified to say that, although, certainly, there have been better and worse times in history, and I certainly have seen my fair share of riots – why, there was even an occasion many years ago, where we ended up fighting against the native troops on some sectarian issue, but one should not exaggerate the problem. His holiness, the pharaoh Apries, knows well that the Greek corps is the most valiant and effective unit in his army, and therefore, he has never allowed us Greeks to suffer any harm. The priests know it, the nomarchs know it, the court officials know it."

"Yes, yes," confirmed Nehurabhed. "You have indeed come to great prominence here. I mean to such prominence that some look at you with aversion, others with envy, and some – with fear."

"But who?!" Diomenes exclaimed.

"The Phoenicians!" whispered Philemon.

"That's certainly true," added Sotion.

"But Phoenicians do not rule in Egypt!" Diomenes said impetuously. "Egyptians rule in Egypt. There may be some occasional neighborly trouble between us and the common people here, but the entire Egyptian administration respects us and protects us."

Nehurabhed shrugged.

"Well, yes. Egyptians rule in Egypt. That is true. Or rather, the Egyptian ministers and advisers of his holiness rule in Egypt. But all of them, or most of them, are indebted to Phoenician merchants and bankers. Or receive a subsidy from them, which is sometimes higher than their government pay. Besides, the picture is far more complex than just Phoenicians. Egyptians themselves do not love you. Many feel that you are cliquish and do business with each other to the exclusion of the natives. They fear your growing wealth and importance. The priests look with a jaundiced eye on your temples, rising like mushrooms on the banks of their sacred river. And the officers of the Egyptian and Libyan units complain that all promotions go only to Greeks."

"This is all true," replied Diomenes. "But it has been so for as long as I can remember. I don't think Kalias is now in more danger for being Greek than he would have been three years ago or thirty years ago. He's just a foreigner who offended Egyptian gods."

"But I happen to think otherwise. I think that it is more dangerous to be Greek in Egypt today than it has been in many years, and certainly far more dangerous to be Greek than any other foreigner," the old man replied. "What I have learned through my work is that, in the current mood, Egyptian priests will not let slip an opportunity to deal a high-profile blow to the Greeks."

"Why?"

But here, Philemon broke in to confirm Nehurabhed's words.

"You, Diomenes," he said, "sit in your camp among your Greeks, loyal troops of his holiness all of you. So, you don't know what's going on here, in the city. We, city merchants, have been talking about this lately – there has been a lot of trouble with the locals in recent months. Egyptians now openly say things they would never have said five years ago. It isn't just words; it's also actions. There have been troubles with workers, theft, and absenteeism. There have been rising cases of arson and vandalism. Trouble collecting bills and rents. We have had reports that messengers have gone throughout the country urging peasants not to buy from Greeks. People in the city seem to avoid our stores. My own sales are almost a third off this year."

Diomenes was silent for a moment but then he continued stubbornly:

"I still think that if only Aeskhines, the commander of the Greek Corps of Heliopolis, were to intercede for Kalias with the noble nomarch of Memphis, he would obtain his release from the priests. After all, he's just an inconsequential stupid Greek who got drunk and acted stupidly in his cups. As you know, I am traveling back to Sais tomorrow. Should I stop in Heliopolis, with Aeskhines? Aeskhines knows me, and he will not refuse an old soldier's request."

But Nehurabhed shook his head:

"I doubt the nomarch would want to speak to Aeskhines now. But, more importantly, Aeskhines is no longer in Heliopolis."

Diomenes smiled dismissively.

"Forgive me, worthy sir, but I, a soldier, should know better than you. The Aeskhines regiment is in Heliopolis, so he must be there too."

But Nehurabhed replied calmly:

"Aeskhines and his regiment marched out of Heliopolis three days ago. They are now on their way to the Sinai."

Diomenes jumped up from his seat.

"What? It can't be! And how can you, a foreigner, know?"

Sotion, who had learned from Kalias who Nehurabhed was, took the old soldier's hand.

"Diomenes," he said, "our venerable guest does not speak in vain. And it is quite possible that he knows more than you, me, and all of us with Aeskhines combined."

Diomenes fell silent and sat down. Nehurabhed continued after a while:

"Aeskhines is on his way to the Sinai as we speak. All Greek troops in Lower Egypt have received marching orders for Arabia."

"And my regiment as well?" Diomenes asked contemptuously. "If you know this, my lord, you must indeed be a great sorcerer."

Nehurabhed took no notice of the Greek's challenging tone.

"Your regiment, Diomenes, belongs to the royal corps and, as far as I know, remains in Sais. However, I expect it will also be ordered to march east any day now."

"What, then, are these sudden troop movements all about?" Philemon asked. "War? War against whom?"

Nehurabhed nodded.

Diomenes jumped up again.

"I do not want to offend you, venerable man, because you are my brother's guest, but your words do not... er... cohere. If there is indeed a war brewing – and there has been some talk of that – then Egypt will need us now more than ever. By Zeus and all immortal gods, the fame of our phalanx[47] is known even in Babylon!"

---

[47] *Phalanx*: a formation of heavy Greek infantry

"Yes," replied Nehurabhed without raising his voice. "Indeed, such would normally be the case. Except if the coming war were of the sort in which your phalanx would be useless to Egypt. Or might even turn out to be a liability."

"What kind of war would that be?" the old soldier asked incredulously.

"A war against Greeks," said Nehurabhed.

Now all three, Philemon, Sotion, and Diomenes jumped up in their seats.

"A what?" they all shouted with one voice.

"A war against Greeks," repeated the old man slowly. "Against Cyrene, to be specific."

There was a long silence.

"This could be," Sotion said finally.

"It's not impossible," said Philemon.

Nehurabhed rose and looked around.

"I'm here," he announced, "not just on the business of Kalias. Of course, we must try to save him, and we still need to talk about that. But there is another matter – your business. The Greeks in Egypt are in danger. You don't want to believe it – I understand. Whether you believe it or not is your business. Based on what I have learned, I am very confident in what I say. Yesterday, I sent a secret warning to the commander of all Greek corps, Symonides. But I know this will be in vain. Symonides already knows what is coming and will do nothing to change the course of events. He does not see himself as a Greek anymore, or even an Egyptian Greek, but as a servant of the pharaoh. His one overwhelming ambition is to become, in time, the commander-in-chief of all Egyptian forces.

"A week ago, he sent packing messengers from Cyrene who had come to him to beg him to intercede with the pharaoh and persuade him to prevent the coming war. All these envoys accomplished was to alert the priests and officials who had already felt they could not fully trust the Greeks and to confirm them in their resolve to rid Egypt of all Greeks. That's why they have decided to send Greek units to the opposite end of the kingdom. And that's why they look distrustfully at everything that is Greek. There are, in fact, discussions of disarming and releasing from service of a substantial part of the Greek corps."

There was conviction and certainty in the old man's words. All were silent.

Only Diomenes spoke again:

"All of this could be true, perhaps, if Egypt indeed wanted a war with Cyrene. But why would Egypt want to make war on Cyrene, a poor little place of the sort Egypt has by the dozen on each bank of the Nile?"

"Cyrene has had some trouble with the Libyans recently, and the Libyans have complained about it to his holiness," said Nehurabhed. "But this is only a pretext. Cyrene lies far beyond the Libyan Desert and bothers the sacred land less than the grains of desert sand blown by the wind."

"And so?" Diomenes muttered.

"And so... Cyrene does not bother Egypt. But it does bother the Phoenicians. The Carthaginians are especially worried about Greek ports being established on the African coast, which, until now, had belonged to them alone. And they hate the fact that ships sailing between Egypt, Crete, Levant, and Carthage, which in the past sailed straight on to them, now call at Cyrene and Barca. Cyrene is only a little town, but it did not exist three decades ago and today has maybe thirty thousand inhabitants."

"So, Egypt will fight for Phoenician interests?"

Nehurabhed nodded.

"The Phoenicians have explained to the ministers of his holiness that this is not actually a war, just a punitive expedition for which just one army corps should be enough. They will finance the war with a large loan, and many in the government will benefit personally from various commissions on the transaction."

"There was talk about such an expedition two years ago," said Diomenes. "But it all came to nothing."

"Because, at that time, several Greek commanders made it absolutely clear that they would not fight other Greeks, and the pharaoh feared a split in the army. That was actually a very bad thing:

it showed the Egyptians that Greek units could not be trusted, that Greek units had divided loyalties. So, this time, it was decided to neutralize the Greek units in advance by sending them out into the Arabian Desert. Or dissolving them altogether."

"But the pharaoh is our friend," Diomenes defended his case.

"He was, yes. But now he is old and sick and has increasingly been ruled by others."

"It's true. That's what everyone says," Philemon whispered.

Diomenes lowered his head.

"Let's talk about Kalias," said Sotion.

"All that I said concerns Kalias as well. I just wanted to explain to you why the position of Kalias is so bad and why any attempt to rescue him will be difficult. Bad times have come for Greeks in Egypt."

There was silence in the room.

"What can we do for Kalias?" Sotion asked.

"We have to try to bribe the priests of the temple of Sobek. Of course, not Mekhroes himself, but his assistants. This will be difficult because anyone who helps an escaping prisoner can be executed in his place. How much money can you collect?" he asked.

Philemon looked at Sotion.

"Kalias is not rich," the old sailor replied slowly.

"How much could his fortune be worth? Remember that this is about his life and that the reverend priests are not used to small sums."

Sotion thought for a moment.

"One *talent*[48], maybe. Maybe one and a half," he said.

"By Mercury! A *talent* is a great sum!" Philemon whispered.

"This is probably the least that can be offered for such a favor. When can you collect it?"

There was a minute of silence. At last, Philemon said:

"I can raise two thousand shekels if Sotion guarantees it."

Sotion peered at him:

"For a year?"

"For a year."

---

[48] *Talent*: a unit of account equal to 6,000 drachmas

"No interest?"

Philemon thought about it.

"What the duce, let it be without interest," he said finally. "I'll do it for you, Sotion."

"That'll do. We can raise the rest among the crew. Everyone likes him, and they will want to help him somehow."

Philemon bit his lip.

"A *talent* is a tremendous sum," he said. "A tremendous sum."

"Let us pray that it is enough and that the saintly priests will deign to accept it," muttered Nehurabhed. "But I am afraid that no money will help this time. Yet, we have to try it because I see no other hope."

And that was the end of the conference. The Greeks promised to raise the money by the evening of the following day. Nehurabhed was to identify likely targets in the Sobek temple who might be willing to take a bribe. On his way out, Nehurabhed addressed Diomenes once more:

"And you, valiant Diomenes, if you are going to Sais tomorrow, please tell your commander, Peleas – his name is Peleas, is it not? – everything you have heard from me."

"I will," said the old soldier. "Do you really think, my lord, that the Greek mercenary units may be dissolved?"

"I pray that things might stop there," replied Nehurabhed.

### Chapter Seventeen

# The Judgment of Sobek

Nehurabhed's fears concerning Kalias turned out to be correct. The temple court decided to take full advantage of the case of the unfortunate Greek to strike terror into the hearts of foreigners and to incite the faithful against the Greeks. Kalias was sentenced to death, and the sentence was to be carried out in a few days. At the same time, his guard was doubled and assigned to trusted temple officers.

All attempts to bribe this guard failed. The temple guards knew well that the prisoner's own fate awaited them if he escaped. And they also knew that there was no place in Egypt where one could hide from the all-powerful priests.

Nehurabhed, having tried all avenues of access to the people in charge of the Kalias case and having made no progress at all, finally decided to go to the high priest Mekhroes himself. In the extreme circumstances in which Kalias now found himself, nothing could hurt his case anymore. But Nehurabhed returned from the meeting in no time, more depressed and gloomy than ever.

To Melicles, who waited for him with a trembling heart, he only said:

"All was in vain."

And he plunged into gloomy silence.

The boy wrung his hands.

"How can this be? How can there be no hope anymore?"

"Where there is life, there is hope," replied the old man.

Then he recounted his entire conversation with the venerable Mekhroes.

"The priests not only want to punish Kalias," he said, "but they want to make his punishment into a spectacle for the common people. When I asked Mekhroes to have pity on the condemned man, he answered me with great unction, that he himself was not offended, but the god was offended, and therefore only the god could forgive him. The prisoner will be put to the test, and only if the god does not kill him will he keep his life and his freedom."

"What kind of test is this to be?" asked Melicles.

Nehurabhed waved his hand doubtfully.

"There is a pond in the grounds of the temple of Sobek, right by the wall of the central shrine. In this pond dwells a crocodile which is said by the priests to be the living image of god Sobek on Earth. Well... the sentenced man must swim across this pond, clear from one side to the other. That's all. The pool is small, but it has not happened in fifty years that a condemned man managed to swim its length. The deity is not usually in the mood to spare a sinner's life, and the crocodile is always very hungry."

"This is terrible!" the boy cried.

Nehurabhed said nothing.

"Lord, what if we arm a dozen sailors and attack the crowd and guards at the pond?"

The old man shrugged.

"Nonsense," he said. "Hopeless nonsense. Don't even think about it. You will lose yourself and others in vain. There is one Kalias already; we don't need a dozen more. Have you taken a good look at this temple? At its inner courtyards? Walls five feet thick and thirty feet high? Great towers on both sides of the monumental gate? Temple guards everywhere? It is more of a great fortress than a temple."

"But Kalias cannot be left like this, my lord!"

The old man glumly rubbed his forehead.

"I need to think about it," he said.

"When are they going to execute him?" Melicles asked again.

"Tomorrow morning."

"O, great Zeus! O, merciful god!" the boy burst out. "Tomorrow! Oh, Kalias, Kalias!"

A violent sob shook his chest; a spasm clenched his throat.

Nehurabhed turned to him impatiently:

"Melicles, go away and calm down. I already told you that I need to think about it, not attend to your histrionics."

The boy left without a word and ran with the terrible news to Sotion and Philemon.

The Greeks were seized by rage and despair. They cursed Egypt, its priests, and every one of their gods and idols. They tore at their beards in powerless anger.

But they realized that there was nothing they could do.

Hours passed. Melicles, unable to find a place for himself, returned to Nehurabhed. If there was any hope, it was in him. The old man was not at home. He didn't arrive until evening, bearing a large bundle under his arm.

"Have you found a solution, my lord?" the boy asked.

"We'll try the last possible way," replied the old man. "Tonight, I will go back to the temple of Sobek to pray to the great god for mercy."

"You want to appease the god, my lord?"

The old man made an indefinite motion with his head.

"I will probably see some priests of Sobek, and I want to convince them about my piety."

"And you will cast a magical spell in the temple?" Melicles asked.

Nehurabhed bobbed his head vaguely.

"What should I do, my lord?"

"You will follow me to the temple gates and carry this bundle."

"What's in that bag?"

"A sacrificial animal, my friend. A fat, delicious goose which I shall sacrifice on the altar of the holy god."

"And you think this will help save Kalias, sir?"

"Everything is in the hand of god," replied the old man.

As dusk fell, Nehurabhed and Melicles left the house. Nehurabhed was not dressed as usual, however: he wore the robes of the priest of the great goddess Baset. He had a white linen loincloth wrapped around his hips, and his chest was bare except for a leopard skin tied around his shoulders and sloping diagonally across his torso. He wore holy amulets on his forehead, neck, and wrists. He looked grand, lavish, and dignified. Egyptians in the streets respectfully parted before him as he walked.

Melicles walked behind, carrying the offering in a sack. He had looked inside and found that it really was a goose, a regular, large white goose, recently killed, with traces of fresh blood still on its feathers.

It was getting dark as they reached the temple. Nehurabhed took the boy's burden from him and said: "You stop here, my boy, and wait for me. You will not try to enter the temple. If I do not return for a long time – well, if I don't return, then you will go to the Syrian priest in whose house we live, and you will tell him that I have not returned. That's all."

"Oh. And also..." he added in a softer voice. "If I do not return, you will go back to your mother, to Miletus, immediately. As soon as you can find any kind of passage home."

Before Melicles could reply, the old man turned and calmly walked through the monumental gate. Temple guards standing at the entrance bowed humbly before him. One of them knelt down on one knee. The old man stretched out his hand over him in a gesture of blessing and walked inside. Peering in from the street, Melicles saw him still walking down the avenue leading to the foot of the shrine.

Just to the right of that avenue, the ground descended in terraces towards a body of water, its edges overgrown with papyrus and surrounded by tall palm trees. That was the terrible pool of execution. But now, he could barely see anything in the shadow of the great palms because the whole courtyard was slowly drowning in the growing night.

Time passed. Night fell. Melicles was overwhelmed with fear for the old man. As he repeated to himself his last instructions, he suddenly realized what the master had meant: that he was in grave danger.

But Nehurabhed returned sooner than the boy had expected, with the same steady, dignified step, past the bowing guards. He motioned to Melicles, who ran behind him, asking breathlessly if the god had accepted the sacrifice.

"I don't know," replied the old man. "In any case, I have done everything to make my sacrifice acceptable to him."

"Did you cast a spell?"

"Er... Yes."

The boy looked at his companion with superstitious fear.

"And Kalias can be saved?" he whispered.

"I don't know. I don't know anything, my boy," replied the old man. "However, I did everything I could. We will see the results tomorrow."

Tomorrow!

Melicles did not sleep at all that night. He imagined what the unfortunate convict might be thinking in these final hours. He remembered his wife and his children, who had been so good to him. He prayed to Zeus, to Poseidon, the protector of sailors, to Apollo, the great god of Delphi.

In the morning, as soon as the sun rose, they went to the place of execution. This time there were no guards at the entrance to the temple courtyard. The grounds had been opened, and commoners had been allowed into the avenue leading to the shrine and onto the terraces descending to the pond so that everyone could witness the judgment of the offended god. Despite the early hour, a vast crowd had assembled already, and more people arrived with each passing moment.

Nehurabhed and Melicles squeezed as close as possible to the terrace by the pond. The fatal pool lay in front of them. It had the shape of an elongated rectangle, several hundred paces long and at most a hundred paces wide. The sides of the pool were laid with stones to the height of a grown man. From the center of the lowest terrace, narrow stone steps descended into the water. Similar steps were on the other side of the pool. The condemned man was to swim from one set of steps to the other.

The water here was calm, clean, smooth as a mirror. But all along both sides, the pool was overgrown with reeds and rushes. Somewhere there, in this tangled thicket, the old river murderer lay in wait, lovingly reared by the priests. It lurked there now, awakened by the extraordinary bustle on the shore – the bustle that had foretold the same event for years: easy hunting for the strange, awkward creature called man.

Nehurabhed bent down to the boy's ear.

"Can you see him anywhere?" he asked in a whisper.

"The crocodile?"

"Yes."

"No, my lord!"

Nehurabhed sighed heavily.

On the other side of the pool was a similar terrace, and right behind it, a small gate in the temple wall. There was excitement in the crowd. There were shouts, wild laughter, and mockery. Melicles did not understand the speech of the Egyptians, but he felt so much hatred for them that his face was burning, turning white and red, and his eyes became foggy.

Nehurabhed had forbidden him to bring any weapon to the execution and forced him to swear an oath that he would keep calm whatever happened. But Melicles could see now with his own eyes how crazy his idea of breaking Kalias out by force had been. There were dozens of temple guards on the steps leading down to the pond and on the lowest terrace around it. And more yet stood by the entrance to the main shrine. They were all armed up to their teeth and dressed especially rich for the festive event. Besides, the crowd of onlookers was so thick that one could hardly stick a needle into it, let alone hope to escape through the middle of it.

A small door opened in the side of the massive temple wall, and a procession emerged from it onto the terrace. Two priests led the way. Eight guards surrounded the prisoner; three black slaves followed with whips in their hands. It was their job to make sure the convict descended into the pool.

All eyes turned to the captive.

Yes, it was Kalias.

He was completely naked. Several days of captivity had shrunk his frame, and his skin had turned sallow. He gazed around him frantically, looked at the pool, then looked at the crowds assembled around the pond. He knew what awaited him, and he knew that there was no help. His eyes seemed hazy. His face was the very image of resignation.

Suddenly, in the general silence, Nehurabhed's loud voice was heard:

"Kalias! Kalias! Trust in the mercy of the great god Sobek and swim calmly. Trust because I am praying for you. Sobek will take mercy on you! Trust and swim, Kalias!"

All eyes turned to him. Nehurabhed raised both hands and stretched them out towards the condemned man as if he were about to bless him. Kalias saw him, too, and something like a beam of light illuminated his face for a moment. At that moment, the guards pushed him towards the steps, and the unfortunate Greek slowly descended to the edge of the water and slowly, gingerly, submerged himself and began to swim.

There was such a silence now that you could hear the splash of water parted by his strong arms.

Nehurabhed closed his eyes. Melicles cast quick glances right and left, looking for the sight of the terrible triangular head piercing the surface of the water.

But there was no sign of the god. All was quiet. Kalias was already halfway across the pool. Suddenly, there was a splash on the right. Everyone jumped, turning their gaze in that direction. But it was just a stone thrown in the water by some impatient hand. At the same time, the crowd began to shout, and the soldiers started to strike their swords against their shields to wake the apparently slumbering god.

Melicles twisted his fingers in rage, panting as if it were him swimming in the pond. The condemned man had already traveled three-quarters of the way, and now, with the opposite bank within reach, he suddenly sped up, kicking the water with his legs and shoveling it away with his arms.

Nehurabhed stood still, eyes tightly closed, hands folded on his chest, his face focused and tight. His eyebrows were furrowed in a terrifying expression.

The crowd looked from the condemned man to him and back.

There was such a silence now that only people's heavy breathing could be heard. Mekhroes, the high priest of Sobek, appeared on a balcony high above the pond to stare in amazement at what was happening below. Or, rather, to stare in amazement at what was not happening – because Kalias was still swimming and there was still no sign of the angry god. Five more strokes of arms, three more, one more. A murmur ran through the crowd. Kalias lunged forward, reached out for the steps with his hands, scrambled ashore, and stood there, naked, wet, dripping. Whole.

Nehurabhed opened his eyes. Seeing Kalias on the far side, he breathed out as if a weight had dropped off his chest. And the condemned man, without looking back, passed among the silent crowd, passed the soldiers standing motionless at the gate. The crowd parted before him. No one in the whole of Egypt would dare lay his hand on a man to whom Sobek himself had just shown his mercy.

Nehurabhed grabbed the boy's hand.

"Let's get out of here. Let's get out of here quickly," he said.

156

When they emerged from the crowd and into the street, Melicles grasped the old man's hand and started covering it with kisses.

"O, lord! You are the best, noblest, and greatest sorcerer, and your god is the most powerful god, and as long as I live, I will worship him."

Nehurabhed did not reply at first, but when they entered the house, he said with a certain severity:

"Ahura-Mazda, the Just One, must always be worshiped because he is righteous and wise and because he gave me a good idea, and he gave the crocodile a good appetite."

"You mean... poor appetite?" the boy corrected him. "The crocodile did not eat Kalias."

"No, I mean good appetite because he ate my goose last night. And therefore, he will eat nothing else ever again."

"Why?" asked Melicles. "Did you not offer the goose on the altar of the god?"

"Er... I preferred, my boy, to throw it into the pool for the holy crocodile to enjoy. After all, I did say that I had done everything to make sure my sacrifice was acceptable to the god, yes?"

Melicles looked at him with puzzlement.

"And that goose, that goose?..." he whispered.

"That goose... that single goose would have been enough to give serious indigestion to the entire crocodile population of Upper and Lower Egypt. Tough luck, my boy, tough luck. The venerable Mekhroes will have to find... a new god."

### Chapter Eighteen
# Swords Come Out

A moment later, Melicles was running headlong to embrace his miraculously saved friend, Kalias. Nehurabhed had forbidden him to breathe a word of how the condemned man had been saved, but he had ordered Melicles to warn the Syracusan that danger had not passed and that he must immediately leave both Memphis and Egypt.

This advice, however, was quite superfluous. Kalias was completely fed up with the gods of the sacred land. Everything had long been ready to go – and within a few hours, the Syracusan ship cast off from its berth, heading north towards the sea and his distant native land.

Kalias, trembling with exhaustion, laughed and cried in turn, hugged and kissed Melicles, bidding him farewell, and blessed and praised Nehurabhed. He pronounced him to be the greatest sorcerer of all time. He also swore by all the gods, demigods, and shadows of his fathers and forefathers that he would *never ever ever ever* again set his foot in this blasted country until his dying day.

Returning from the port, Melicles found his master also ready for departure. Nehurabhed feared that his dealings with the reptilian shadow of god on Earth might come to light and the vindictive priests would find a way to lay their hands on him. He guessed what rage the venerable high priest of Sobek must have felt throughout the affair, and he trembled to think how he might now react to any revelation of the true causes of the crocodile's demise. He realized that the high priest would easily guess who had caused this mischief. Even if he could not prove it or even publicly accuse Nehurabhed of the nefarious deed, venerable Mekhroes would surely seek to exact revenge.

Therefore, Nehurabhed preferred to vanish.

The best thing would have been to leave Memphis altogether and hide in Sais, teeming as it was with foreigners. But the old man did not want to leave just yet because secret councils were taking place here and momentous political decisions were coming to fruition.

The councils took place in utter secrecy, but Nehurabhed felt that, with the help of a few friends, he stood a good chance to learn some details. And so, for the moment at least, he wanted to remain in the city. But they moved to another house that evening, a house located at the edge of the city.

The house was small, two-story, surrounded by an old, neglected garden. Meadows and fields began just beyond its crumbling wall. Apart from the host – an old Chaldean friend of Nehurabhed's from his days in Babylon – and his elderly maid, no one ever came to this secluded place.

Nehurabhed had chosen a good refuge for himself.

He and Melicles moved into a small room on the second floor, whose walls were lined with shelves. On the shelves lay neatly stacked rows of clay tablets covered with dashes, dots, and seals – the cuneiform script of the Chaldeans. It was the library of the host who was all in one person a philosopher, an astronomer, an astrologer, a soothsayer, and, mainly, a very serious crackpot. Apart from the shelves of tablets, the most crucial piece of furniture in this room was a ladder leading up to the flat roof where one could cool off in the evening. The learned Chaldean spent all his nights there, looking at the stars, watching their movements, and writing down his observations.

On their first day in the evening, he took Nehurabhed up on the roof to show him his instruments: various sticks and wheels with which he measured the direction and rotation of the heavenly bodies. He took a long time explaining to his visitor the universe's great mysteries encoded in the starry sky.

Nehurabhed listened curiously, sometimes nodding, sometimes quibbling. The lively conversation lasted a long time. Then the host, glad to be able to show off his knowledge at last, tried to interest Melicles in the study of the divine science. When the boy came out on the roof, he began to explain to him as accessibly as possible the names and strange customs of the greatest stars and planets.

At first, Melicles looked at the starry sky with delight, but soon, a completely different matter absorbed his attention: there was a large plane tree right next to the cottage. One of its mighty limbs reached down to the roof, and two cats chased each other on it. They jumped from branch to branch, ran around the trunk, disappeared, and reappeared again.

Their fur was light-colored, so it was possible to see them in the starlight. The chase continued for a long time, and the boy's interest grew. The bigger cat was just about to catch the smaller one when, with a graceful leap, it got away by jumping onto the roof. The other cat followed, and the two now chased each other among the astronomical instruments until finally, the smaller cat leaped back onto the tree again. This brought a smug smile to Melicles's lips because, of course, he was wholeheartedly on the side of the smaller cat.

The learned Chaldean looked with dismay at this display of pleasure because he had just been explaining the habits of the most terrible star, Hathor, which was the source of all the evil on Earth and caused wars, plagues, earthquakes, and such like. Nehurabhed smiled mildly, but the astrologer was scandalized.

And thus, the first and last attempt to educate Melicles in the most sacred of all sciences came to nothing.

A few days passed quietly. Melicles was bored out of his wits because Nehurabhed forbade him to leave the grounds. Nehurabhed did not go out during the day, either, but went out at night, every night. He returned shortly thereafter, and each time he returned with a more troubled expression.

Once, late in the evening, the Syrian priest with whom they had stayed before came to visit them. After his departure, Nehurabhed said to Melicles:

"Tomorrow, I will know all there is to know. Then we will leave Memphis."

After a moment, he added thoughtfully: "And Egypt too."

Nehurabhed was strangely restless throughout the day. With nightfall, he wrapped himself in his cloak, pulled the hood over his face, and was on the point of walking out when, on the threshold, he practically ran into the Syrian.

The latter rushed up into their room. His face was pale and agitated, his eyes flashed with panic. He related some news to the old man in a hurried whisper. Melicles did not understand the words, but he could see from Nehurabhed's expression that it was bad and that they were in great danger.

Suddenly, the conversation broke off.

There was a rapid patter of feet under the windows, muffled noises, and calls of a dozen voices. The Syrian jumped up and grasped Nehurabhed's arm.

"They've followed me here!" he whispered.

Nehurabhed looked out the window. In the dark, he made out the figures of several Egyptian soldiers at the garden gate. From the host's apartment below, they heard noises, voices, struggle, a sudden cry. Footsteps ran up the stairs.

Melicles and Nehurabhed slammed the door shut, barred it with a heavy box of clay tablets, and stared at each other with horror. They were breathing heavily. Someone violently hammered on the door. Melicles snatched his sword, which he had kept under his sleeping mat.

"We're dead," whispered the Syrian.

"We're dead," repeated Nehurabhed.

But Melicles, grabbing the old man by the hand, pulled him behind him.

"This way, my lord, this way!"

They climbed onto the roof and pulled the ladder up behind them. Melicles rushed to the place where the limb of the plane tree almost touched the walls, and with the agility of a cat, he grabbed a hanging branch, bent it low, and in an instant slipped onto it.

Nehurabhed hesitated. From below, he could hear the crash of the door and of the shattered clay tablets. There was no choice. Somehow, with Melicles's help, he managed to get up onto the tree. The Syrian followed. Then, in an instant, they slid down the enormous trunk and into the darkness of the garden.

At the same time, however, there were shouts upstairs, and one of the guards at the door of the house heard the noise they had made in the branches of the tree and sounded the alarm. Soldiers rushed out of the house, and a disorderly chase through the garden followed.

The refugees ran from one clump of trees to another and were already reaching a breach in the garden wall when three guards cut off their way. One of them, jumping out of darkness, struck the Syrian clean on the head, killing him on the spot. Melicles slashed him across the face with his sword; the guard screamed and fell to the ground.

Another soldier, nicked by Nehurabhed's dagger, jumped back, and the third, seeing that the pursued were armed and could fight and kill, also jumped back and began to yell for help.

Melicles and Nehurabhed jumped through the breach in the crumbling wall and rushed blindly into the darkness of the night.

They ran down the meadow towards the river, jumping over brushwood fences and irrigation ditches in their path.

The shouts of guards followed them. Half a dozen torches flashed in the distance. The old man was panting and stopped from time to time to catch his breath, then ran on again. Having reached a larger canal, they waded across it with difficulty, and once on the other side, he sat down and could no longer move. He had no more strength.

"I can't go on," he said in a broken voice. "Leave me, Melicles. You run."

He was trembling with effort, gasping for air. Melicles stood over him, helpless.

"Run!" whispered the old man. "Run! Go, find our Greeks and tell them – tell Philemon, tell him..." he could barely talk for shortness of breath. "Tell him that the Greek corps will be dissolved. But – listen carefully – first, the families of the soldiers will be taken hostage, so that..."

The old man could no longer speak.

The cries of the manhunt sounded very close. Torches flickered a few hundred paces away.

"Let's run, my lord," the boy whispered.

He lifted the old man, and they set off again. Now, they entered a thicket of shore reeds and waded ankle-deep in the water, then crawled on all fours. When they emerged on the other side, they saw in front of them the immense calm, gleaming mirror of the river slithering under the stars. It was cool, damp, and silent.

To their right, a few dozen paces away, a few fishing boats lay on the bank. This was the beginning of a vast fishing harbor that stretched for miles along the shore. Melicles leaped in that direction without hesitation. He ran, but every now and then, he backtracked, took hold of Nehurabhed, and pulled him along.

The manhunt was getting closer. Apparently, the guards had now summoned the entire population of the suburb because calls were coming from all directions and the whole coast flared up with lights. From a distance, they heard the barking of dogs.

"Dogs! They will track us down!" said the old man.

But Melicles already knew what to do. Reaching the line of boats, he searched out a small fishing skiff and pushed it out onto the water. Nehurabhed came to his aid. Another moment, and the small boat, pushed from the shore by the boy's strong arms, slipped quietly into the calm current of the river, lifting the fugitives into the night. At first, Melicles rowed the boat straight into the middle of the river, and only then, when he lost sight of the shore and therefore knew he could no longer be seen himself, turned north.

For some time yet, they could see dim lights flickering on the coast and hear shouts and barking dogs. And then everything fell silent. In the utter silence that enveloped them now, they could hear only the splashing of their oars and the steady gurgling of water under the boat.

His voice still trembling with exhaustion, Nehurabhed said:

"Melicles, you have just saved my life for the second time."

Then, after a while, he added:

"Though this time, we are still far from safety."

"Do you think the guards will be after us here too?"

"Here, and on land, and everywhere throughout this whole country. There can be no rest for us now, no respite, and no mercy. City guards, and police, and temple soldiers, and all the native troops in Upper and Lower Egypt, and the Phoenicians, and the peasants, everyone – everyone will be looking for us. Everyone. They will hunt us like wild jackals. They will spare no effort to capture us. There will be a huge price on our heads."

"But why, my lord?"

"Because tonight we alone know a terrible state secret: a state secret that can shake the foundations of this country. The unfortunate

Syrian priest paid with his life for this knowledge, but he managed to pass it on to us. And now we know it, and they will try to kill us, too."

Melicles shuddered.

"My lord," he said. "You were telling me strange things when you lay breathless by the canal. But I understood nothing. I only thought about how to get you to run again."

"Yes, Melicles! You must know this, so listen carefully. And know that the lives of thousands of people depend on this. You must know everything because our life now hangs by a hair, and the one of us who survives – if he manages – must take this message to the Greek troops in Sais. Do you hear, Melicles?"

The boy nodded while he continued to row.

"Last night, the high council met in Memphis. It decided first to disarm and then disband all Greek troops still present in Lower Egypt. And since every other Greek unit is already in the Sinai, this really just means the force in Sais. Since various promises have been made to these Greeks, since they have served his holiness, the pharaoh, for decades, and since they have been up to now the most privileged part of the army... Therefore, the priests expect, and rightly so, an outburst of anger and despair when these Greeks are now suddenly deprived of their posts, titles, honors, wages, and jobs. Or, in fact, any means of making a living. So, naturally, they fear that the corps might mutiny. To protect themselves against such a possibility, the priests came up with a plan that the terrible god Sobek himself must have whispered into their ears.

"Listen, Melicles! In the city of Sais, there are thousands of wives and children of the Greek officers from that corps. By regulation, they cannot reside in the camp, so they live nearby, mostly in the city. These families are to be rounded up, interned, and held hostage to ensure the soldiers' obedience."

Melicles froze.

"And the pharaoh?" he shouted. "The pharaoh agreed to this?!"

"The pharaoh is old, sick, isolated in his palace, surrounded by doctors and soothsayers, and probably knows nothing. Or very little. He gave his consent to the dissolution of a part of the Greek corps because it was recommended to him by none other than Symonides. Symonides hates Peleas, and here is his chance to get rid of him. Of course, he would recommend the dissolution of his command!

"I cannot be sure, but I suspect that the pharaoh knows nothing of the planned internment of the families. The priests do a lot of things behind his back these days. To justify the internment, they will accuse Peleas of conspiring with the Cyrenians and planning a mutiny. It's not true, but the priests will produce proofs and witnesses, and the king will believe them, not Peleas. And, of course, Symonides, whom the king trusts, will confirm these accusations.

"So, after all has been done, the advisors of his holiness will easily convince him that taking the hostages was necessary to nip in the bud a dangerous plot and that the families will be released once the corps lays down their arms."

"And what if the corps does not lay down their arms?"

"Ah! Here is the devious part! It does not matter what the corps does! The plan is to keep the hostages until the end of the war with Cyrene – and then sell them into slavery, one way or another. Once the corps lay down their arms, no one will be afraid of them anymore. They will cease to count."

Melicles shuddered. He stopped rowing and put his hands over his eyes. Anythe, beautiful Anythe, came to his mind. She was now in Sais, and she was an officer's daughter. And now she would be detained, held hostage for months, then sold into slavery. She might find herself at the slave market in Carthage. The horror of the thought raised the hair on his head. His hands clenched with fury.

Nehurabhed continued:

"To the eternal shame of Egypt, all the royal dignitaries have signed this order. Only the nomarch of Elephantine, the old chief, refused. I was in communication with him through our unfortunate Syrian. He demanded to hear the order to take hostages directly from the pharaoh's lips and swore and cursed that his job was to fight men, not children. For this, he was arrested this morning in the palace, along with all his retinue. Our Syrian friend heard of this from one of the nomarch's servants and rushed to us to tell us about it, but someone had seen him. He was followed to our house – and the rest you know!

"So, now, you see, we have the fate of the Greek families in Sais in our hands. If we can warn Peleas in time, perhaps he can evacuate the families to the camp and appeal to other Greek units for protection. If this happens and there is a stand-off, then there is a chance that the pharaoh will intervene and the scheme will be called off. If we can get to Peleas in time before these plans are put into effect. And if we can somehow slip through the manhunt which has just begun. Do you understand, Melicles?"

Instead of answering, the boy grabbed the oars and began to paddle with renewed energy. Their boat flew like a bird.

"Do you think," said the old man, "that our boat has been seen? Are they pursuing us by water?"

"No, my lord, I don't think so. It was too dark. I don't think anyone has seen us. Besides, we would hear voices, and we would see lights on the water."

"So, perhaps they are still looking for us in the reeds along the shore. We have a little time. How far can we go before daybreak?

Melicles looked at the water then at the distant shore.

"Since we are going with the current, perhaps as much as twenty miles? Maybe twenty-five?"

"Good. We need to hurry – we must pass Heliopolis before daybreak."

But Nehurabhed did not need to hurry the youth. Melicles felt the responsibility laid upon his shoulders. He realized perfectly well how much now depended on him. He focused his mind, tightened his muscles, and rowed. A son and grandson of sailors, grown up with water and oars, he had taken part in races of endurance many times in the past, and he knew that he had to stay calm and steady and preserve his strength. He did not row frantically but rhythmically and methodically. Each of his movements was deliberate and composed.

He rarely rested. When he did, sometimes Nehurabhed replaced him at the oars, sometimes the boat just floated on its own, carried by the current. At such times they became enveloped by such silence, such total calm and peace that Melicles was overcome with a sense of wonder.

The whole world – with all its dangers, terrible news, chases, fighting, killing – now suddenly seemed distant, unreal, and untrue.

As soon his heart rate slowed down a little, he picked up the oars again and rowed on. The thin crescent of the moon slowly rose in the east and steadily climbed into the sky overhead, illuminating the river. All they could see in its glow was the black body of the river around them, merging at a distance with an even blacker outline of the land.

Then, against the background of a pencil-thin line of the horizon, separating the black darkness of land from the navy-blue darkness of the sky, they saw the silhouettes of great triangular mountains glittering in the moonlight, jabbing their teeth into the sky.

"The pyramids," whispered Nehurabhed.

Melicles looked at them with awe. A kind of frozen terror emanated from that dim, ghostly glow. The boy knew that these were tombs of long-dead pharaohs, and he knew that these tombs were the work of human, not divine, hands. But he had also heard it told that these posthumous palaces were guarded by invisible, hungry ghosts. It occurred to him that perhaps the souls of these dead kings were watching them now, from the tops of these high mountains raised by inhuman pride. Perhaps, at this very moment, they were looking down on them: two puny, miserable foreigners who dared disturb the peace of the eternal land.

He had heard it also told that some of these stone structures played a ghostly song at certain times, and it now seemed to him from time to time that he could make out, in the silence of the night, a strange, barely perceptible melody, like a groan of death. He rowed continuously, with long, powerful strokes, eager to get away from this haunted place. In his mind, he prayed to his own solar gods – to Zeus and Apollo – that they might keep him and protect him from the evil intentions of these mighty alien spirits, with their heads of vultures, jackals, and bulls.

The shadows of the pyramids slowly moved past and receded into the low-lying predawn mist. Again, they were surrounded only by water and darkness, and the sky full of stars and glowing with the silver dust of moonlight.

Long hours passed this way.

But as they rowed, runners went out from Memphis to the four corners of the sacred land with orders to all branches of the army, guards, river police, officials, and the population of towns and villages to capture and imprison two dangerous foreign fugitives

Chapter Nineteen

# Dog Magic

Before dawn, as the sky was still barely beginning to turn pale in the east, they saw ahead of them several smaller and larger boats standing still in the middle of the river. Melicles became alarmed, thinking that the Egyptians had already set up a cordon on the river and were waiting for them to approach. Soon, however, from the calm and careless movements of the crews, he realized that they were just ordinary fishermen, busy with their own affairs.

He then worried that maybe their little boat with two foreigners would attract attention, but he was wrong about that, too. Despite the utter stillness of the night, ordinary water traffic was waking up. Gradually, more and more boats from neighboring Heliopolis came out on the river in pursuit of fish. One more boat, the crew of which no one could make out in the dark, did not attract attention.

They passed by the city of Heliopolis just as a tiny crack of orange light appeared on the eastern horizon. The vast port, with its shining fires, slipped behind them. Melicles, steadily rowing, pushed himself hard to reach as far as possible past the city before the day broke. This last effort exhausted him, and he needed to rest.

Taking advantage of the morning mist which now enveloped the river from bank to bank, they came ashore. They found an isolated spot overgrown with coastal reed and hid their boat within it. Then they climbed somewhat higher onto the dry shore – sleeping on the water was a breakfast invitation for crocodiles. They found a stretch of a lush meadow covered with tall grass, and Melicles, unconscious with exhaustion, threw himself to the ground and fell asleep instantly.

When he awoke, the sun was already past its zenith.

He stretched his aching bones, sat up, and looked around.

There was the huge river in front of him. Or, rather, one arm of it, since the greater part of it had branched off and turned east just past Heliopolis. He could see both the city and the great fork in the sacred river from the spot where he sat. This was the place where Upper Egypt ended and Lower Egypt began – the most fertile part of the great country. Lower Egypt was embraced by the river delta and changed every autumn, during the annual rise of the Nile, into one huge lake with thousands of islands and islets, little groves of trees, sometimes even individual houses all surrounded by high water.

But by now, the Nile had been falling for several months. In place of the great seasonal lake, there now grew rich fields of grain and meadow, richest in the world, and on the horizon, behind this riot of gold and green, thick forests of palm trees swayed in a gentle wind. But even now, this gold and green world was cut in all directions by a network of countless branches of the life-giving river, both natural and artificial channels. A boat was more useful to a traveler in this country than either a horse or cart.

Melicles turned his attention to the river, full of boat traffic going in all directions, like a busy highway. He studied different shapes of Egyptian boats, many of which looked like the crescent moon lying on its side, with the ends turned up skyward, a small sail in the center, and a long, thin rudder oar far beyond the boat's aft end. In time, his attention was drawn to a strange movement farther upriver, in the direction of Heliopolis. Boats filled with soldiers intercepted other boats going north and diverted them ashore.

Nehurabhed, who had also woken and now sat by his side, watched the curious sight and smiled.

"They're looking for us there. The net, as you can see, has been cast. What a pity that the fish have already slipped through."

"But they can set up barriers farther downriver, too, between here and Sais."

"And they certainly will, and that's why we can't follow the normal route to Sais. We have to do something they do not expect. Right around the bend in the river, which you see over there, we will take a smaller branch. That branch also goes north and flows near Sais, but somewhat east of the city. Our pursuers are less likely to look for us there. But we will have to proceed with the utmost caution because the river police along that canal will also have been alerted."

At nightfall, the runaways resumed their journey. Everything went well for the first few hours: the night was dark, and the river was empty. They found the branch of the Nile that Nehurabhed had spoken of without difficulty and turned onto it.

But they were moving more slowly now because the current was weaker, the watercourse was narrower, and the banks closer together. They often stopped in the middle of the river and listened to the silence around them. And if they heard any murmur or rustling from the shore, they froze up, wondering whether perhaps it might not be the sound of pursuit. They held their breath and only after a long while, having calmed down, continued on. And the entire time, they stared into the darkness in front of them, looking for a chain that the river guards may have stretched across the water.

And so, they proceeded very slowly. The night was unusually dark; the moon had not yet risen, and this also made the journey more difficult – the more so because Nehurabhed did not know the way well.

The river sometimes spilled wide, sometimes ran narrow under canopies of giant palm trees. Finally, they entered a great, shallow lake from which numerous branches and canals radiated outward. Guided only by stars, Nehurabhed chose one of the branches going in what seemed like the most northerly direction. But after a couple of miles, they realized they must have taken the wrong channel. The river was quite wide here but shallow and getting shallower. Clumps of reeds and rushes blocked their way, and they had to go round them looking for passage. Melicles had to jump out and push the boat through the reeds several times. At first, they considered turning back, but Nehurabhed decided to continue, thinking that perhaps their canal might join the main arm of the river farther on. And so, they continued.

Melicles felt more and more tired.

He had had nothing to eat for thirty-six hours now except a few bird eggs, which he had found in the meadow during their day of rest. Hunger also meant flagging strength, and the tangle of reeds and brambles and roots and mud slowed their progress to a crawl.

After a few hours of this struggle, the moon rose and illuminated their way. The watercourse became deeper, narrower, and swifter. But it also turned more clearly east, meaning that it was now running straight away from the main course of the river and away from their goal.

Nehurabhed decided to stop.

Before them lay a large clump of reed. As they approached, they saw that it was, in fact, a tiny island. They decided to stop there to rest and try to orient themselves better with the arrival of daylight.

Suddenly, in a dense grove of several dozen fan-shaped palms, they saw the outlines of a small house. They lowered their voices and took a moment to discuss what to do. By Nehurabhed's reckoning, they were still nearly two days away from Sais. It was simply not possible that they could survive those two days without any human assistance. Above all, they needed to find food. They hadn't been able to do this anywhere along the way because all the coastal villages they passed could easily have been notified about the manhunt, and any resident there could have turned them in to the river police.

But here, to this lonely island, surrounded by watercourses and a sea of reed, perhaps the news may not yet have reached. Of course, the sudden appearance of foreign travelers at this hour of the night would raise suspicions, but there was no avoiding it. Nehurabhed decided to impersonate a priest in charge of supervision of waterworks, traveling along the river to make measurements.

After a short hesitation, having tied their boat ashore, they set off on foot towards the unknown house. They were greeted by the fierce barking of a mean-looking dog. After a while, the owner of the clay hut emerged to meet them. He was a small, frail, toothless old man. Seeing the two strangers in the middle of the night, he froze with terror and amazement, trying to decide whether to run or stand and prepare to defend himself.

Immediately, however, Nehurabhed explained to him about being a priest and making measurements. He spoke in the hard, commanding tone of voice priests always used to speak to peasants in this country. He did not ask but demanded lodging and food for himself and his servant, and, he said, in the morning, the rest of his retinue would arrive.

The peasant fell on his face in front of the great dignitary, groaned, and complained about the hard times, the crop failure, the crushing poverty. He excused himself that he had nothing worthy of such important guests, but, at length, with the help of his hunchbacked woman, he got out a barley cake, a piece of fish, and a handful of dates.

The fugitives ate eagerly. In the light of a weak torch, they looked around the small room. It was really no more than a clay hovel, with a low door for its only opening, hung with a tattered reed screen.

The farmer, a dark-skinned peasant, watched them suspiciously. When Nehurabhed promised him a generous reward for food and accommodation, his humility turned into obsequiousness.

He gave up his bed for his visitors for the rest of the night – actually a straw pallet – and amid constant prostrations, he and his wife left the room. Nehurabhed accepted it as a matter of course and pointed out the bed to the boy. Without a moment's thought, Melicles threw himself upon the bed and fell asleep instantly. Nehurabhed put out the torch but did not lie down: he remained on his small stool. Fatigue and sleepiness overwhelmed him, too, but he did not allow himself to rest.

He had not liked the look of the peasant. A lifetime of experience had honed his rare native gift to judge human character from simple signs. That is why he had liked Kalias immediately, and his instincts did not fail him. And now, that same instinct told him not to trust this Egyptian.

He listened. He could hear some whispering behind the curtain and a muffled sound of heavy objects being moved. Apparently, the host was preparing his bed against the wall of the house. After a while, everything was quiet. Silence and darkness and peace prevailed. The old man swayed on his stool – he felt he was falling asleep. He got up with effort and started pacing the room. Finally, he went to the door and pulled back the curtain.

But instead of the night, palm trees, and sky, which he had expected, he saw in front of him a wall! He froze in place with surprise. The door had been barred with solid wooden planks! He pushed them. They did not budge. They did bend backward a little at the top, forming a small opening through which he could see the stars, but the bottom was fixed solid. Apparently, the planks were held in place by something heavy. Nehurabhed restrained the shout of surprise which pressed itself on his lips.

They had been captured!

He woke Melicles immediately.

The boy, upon hearing what had happened, sobered up in an instant. Together, they tried to push at the boards again. The boards creaked and bent near the top but did not yield. Melicles snatched his sword, pushed it into the gap between the boards, pried them apart, then jerked once, twice, three times. There was a crack, and two planks broke off near the top, creating a wider gap.

The boy pushed through the opening and climbed out on the other side. He breathed out. He looked around. The islet was empty: the peasant and his wife had fled. Only the dog remained, barking and jerking on its rope.

Melicles paid him no attention and began to remove the planks blocking the entrance.

The boards which blocked the door turned out to be a kind of raft, probably something built to transport hay. At the bottom, the raft was held in place by a heavy log of an untreated palm. Melicles rolled the log aside, and Nehurabhed stepped out of his prison.

They were free – for the moment. They rushed towards their boat, searching frantically in the dark... but the boat was gone. They walked all around the island. Nothing – there was no sign of it. And yet the treacherous peasant must have had his own boat to go ashore and back. The rogue had apparently anticipated that the runaways might break out from their prison and decided to cut off their escape from the island by taking their boat away.

Melicles cursed. Nehurabhed bit his lips in silence. Time passed. The Egyptian was undoubtedly already summoning his neighbors or the river police. Every moment was precious.

It occurred to Melicles that perhaps they could use the raft with which the peasant had tried to bar them in his hovel. The raft was made of a few thin planks, but it was quite wide and could perhaps serve as watercraft.

So, without wasting time, they rushed towards the cottage and dragged the raft ashore. Melicles found a pole with which to punt it. Carefully, slowly, so as not to upset it, they crawled onto the frail craft.

Here, however, difficulties began. The thin strips of wood bent under the weight of the two men, and although the raft did not sink, it kept slipping from under them. Nehurabhed and Melicles found a way to hold the raft together with their hands while kneeling on it, but this way, they could neither paddle nor push themselves with the pole. Melicles wasted a lot of time trying to find a better position; finally, he sat up, grasped the pole in his hand, and pushed them away from the shore.

The raft, three-quarters underwater, moved slowly, dragging rather than floating. They managed only a few strokes of the pole when, suddenly, Melicles having pushed a little too hard, the raft swayed and wobbled. Nehurabhed shifted sharply, the raft leaped from under them, and both fugitives crashed into the river.

Melicles surfaced immediately. He was a good swimmer and floated like a duck. He looked around. Nehurabhed was flailing in the water, beating it helplessly with his hands, desperately trying to stay afloat. There was terror in his eyes. He was trying to shout but kept choking on water.

Melicles grabbed the old man by the hair and swam with all his might back towards the island. It was not easy because the old man struggled, and reeds obstructed movement. Soon, however, he felt the ground under his feet, made his way through the clumps of reeds, and came ashore, dragging Nehurabhed behind him.

They were back on their prison island.

They sat helpless and breathless. A dozen or so steps ahead of them, the raft swayed on the water, carried gradually away by the lazy current.

Melicles threw himself on the ground. He gave up. The fight had gone out of him. He didn't care anymore. All his energy was completely spent. If he had been alone, he would have crossed the river without hesitation, although such a trip through the water at night, water perhaps teeming with crocodiles, would be dangerous even for a strong swimmer.

But with Nehurabhed? The old man could not swim, as he had just clearly demonstrated, so he would have to stay on the island. Melicles didn't even want to think about it.

"What to do?" he whispered helplessly.

"Wait, Melicles, I need to think carefully," said Nehurabhed.

The boy had learned to appreciate those words from his master. They cheered him a little.

"We have to hide," Nehurabhed said slowly.

"This is a tiny island, my lord. They will find us easily."

"Naturally. So, it is better if they don't look for us."

"How do you mean?" The boy was surprised.

"Well, we need to make sure that they do not look for us. Or that they look for us badly."

"Badly?"

"Yes. You search badly if you believe that the person you are looking for is somewhere completely different. Or perhaps does not even exist. Listen, Melicles, do you see that raft on the river?"

"Yes."

"Yes, well, the Egyptians, when they come here, they will see it too."

"Yes."

"They'll go there, and they'll probably find your pole, and maybe my hood. I already feel bad about losing it."

"Yes?"

"Okay... So, now, Melicles – do you think you might know how to... scream horribly, blood-bloodcurdlingly, as a drowning person screams? So horribly that the listeners can feel the terror experienced by a dying man? I'll try to scream like that too."

Melicles nodded. He was starting to understand Nehurabhed's plan.

"Okay. Well, the Egyptians – some Egyptians – must be nearby. When they hear our screams, they will understand that we are drowning. As soon as they see an empty raft far away on the river – they will believe – they must believe – that we have drowned. The day will break in half an hour, and the raft will be clearly visible."

"But the dog, my lord!" Melicles suddenly cried out. "The dog! You forgot the dog! The dog will betray us!"

Nehurabhed shook his head.

"No. The dog will help us," he said.

He got up from his seat and walked quickly towards the house.

And now, Melicles witnessed true witchcraft for the first time in his life.

The old man brought a burning torch out of the hovel and sat down a few steps in front of the dog, which was straining at its string, choking with rage.

The old man stared at the dog's bloodshot eyes with a calm and indifferent gaze. The flame of the torch illuminated his still face, now expressionless as if it were hewn in stone. The dog bristled but stopped barking, never taking his eyes off Nehurabhed. After a while, it began to squint its eyes, calmed down, then lay down, and finally closed its eyes. Then it briefly tensed its body – and went completely limp.

Nehurabhed rose, approached, touched the dog's eyelids with his hands, and lifted each in turn. The dog sat up and licked Nehurabhed's hand. The old man spoke a few words to him in a calm, serious tone and then summoned Melicles. The dog sniffed the boy, wagging its tail amiably. Then, on Nehurabhed's command, it walked away into a corner against the fence and lay down obediently.

Melicles watched the whole performance with wide-eyed astonishment.

"This dog will not notice us now, or hear us, or feel us, even if he is but a step away from us," said the old man.

"So, my lord, you are a sorcerer, after all!"

The old man waved his hand dismissively.

"Every serpent is just such a sorcerer," he said. "But enough of this. The day is breaking. It is time for us to drown."

They walked to the end of the island, close to where the raft jammed on a clump of papyrus in the river. Melicles took a few steps into the canal so that his voice might carry better on the water. A moment later, desperate screams of a pair of drowning unfortunates pierced the peaceful silence of the night. The screaming then turned into howling and then into a muffled, gibbering yelp. It lasted a long, long time. Then, there was a moment's pause and again, one single howl, more horrible yet broken, short – and that was that. Silence. It was all over. The unfortunates had drowned.

Now, Melicles and Nehurabhed walked to the other end of the island, searching for a place to hide. They hurried because they saw a few lights on the nearby shore, and, simultaneously, they heard the confused voices of a dozen people.

"They're here," whispered Melicles.

Hurriedly, they climbed into a dense stand of reed, went waist-deep into the water, and knelt in the mud.

It was high time. It was now broad daylight. The commotion of the approaching party was now upon them. A moment later, two boats emerged out of the morning mists carrying half a dozen peasants and three soldiers. They jumped ashore and ran towards the house.

The fugitives held their breath. They listened. From the house came shouts, there were questions, answers, orders. Melicles didn't understand any of it, but Nehurabhed could catch individual words.

"That's what I expected," he whispered. "They noticed that the raft is gone and followed it to the shore."

Indeed, the raft had left a clear mark in the ground where they had dragged it. Then, in a moment, the shouts broke again. The raft on the river was spotted – far off, near the opposite bank.

Both boats set off immediately for the other side. And from then on, everything happened as Nehurabhed had predicted. The Egyptians had heard the terrible screams of the drowning men; they saw the empty raft on the far side; then, after a short search, they found the punting pole stuck in the reeds on the far bank. This convinced the Egyptians that the catastrophe had taken place there. So, they now searched the far shore.

And, as it usually happens in such situations, the first searcher found no footsteps; the second found the footsteps of the first; the third found the footsteps of the first and the second; and, in the end, no one could say for sure whether any footprints had been there or not. But it was generally assumed, judging from the horror of the screams, that the fugitives had drowned.

Just in case, they searched the coastal reeds carefully, but all that searching took place on the other side of the canal. The islet itself was left in peace.

Admittedly, on the orders of the guards, the peasant did take his dog off its string and walked with it around the house, but, as he did it, he watched the proceedings on the other side, and the dog was mainly interested in chasing lizards. Having done his job, the peasant tied the dog up again and went quickly to the other side to take part in the search.

Melicles and Nehurabhed huddled motionless in their hideout. They could see nothing but guessed from the direction of the voices that the Egyptians had thrown themselves full force into the pursuit of the false lead and clung to it stubbornly.

Hours passed. The position of the fugitives was still terrible. They were still in danger of being discovered by accident. Fear and uncertainty combined with hunger and inhuman weariness; mosquitoes and giant water spiders bit them painfully on hands and faces, and the dense reeds filled them with foreboding. They knew well that crocodiles liked to lurk in just such coastal thickets, and Melicles listened to every rustle of the reeds with perhaps even more anxiety than to their pursuers.

His fears proved partly justified because, at one point, they saw a baby crocodile poking around in the reeds. The animal was tiny and completely harmless. Seeing the two men, it quickly scampered into the bush. Its very appearance, however, was a serious warning, and the two wondered for a moment if they should return ashore as all seemed calm again.

But just at that instant, there was a new commotion: a new boat arrived, carrying more soldiers. The new arrivals immediately followed in the footsteps of the first group and set off for the opposite side of the river. They stayed only a short time, promised a reward for catching the fugitives or dredging up their bodies, and went away.

Noon passed, and the search continued.

Encouraged by the promise of reward, the peasants carefully poked with sticks along the bottom of the canal, and at last, they fished out Nehurabhed's hood. This gave them renewed encouragement, and they redoubled their efforts. By evening, however, their enthusiasm began to flag. The guards were the first to leave, assuming that the crocodiles had gotten to the drowned men. The peasants soon followed suit, and by dusk, deep silence reigned around the island again.

The fugitives waited for darkness to fall.

Then they crept slowly ashore, stretching their bent backs and stiff, aching bones. They looked terrible. Smeared up to the eyes in black mud, their hair caked with it, their faces swollen from the bites of the mosquitoes – they nevertheless looked at each other with triumph. They were free and had shaken their pursuers.

"Melicles," the old man whispered, "do I look as bad as you?"

"You look monstrous, my lord!"

"Ah, well, then we look the same!" said Nehurabhed.

They crept in darkness until they found a boat on the shore. Not their own – because that one, along with Nehurabhed's hood, had been taken away by the guards – but a local fishing boat.

They paddled away quietly, moving on down the river.

### Chapter Twenty
# Sigma! Gamma!

After only a couple more miles, Nehurabhed ordered the boy to take them ashore. Then, after rinsing off the mud from their hands and faces, they carefully hid the boat in the rushes and continued their journey on foot. They walked on the right bank of the river – that is, the one opposite from the side where the unfortunate raft had become stranded – and they walked quickly because they did not expect a search party here. And because they hoped that, after the news of their drowning had got abroad, the search may well have become less intense.

But, most importantly, there was no time for further hiding. Two days and two nights had now passed since their flight from Memphis. The secret orders to seize the hostages and disband the Greek corps must already have reached Sais, and action might begin at any moment.

This thought troubled Nehurabhed much and made Melicles tremble.

Soon, they were on a road leading in the right direction: straight north. The country through which they now passed was rich and densely populated; many villages and estates lay among the fertile fields covered with ripening crops. These farms and the numerous human settlements were the largest obstacles on their journey because they had to avoid them, go around them, then find their way back onto the road. Melicles led the way. The old man followed him with a steady pace, with admirable perseverance.

"We must be with Peleas by tonight," he repeated firmly.

However, after a few hours of their march, they realized that they could not possibly continue without rest. When they saw a few haystacks in a meadow by the side of the road, they crawled into one of them and went to sleep.

The rising sun, however, found them on their way again. They were now meeting people hurrying to work. Melicles was worried about this, but the old man paid no more attention. He had a plan.

When he saw a plowman working in a field with a pair of horses, he went up to him. First, he questioned the man about the road ahead and directions to Sais. Then he inspected the horses, their teeth and legs.

"Young, strong horses," said Nehurabhed.

The Egyptian nodded.

"Good," said the old man, "then I'm buying them."

And he started to untie them from the plow.

"They are not my horses!" cried the terrified peasant. "They belong to his eminence, the deputy scribe of Bubastis!"

Nehurabhed paid him no attention.

"Melicles," he said. "Use your sword to cut the horses loose and hold them for us."

Then he turned towards the peasant:

"And you, my man, you tell his eminence, your lord, that we were in a hurry and had no time to deal with him. You will take this payment to him." He shook a handful of golden crumbs from the bag hanging from his neck into his hand. "You can buy four horses with this money," he said. Then he shook two crumbs more. "And these are for your trouble and flogged back."

The peasant stared with amazement. He was going to object, but the sight of the sword terrified him. He fell on his knees before them, whimpering.

But Nehurabhed, having mounted the horse, said:

"Keep quiet, man, if your life is dear to you. Keep quiet until we disappear behind that copse of trees. Then you can shout all you want."

And, throwing the gold on the ground in front of the stunned man, he kicked his horse with his knees and took off. Melicles, mounting his, hurriedly followed Nehurabhed. They flew like a whirlwind through the field, through the small palm copse, and rushed out onto the great road to Sais.

They passed passers-by, carts, farms, and villages, followed everywhere by astounded gazes. The horses were strong indeed, and Nehurabhed was an excellent rider. But things were far worse with Melicles. He had had little to do with horses in his life. He had spent his life at sea, near nets, in ports. He was holding on somehow to his horse's mane, holding on with both hands for dear life, but he was panting hard with the effort and could barely keep up with Nehurabhed.

The old man came from the land of the best horses in the world, and the world's best horsemen and was in his element. He now stared in amazement at the jerky, graceless movements of his pupil. When they slowed down a little, he said with a certain severity:

"Melicles, you ride a horse like a drop of oil rides a knife."

The boy wanted to say something but nearly bit off his tongue when his horse jerked suddenly. All he managed to say was:

"Lord, I ride a horse like you ride water."

Nehurabhed laughed uproariously.

"That is true," he admitted and whipped his horse.

After about an hour of crazy riding, they saw a big town in front of them – Chersois, of which the peasant had told them. There, they turned right, rode around the town on small country paths, waded across two canals, and, coming onto the main road again, they sped north. They looked back from time to time for signs of pursuit but saw none. Before any pursuit could begin, they had gone far and turned onto a sidetrack.

Now, they slowed to a trot because their horses were covered in foam. Nehurabhed was of good cheer; they had covered half the remaining distance to the Greek camp in less than two hours.

Everything had gone well so far; the path continued straight north, bringing them closer to their goal with every step. When they saw before them a line of tall palm trees growing along a canal, they decided to give the horses a break and rest a little in the shade of the trees.

But they barely made it across the canal when a group of armed horsemen appeared directly in front of them. They must have seen them from afar and now fanned out to block their way.

Melicles screamed, grabbing his sword; Nehurabhed spurred his horse and jumped into the field, yelling: "Follow me!" Melicles followed, and they crashed ahead like a storm. The eight horsemen galloped after them.

The outcome of the race was clear from the beginning.

Their horses were tired, going on their last breath, while those of the soldiers were rested, and, in any case, they were proper warhorses, not plowing nags. After the first desperate dash, during which they managed to put a little distance between themselves and their pursuers, their mounts began to flag. After half a mile, they entered a freshly plowed field. The soft, sinking ground sapped the rest of their horses' strength.

Finally, Melicles's horse slipped and fell, taking Melicles down with him. Nehurabhed stopped his horse and returned to where the boy had fallen. He couldn't keep going anyway. Ahead of them was the river.

The soldiers caught up with them, disarmed Melicles as he struggled to get out from under his horse, and surrounded Nehurabhed. The fugitives could now see them up close and realized

OUT OF THE LION'S MAW

that the men were not Egyptian but Libyan – they were from the Libyan mercenary regiments in the pharaoh's service.

It was all over. After all their effort and struggle, all their hardships, after all the dangers, the hunger, and the terrible exhaustion, after traveling nearly a hundred miles in three days, by boat, on foot, and on horseback, and within just a few hours of their goal, they had been caught at last.

And now, there was no more hope of salvation.

Melicles looked around for help, but Nehurabhed was pale and calm. Sweat ran down his face. He trembled with the exertion. The Libyans were also tired – their horses were covered with foam, and the riders breathed heavily.

Nehurabhed turned to the commander of the detachment and offered him all the gold in his possession to let them go.

But the Libyan would not hear of it. Though he took the gold eagerly, he began to mock the old man. Then he ordered everyone into the shade of nearby trees. The soldiers rode, and the prisoners walked. Once they arrived by the edge of the water, the soldiers dismounted and took the horses to drink. They were breaking for a siesta through the hottest part of the day. It was noon, and, beyond the shade of the trees, the sun's heat was unbearable.

Nehurabhed asked for water. One of the Libyans drew water in a leather pouch and tried to hand it to him, but the commander knocked it out of his hand. The Libyans laughed.

Nehurabhed remained calm. He sat down, crossed his legs – as priests do – closed his eyes, and prayed. Melicles sat down beside him. They were left alone. The Libyans did not tie them: they were defenseless, and, with no horses, they had no chance of escape.

The soldiers went about their own affairs, watered their horses, cooled themselves off by splashing each other with water, and broke out cakes and dates to eat. Then they stretched out on the ground, waiting for the heat of midday to dissipate a little and the horses to rest before moving on.

"Melicles," the old man said gently, "I'm afraid this is it. Forgive me, my friend."

Melicles sat down beside him.

"What for?"

"For taking you from Syracuse, from Kalias. Had you stayed behind, perhaps you would already be in Miletus by now. Perhaps, at this very moment, you might be sitting down with your mother to a midday meal. And now... I should have left you in Syracuse."

"Lord, do they know who we are?"

"I don't think so. But they'll take us to their commander, and he will know for sure."

"Do you think we are going to die?"

"I... well, I am going to die for sure. But you... your fate may be worse. You may go back to your former state."

"My lord," said Melicles upon reflection, "I could try to save myself even now."

"How?"

"Simple: jump in the river and swim across it."

"They'll catch up with you."

"They won't catch me on the river. Horses aren't good swimmers. There is no boat here, and the river is wide and deep. If I can make it to the other bank before they shoot me, I might be able to get away".

Nehurabhed perked up.

"My friend, this is a very dangerous idea, but I will not dissuade you from it. Why don't you give it a try? I assume that nothing worse than return to slavery can happen to you, whatever you do."

Melicles stared straight ahead, thought for a moment, then replied firmly:

"No, I will not abandon you, my lord."

The old man whispered impatiently.

"Oh, but this is not about me! It's not even about you! It's all about those Greek families in Sais! If you save yourself, you stand a chance to save them as well!"

"And you, my lord? What will happen to you?"

"Oh... It doesn't much matter now what happens to me. And it will be all the same with me whether you run or not."

Melicles shook his head.

"Melicles, my friend, will you do this for me? For me. You will leave me now. If you do, you will give me hope, at least, that not all has been lost. Hope that Peleas can still be warned in time. Hope that we have not done all of this in vain. Don't you understand what this means to me, Melicles?"

The boy made no reply. Only his eyes began to tear up.

"No, my lord," he said. "I will not abandon you if the whole world depends on it. You saved my life. I am not going to leave you."

Nehurabhed turned his head. They were silent for a long time, then, finally, Nehurabhed said quietly:

"I suppose it was not a good idea, really. After all, the Libyans have bows, and they are excellent shots. Yes, well, I guess all is lost now."

And again, they were silent for a long time, looking at the eternal river slowly gliding past them as it had done for thousands of years.

That was how the heavy, hot midday passed.

Suddenly, there was a commotion among the soldiers; they dragged their horses away from the water, tightened their straps, jumped on their backs. The commander approached the prisoners and ordered them to get up. This time, the Libyans threw nooses around their necks, tying the end of each to a horse. And so, surrounded on all sides by riders, ropes pulling at their necks, they set off on foot towards the road.

There was a thick cloud of dust far out on the road: a column of troops was approaching. The captives looked at each other: the inevitable was upon them. This was the end.

The squads' commander poked them with his riding crop and hurried them on.

"Hurry up, you dogs! What do you prefer, choke on your rope or swing from a tree?"

They marched swiftly, almost running, stumbling on the plowed, sticky ground, trying to steal a peek under the horses' bellies at the approaching troops. The old man was soon out of breath and fading. His hand was on the rope around his neck, now dangerously taut.

Then Melicles saw it. Right in front of him, a few hundred paces away, in a cloud of dust. He first spotted the gleaming armor: shields, helmets, breastplates, spears. And then the standards.

"My lord!" the boy cried. "My lord! These are Greeks, aren't they? Look at the standards! Sigma! Gamma!"

Nehurabhed raised his eyes. Yes. There could be no doubt. Now, no one needed to spur them on. They ran fast, light-footed, right alongside the trotting horses. This was a Greek regiment! These were the Greeks of Sais! They stretched out their arms, cried with hoarse voices, and ran headlong along with their captors.

The commander of the Libyans pulled his horse to a stop within a few strides of the first unit, jumped off, and, finding the commander of the Greeks, began to enumerate his titles, name, rank, and the unit number of his soldiers. They were the fourth guard unit of the regular third mounted auxiliary of the left bank army of his holiness, the pharaoh. May he live forever.

By the time he finished, the prisoners already knew that this really was a unit of the Greek corps of Peleas; and that the *lochagos* Diomenes was following in the second column, at the head of the second hundred. Shortly, Diomenes was by the side of the prisoners. He could barely recognize them, especially Nehurabhed.

A hungry, dirty old man in torn rags, barefoot, with puffed-up face, he looked nothing like the dignified priest Diomenes had seen at Philemon's house in Memphis. The *lochagos* quickly dismissed the Libyan who was babbling something about bounty. He took the old man by the arm, and, learning the news the fugitives had brought, he froze stiff with horror. He looked at the two, now one, now the other, unable to speak.

He believed Nehurabhed wholly, for every single prediction the old man had made had come true. Moreover, the very appearance of the old man convinced him that the two had not made their journey on a whim: the old man's eyes burned feverishly in their sunken sockets. He also believed Melicles because he trusted the young man's sincerity. The old soldier knew his people. He knew that a young boy with such a bright, open face could not be lying. He stopped his column and rushed quickly to Peleas.

And here, their difficulties began.

Peleas, although he had already heard about Nehurabhed from the stories of Diomenes, refused to believe the terrible news. He allowed that such a plot might well have been hatched. He knew that he himself had long been in disgrace. But he believed that the conspirators would never dare to put into practice such a heinous plan without the pharaoh's consent. Rumors of the sudden imprisonment of the nomarch of Elephantine had reached him, however, and he now found an explanation for them in the old man's words.

Peleas stared at Nehurabhed searchingly, rubbing his forehead with his hand. He was troubled and angry. He hesitated. To bring the officers' families to the camp, causing panic among them and the troops and to do so on so little evidence... all this seemed to him too reckless even to consider.

"When we complete the present exercise, I will be with his holiness and will be able to ask him just what all these rumors mean," he said slowly.

"If they let you see him," whispered Diomenes.

"And if it is not too late," added Nehurabhed.

Then, looking sharply at Peleas, he asked:

"Why, worthy commander, are you with your regiment on the march and not in your camp near Sais?"

"Because I have orders to march to Chersois for a two-day military exercise."

"And when did you receive this order?"

"This morning."

"This means that, in the next two days, your children will be imprisoned. They want to send you away from Sais for that critical time."

Peleas became lost in thought, and, for the first time, anxiety appeared on his face.

Diomenes folded his hands in prayer.

"Commander," he said. "I believe this man. Every single thing he has said so far has worked out exactly as he has said it would."

At that moment, a tumult arose among the soldiers standing nearby. Several Egyptians from the neighboring village begged to see the noble commander. Peleas rode over to them. They were local boatmen who rented themselves out to ferry grain and vegetables across the river in this season. They had been contracted by the manager of a large temple farm and had already prepared barges for the task. But now, river police turned up and told them to drop everything and send the empty barges to the other side at once.

Peleas frowned and ordered the policemen to be summoned. They showed up immediately.

"Why don't you let these people do what they set out to do?"

"We have received an order to seize all watercraft on this side of the river and move it to the other side immediately."

"But why?"

The guards shrugged.

"We don't know, commander. We receive orders; we obey."

Peleas looked at them for a long time; there was a strange flash in his eyes.

"Ixion," he said to one of the officers, "detain these men."

And after a while, he turned to another:

"Aristarchos, you will go to the riverbank at once with two dozen men. It will be your job to make sure that not a single craft crosses to the other side. You will seize as many as you can, crew them with our men, and take them downriver to our camp. And you, Diomenes, will order all units to turn around and proceed immediately back to camp."

Diomenes lowered his voice.

"Have you decided to trust our friends, my lord?"

Peleas hissed through his teeth:

"Oh, yes! Now I understand everything. These scoundrels want to lock us up in the fork of the river and prevent passage in either direction. By all immortal gods, we have to hurry."

The entire column now turned northward. Melicles walked between two units, holding his horse by the bridle. A young soldier approached him.

"Melicles the Milesian? My father has told me to look after you."

"Who's your father?"

"I am Polynicos, son of Diomenes the *lochagos*," said the soldier with some pride.

Ha! Here was the brother of Anythe, thought Melicles, and his heart skipped a beat. He looked closely at the young man. Polynicos was long and thin like a stick, but his face was completely childish. He did not seem older than Melicles.

"Are you a soldier, Polynicos?"

"No! I have not yet been commissioned. But my father brings me along with him to learn the craft."

Both boys looked at each other curiously.

"So! You are Melicles. That Melicles!"

"I suppose so."

"I heard a lot about you."

"About me? From whom?"

The boy was surprised.

"From Anythe, my sister," explained Polynicos.

Melicles was suddenly confused.

"How could she know anything about me?"

"I don't know. Maybe from Kalias, or maybe from Philemon."

"Have you heard about Kalias?"

"Oh, yes. It was hard not to!" he laughed. "In fact, I even saw him. Kalias came to see my father when he passed through Sais on the way to Syracuse. He stopped by to thank him for his efforts in

Memphis and told wonders about his salvation. He praised your lord, that foreigner, the priest and sorcerer with a strange name, but he also praised you, saying that you did not abandon him in his misfortune."

And the conversation went on from there.

Melicles was surprised to learn that all his adventures were known to the young Greek and that he looked at him with admiration and even with a certain degree of envy.

"How old are you?" Polynicos asked suddenly.

"Eighteen," lied Melicles swiftly, because the last thing he wanted in his life was to be taken for a child by the brother of Anythe.

"Just like me," sighed Polynicos. "But nothing interesting has happened in my life so far. I had no adventures, nothing. And you have already fought with pirates and escaped from Spartan captivity. And now you must have seen a lot on your way here."

Melicles nodded.

"You will have to tell me all about it! You're so lucky, Melicles! And, you know? I just heard Peleas say to my father that if what this foreigner says should turn out to be true, he will reward you both handsomely."

"Do you know what news we brought, Polynicos?"

"I know that my sister and the other Greek families are in danger. Peleas sent Eutychios ahead with some soldiers. They are supposed to bring the children of Peleas, my sister, and other officers' children to the camp and warn all others to do the same."

"And where is your sister, Polynicos?"

"She is not far from the camp. She is staying with the children of Peleas in a house just across the river from the camp. We can see the house from the camp and wave to each other across the water."

Melicles calmed down, and Polynicos continued:

"As soon as Peleas found out that my father wanted to bring Anythe to Sais, he proposed it himself. Peleas and my father have served together for many years, and I think Peleas likes my father. And he loves Anythe."

"Philemon's children liked her, too," said Melicles.

"Everyone likes her," said Polynicos proudly.

Melicles blushed.

"So, it's close?" he asked quickly.

"If it were still broad daylight, we'd already see the trees in their garden across the river."

The sun had already set, and it was getting darker by the minute.

"You will see it tomorrow."

"Will Anythe be able to come to us before nighttime?"

"Oh, yes! Eutychios must have already reached them. Before the children dress and pack their things – well, it may be an hour or two, but they will be in camp by tonight. They will have to cross the river in the dark, but it's not difficult. The river here is wide but shallow and calm, and Eutychios knows every pebble of that crossing. We will see them soon."

Melicles sighed a sigh of relief. Polynicos's assurance calmed him down. Anythe was now no longer in danger. And in a little while, he would see her, at least from afar. He smiled at the thought.

The sky to the west was now barely pale; the red of sunset had turned to purple, then dark blue. First stars flashed in the sky. A quiet night descended on the world, bringing with it cool respite after the blazing heat of the day. A cool breeze blew from the river.

It was completely dark by the time they entered the camp. As they passed the commander's tent, they saw Peleas talking to Nehurabhed and several officers in the illuminated interior.

At that moment, a tumult arose in the camp. A man came rushing down, and he ran straight into the chief's tent. Polynicos grabbed Melicles by the arm.

"It's Eutychios," he whispered in surprise.

They stopped under the wing of the tent.

"They have been kidnapped!" Eutychios blurted out.

"By the immortal gods! What are you saying?"

"Kidnapped, commander! Half an hour ago, less, even."

Suddenly, terrible cries were heard across the camp:

"My children!"

"Yes, commander, your children, the children of Diomenes, and Aristarchos, and the children of all the other officers – everyone on the farm, all of them! The kidnappers left two Egyptian guards on the farm to prevent anyone from leaving with the news. I arrested them and brought them here with me. They say the children were taken to the old Assyrian fortress in Sais. They say that our families in Sais are also being rounded up and taken to the fort."

"O, merciful Zeus!"

Polynicos and Melicles came even closer.

The officers stood pale, speechless. Peleas looked terrible. There was a look of astonishment in his eyes, and it gradually turned to fury. Suddenly, he pulled Aristarchos close to him and grasped him convulsively in his arms.

There was a long silence all around.

Peleas looked up.

"Call the men to the square," he said in a low, terrible voice. "Immediately."

But the soldiers were already assembling. The news was circulating already from mouth to mouth. The crowd grew bigger and bigger and surrounded the commanders' tent. Swords and shields flashed in the torchlight.

Peleas emerged from the tent and climbed onto the platform, from which he usually addressed his army. Torches illuminated his face.

The noise of voices died down.

Peleas raised his hand.

"Soldiers! We've been together for twenty years. You have seen me in victories and defeats, you have seen me in pain, sorrow, and despair, but I swear by all gods, you have never seen tears on my face. But now, I am fighting back my tears.

"Men! You are no longer soldiers! You have been dismissed from service! Officers! You, too, have been dismissed! I myself, I, your general, I, too, have been dismissed! We are getting kicked out of service like worthless, mangy dogs!

"Our corps has been disbanded!"

A wave of shouts rolled through the crowd.

"For the twenty years of our service! For the blood we have shed in the wars against Babylon! For the thousands and thousands of our brothers, who laid down their lives in battle and died of thirst in the deserts of Arabia, for all our toil, all our suffering, for all our faithful service – we are told today to lay down our arms – and get lost!"

"Boo! Boo!" roared the crowd.

"Boo is right! We are accused of treason, of plotting with the enemies of Egypt! O, comrades! On Zeus, and by all the immortal gods, by the shadows of my fathers, by the shadows of our brothers fallen on the Euphrates, I swear to you that the thought of treason against his holiness, our pharaoh, has never even crossed my mind. I have sworn my eternal allegiance to him because he has been like a father to us all.

"But, o, Greeks, that is no more! Today, we are dismissed!"

"No dismissal! No dismissal!" shouted the soldiers.

"But, listen, men! That is not all!

"As if that were not enough, as if the omnipotent priests could not be content merely with the shame with which they now cover us and the misery to which they now condemn us, they have taken our families, also. Our wives. Our children. Yes, our children were snatched from us tonight! Mine! And yours, Epictetus! And yours, Aristarchos! And yours, Aeneas! And yours, *lochagos*, officers, and non-commissioned officers. They were taken to the old Assyrian fort, where they are held hostage lest we Greeks dare to flinch under the whip of our lords.

"You hear, Greeks? Our children! They are even now being dragged to the dungeons, under the guard of temple soldiers. And tomorrow? Tomorrow they might be in the hands of executioners or slave traders. For gods' sake, am I dreaming this? Could this be true?! Our children are calling to us – us, their fathers, to come and rescue them!

"Shall we give no response? Shall we accept this? Shall we take this lying down?"

"No! No! We will not take this! No!" shouted the men.

"My men! The priests of this land have declared that we are no longer in the pharaoh's service! Well, if that is the case, then it is impossible for us to mutiny! And, therefore, nothing prevents us from doing what every father should do: get up and go rescue our children. And so, I do not command you as your general, but as a father. I stretch out my hands to you, and I implore you: let us not allow this to happen. Let us save our children. Let us go and save the children! Yes, by doing this, we are going against the whole might of this kingdom, all of its Egyptian, Libyan, and Ethiopian regiments. And perhaps our brothers, the other Greek units, will not come to our aid.

"But, by all gods, we are not pushovers. And we will not let anyone take our children from us without a fight. What do you say? Are your swords and spears ready? Shall we go to Sais?"

One cry answered him, one cry from a thousand breasts:

"To Sais! To Sais!"

## Chapter Twenty-One
# The Old Assyrian Fort

The corps began to cross the river within a quarter of an hour.

When Nehurabhed first heard that the hostages had been taken, he fell into deep despair, thinking that all his efforts had been in vain. Yet now, he realized that the opposite was the case.

Their flight from Memphis had compromised the plot. The fact that the secret of the Memphis meeting had slipped out forced the conspirators to speed up the execution of their plans and to carry out the kidnapping much earlier than they had planned, before everything was ready and all their regiments were in place.

Most importantly, Peleas found out about the kidnapping a full twelve hours earlier than would have been the case and found out about it not in the distant Chersois, to which he had been sent, but back in his camp, less than an hour's march from the city gates. And it was only thanks to Nehurabhed's warning that Peleas had guessed and foiled the plan to strand him on the right bank of the river by depriving him of watercraft.

And so, when about midnight, the leaders of the conspiracy in Sais received the eagerly awaited news that the kidnapping of hostages had gone without a hitch, none of them suspected that the entire Greek corps was already on the left bank of the river and marching fast on the city.

So, they calmly gave orders to the royal regiments standing on the right bank to occupy the empty Greek camp and, to complete the encirclement of Peleas (as they thought), sent out Libyan cavalry to guard the other fork of the river

Meanwhile, within an hour of the arrival of the last hostages at the old Assyrian fort, the Greek corps was already at the city gates.

In those days, Sais was the largest city in Egypt and the beloved seat of the pharaoh. It consisted of two parts, one on each bank of the river. Right-bank Sais was known as the Royal Sais. It was magnificent, brilliant, rich, bathed in green parks and gardens, filled with palaces of the elites. Left-Bank Sais was the city of the poor: lively, teeming with people, the site of a busy port and a busy market.

In Royal Sais, the most prominent structures were the magnificent temple of Amun[49], which was the seat of priestly power; and the palace of the pharaoh, the seat of royal power. In Left-Bank Sais, the main building was a prison that also served as the barracks of the river police and was commonly known as the Old Assyrian Fort.

It had indeed been built by the Assyrians a hundred years earlier, during their short reign over the land of Egypt. It served at that time as the headquarters of the Assyrian army.

The fortress was universally hated. After the pharaoh Psametych chased out the Assyrians, an enraged Egyptian mob broke down the fortress walls. Later, the fortress was partly restored and turned into a barracks and a prison.

---

[49] *Amun* or *Ammon*: Egyptian god of the sun, the most important deity in the Egyptian pantheon

This dark, foreboding structure was located just south of the main city fortifications, on the banks of the Nile, so that the Greek corps did not need to enter the city to stand directly under its walls. Within a short time, they surrounded the fortress, cutting off all approaches by land.

But approaching the fortress and surrounding it was one thing; taking it was quite another. The gates had been closed. The enormous crenelated walls rose high up over the heads of the arriving soldiers. Guards were on watch on the walls: as soon as the first Greek units were noticed, the entire garrison mounted the defense of the wall. Great blazing fires were lit on the towers. A red, flickering glow illuminated the crowd of Greek soldiers below.

There were over two thousand Greeks, battle-hardened men, each one a veteran of several campaigns. And there were perhaps two hundred Egyptian guards, and the only combat experience they had ever was at most to face their own defenseless population, putting down a city riot somewhere, or enforcing tax collection – if that. But the walls defended them and defended them well. And the Greeks had no siege engines, not even ladders.

Peleas immediately sent scouts to search the suburbs for ladders. They had barely brought a few when, having lashed them together, men began to scale the walls. It was a furious attack, but it failed. One of the ladders was crushed with a boulder thrown down by the Egyptians; others were quickly pushed away.

And so, the first assault was repulsed. The Egyptians suffered almost no losses.

Peleas ordered his troops to wait until more ladders could be brought from the neighboring suburbs, and only when a dozen or so were gathered did he renew his attack. But these flimsy civilian ladders bent and broke under the weight of armed soldiers. The Greeks, hit from above with arrows and stones and burning coals thrown in their faces, slid down one by one. The second and third attacks were repulsed, too. The inaccessible walls mocked the besiegers.

Peleas tugged at his beard in a fury. He understood that, without more ladders, which might enable the simultaneous attack of the fortress in several dozen places, the capture of the fortress was impossible. Entire units were sent immediately in search of more ladders; those that had already been brought were now tied together and strengthened with spears.

If the Greeks had time, conquering the fortress would not have presented difficulty – it would have been only a matter of time. But time they did not have. The Libyan regiments now standing somewhere in the south might arrive at any hour. The Egyptian troops on the other side of the river might begin crossing to this side at any moment. The fortress garrison could expect relief by daybreak, at the latest. Both the Greeks outside and Egyptians inside were aware of this. And precious hours passed. The Greeks renewed their attacks from time to time regardless of their losses, but all these attempts were failing.

Melicles and Polynicos took part in the first attempts to storm the fortress. They tried to scale the walls, hold up the falling ladders, squeeze in among the storming troops. But Diomenes caught sight of them and flew into a fury.

"This is just the place for puppies like you," he shouted. "These are my best soldiers. They have been doing this for decades. Do you think you are helping? Away with you!"

Polynicos was red with shame; Melicles paled with rage. They had to retreat. A moment later, Eutychios found them.

"By the orders of Diomenes, you are now attached to my unit."

"What is your unit doing, *lochagos*?"

"We guard the eastern side of the fortress."

Polynicos obediently followed Eutychios, but he swallowed tears of humiliation.

"Do you know, Melicles," he whispered, "what unit Eutychios commands?"

"No."

"A squad of veterans and the handicapped! Old soldiers who are no longer fit to fight and are mostly used to dig latrines and guard the kitchen supplies. And we are now assigned to that unit! Melicles! See for yourself how it is with my father. How can I ever hope to get ahead? To prove myself? To gain fame and experience? I just joined the cripples' squad! Merciful Zeus!"

Melicles shared his frustration and looked, scowling, at his new commander. Eutychios was indeed a fit commander of veterans and invalids, for he was both old and handicapped. He was close to sixty and missing his left hand. People called him the One-Armed Eutychios.

However, despite his disability and his sixty years, he was still a feared commander. He had once been the strongest man in his regiment, and he could still knock out a horse with one blow of his one remaining fist.

The detachment of veterans stood in two groups at the eastern wall of the fortress. Here, the peace was complete. The walls reached almost down to the river, separated from it only by a narrow strip of land. The ground was boggy, silt-covered, and overgrown with a dense thicket of stiff marsh grass; all of this made it difficult to move here. And the proximity of the river made it impossible to bring a larger unit to bear. Because the shore sloped a little, the walls here were taller than anywhere else. No attack from here was remotely possible.

The Egyptians realized this and left only a few guards on this section of the wall. Their job was merely to raise the alarm in case any Greeks turned up with ladders. Without ladders, the unit was no threat to the fortress.

Eutychios' entire task was to make sure that no one left the fortress from this side and that no one from the river got into it. It was not a very challenging task – the entire squad of forty men had really nothing to do.

Melicles was desperate and angry. The thought that here he was, obliged to remain idle while everyone else was fighting, burned him like a branding iron. He briefly considered how to slip away from Eutychios, but in the end, decided not to endanger Polynicos – all the more so that he had to admit that Diomenes had been right: there really was room only for the most experienced and strongest soldiers on the few ladders they had, and he did not even know how to cover himself with a shield.

The soldiers of Eutychios, without exception old practitioners who had experienced many sieges, were calm and patient. Listening to the sounds of the fight on the other side of the fortress, they talked in an undertone about old battles. One of them, an old man with sharp vulture features, remembered the fortress from the time when the Assyrians were leaving.

"The walls were even higher then," he said, "and the river reached right up to the wall. There was a gate in the wall on the riverside, at water level, so that boats could go in and out. Later, everything changed: the walls were first partly taken down, then rebuilt, and the river must have changed its course and backed away from the walls. And so everything is different now."

Melicles did not want to listen to these old tales. The calm of these old soldiers irritated him. He didn't know what to do with himself. He couldn't stand inactivity. He finally decided to creep along the wall and see for himself if any trace of the old water gate remained.

Upon learning of this, Eutychios shrugged. He had known these walls since childhood. There were no traces of the old water gate; he could vouch for that. He was not opposed to letting the boy investigate, though – he only warned him to go carefully and not expose himself to a random shot from the wall above.

So, Melicles set out – or rather they both set out because Polynicos joined him eagerly. They crawled on all fours among the thick grass, right by the wall of the fortress, practically rubbing their shoulders against its stones. They went the entire length of the wall this way, carefully examining the stonework overhead.

Nothing.

There was no sign of a walled-up passage, only a smooth, even brick wall. It was not too dark to see since the night was illuminated by fires blazing on the walls and reflected in the river – and the wall was clearly visible. It was straight and smooth.

Discouraged, they turned back.

And then, suddenly, Melicles, still crawling on all fours, nudged his elbow against a protrusion in the masonry. He stopped. Right at ground level embedded in the wall, there was a kind of stone beam, like a narrow step. Melicles stopped to look.

Above the beam, there was the plain wall again, as everywhere else.

He was about to move on when a strange thought occurred to him. Such beams – were they not sometimes placed above doors? Was that not called a lintel? What if the door they were looking for was not above but below? He pressed his hand under the beam, easily parting the muddy ground. The hand did not hit any obstacle. There was no wall beneath the beam. After a while of groping around, he felt a rusted bar with his fingers. He had found the old water gate.

The grille he now grasped was completely corroded; it crumbled in his hand. With Polynicos's help, he easily yanked out a larger shard of the rusted iron. It had offered no more resistance than a rotten branch. Both boys were trembling with excitement. They understood the importance of their discovery.

Melicles now understood why, according to the old soldier, the walls used to be higher, and the water gate had once opened straight onto the river. Why! The wall had not shrunk, but the earth had risen! Year after year, the Nile had tirelessly deposited new layers of brown silt, slowly but surely lifting its banks. Lush grass grew on this fertile ground, hiding from view the remains of the brickwork of what had once been the water gate.

Melicles and Polynicos looked around, then back towards their companions and up towards the tops of the walls overhead. They saw nothing. No one could see them here, tucked into the corner at the foot of the walls, hidden in a thicket of tall grass. They set to work frantically. They dug away the soft, half-liquid mud with their bare hands until they made an opening big enough for a man to squeeze through. They broke one more rusty rod out of the old grating. The hole grew bigger.

Melicles slid into the passage, first his arms, then his head, then his shoulders, then his entire torso. He crawled on in the dark, rubbing his head against the stone that used to be the ceiling of a corridor, his breast pushing aside the greasy mud. After crawling a few feet, he felt the passage begin to rise above his head. Another foot and the space opened up. He could already raise his head and stand on his fours. Overhead, just a few steps away, he saw numerous gaps through which light shone.

It was now possible to stand and straighten his back. Polynicos crawled in right behind him. It was even easier for him because he was thin and long like a snake, as if he'd been made to crawl through narrow passages.

They stood side by side, not daring to speak. They were undoubtedly in a corridor leading from the former water gate to the main courtyard. The vault above them was of the old staircase. In front of them was the main prison yard.

Melicles put his eye to the gaps in the barrier ahead. Yes, he could see it now: this was where the courtyard began. Confused shouts and sounds of fighting came from there. They were separated from the yard only by a few planks with which the old passage had been boarded up.

Melicles tried to move them. The planks were weak, rotten, swaying. They could easily be torn off or broken. If he only had an ax or even a solid stick, Melicles could have dealt with them in no time. But the breaking of the boards would undoubtedly draw the defenders' attention.

The boys conferred in whispers.

They both felt a strong temptation to slip into the besieged fortress without the knowledge of their own army, but both Melicles and Polynicos understood that they were not allowed to do this. They were not participating in a heroic adventure but in a battle to free the hostages. The discovery of the passage could decide their fate; they could not risk it for the sake of empty heroics.

Polynicos immediately crawled back to their commander, and Melicles set about widening the passage. Eutychios arrived shortly afterward and, barely managing to squeeze his enormous body through the narrow opening, looked around and exhaled with satisfaction.

"Wait here, boys," he said. "More of us will be here in a minute. And, by all the gods, make no noise. Do not alarm the defense."

Returning to his squad, he sent a messenger to Peleas, asking him to redouble his attacks because the veteran squad had a good hope to engage Egyptians on the eastern side. He then chose twelve soldiers, equipped them with axes to break the barrier, and led them back along the wall towards the passage. Soon, the passage began to fill up with soldiers. They could barely all fit in – the twelve men, Eutychios, and the two youths – fifteen men in total.

They placed their axes and swords in the cracks of the barrier, leaned against it, and waited silently. When renewed shouting and running told them that the new attack on the west and north walls of the stronghold had begun, Eutychios gave the command to proceed.

A dozen arms strained with effort, a dozen swords pried out the creaking boards, and the barrier collapsed with a loud crash. The Greeks rushed inside.

Several Egyptian guards on the wall nearby gave a terrible cry, but it was too late. The Greeks ran into the courtyard, flew through it like a whirlwind, and rushed up the stone stairs leading to the north wall. At their head ran the long-legged Polynicos, his hair flowing, his face flushed with joy. Behind him, barely able to keep up, ran Melicles, followed by the giant Eutychios and the others.

And then, a strange thing happened. The Egyptians waging a fierce battle against the troops of Peleas on the northern wall did not notice the runners. Or, rather, did not notice them until the last moment when they were already upon them. The attack was so unexpected, the surprise so complete and the shock so terrifying that this first group of guards threw down their weapons and fled as if they had seen a ghost.

A few other Egyptians on the wall did put up a fight, but Peleas's men were now jumping over the crenelations – first two, then four, then eight, then twelve. Seeing that their men had gained the wall, the Greeks below gave a shout of triumph and raised more ladders.

And then, the Egyptians no longer resisted. Panic seized them like wildfire. Screaming with terror and throwing their weapons, they jumped off the wall and into the courtyard.

The fortress was taken.

Melicles stood near the door leading to the dungeon but had no chance to squeeze through. A crowd of men surrounded him on all sides. The hostages were emerging in ones and twos. Confusion was general. There were shouts and crying, crying and shouting as men were reunited with their families.

At one point, Melicles saw in the passage the tall figure of Diomenes clasping Anythe to his chest. The girl was pale and trembling, and her face was bathed in tears, but she was smiling through them. Polynicos ran up to her. Melicles wanted to join them but hesitated; it was their moment, and the crowd was blocking his way.

Then, Peleas's voice was heard from inside:

"Diomenes, tell the soldiers that all the children are safe and sound. No one is hurt!"

Diomenes repeated the chief's words loud and clear for all to hear.

There was such shouting that the light of the torches swayed as if from a gust of wind.

"Glory to Peleas!" they shouted. "Long live Peleas!"

Then Peleas continued:

"Diomenes, find out who was the first on the wall!"

And again, Diomenes's loud voice was heard:

"Soldiers! The commander wants to know which one of you was on the wall first!"

A silence ensued, in which the calm words of Eutychios came loud and clear:

"Polynicos, son of Diomenes; Melicles, volunteer from Miletus; and Eutychios of the veterans!"

Diomenes was struck speechless for a moment, but, having recovered, shouted out exactly the same words. Peleas tore his sword from its sheath and raised it high above his head.

"Glory to Eutychios!" he cried. "Glory to the veterans! Glory to Polynicos and Melicles!"

A thousand swords went up, and a cry like thunder roared from a thousand mouths.

Melicles stood half-conscious. He saw upraised swords flickering in the torchlight; he saw faces quivering with emotion; his mouth was open in a shout; he heard his name repeated by a thousand mouths. His face burned with blood; a haze of intoxication obscured his vision. He kept his arm upraised; tears ran down his face, and in his ears rang out the most beautiful, the most magical word in the entire Greek language: *kleos*[50] – glory.

---

[50] *Kleos*: an ancient Greek word meaning "fame or glory attained through good deeds and hard work." The heroes of ancient Greece strived to earn their *kleos*

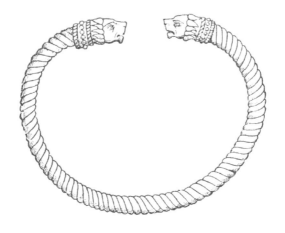

### Chapter Twenty-Two

# The Silver Armband

At sunrise, Peleas left Sais with his entire army.

The troops marched in battle formation, ready at any moment to repel an attack. Between the marching columns traveled the families of the troops and many other Greeks from Sais who decided to flee the city along with Peleas. Some traveled on foot, and others rode in carts.

Just outside of town, a small entourage of well-dressed riders caught up with them. At the head of the retinue, in gilded armor and helmet, rode Amasis, an envoy of his holiness, the pharaoh Apries, and the old king's most trusted advisor. Amasis was popular with the Greeks because he had a good command of the Greek language, knew Greek customs, and sometimes even dressed in Greek fashion.

Peleas received him respectfully but did not order the columns to stop. Amasis was extremely agitated and reproached Peleas for his impetuosity. He was indignant at those who had ordered the taking of the hostages. He swore by all the Egyptian and Greek gods that his holiness had known nothing of it. The pharaoh, he said, was furious with his ministers and ready to forgive the Greek corps for its mutinous step.

However, all his assurances were in vain. Having experienced what they took to be treachery, the Greeks were now unwilling to trust any new promises of a minister of his holiness. On the contrary, they feared it was all just a trick and would be followed by revenge and punishment. The blood spilled at the old Assyrian fortress would not be easily forgotten nor forgiven now by either side.

So, the envoys left with nothing. Amasis only managed to obtain the release of the captured prison guards. By releasing them, Peleas hoped to appease the pharaoh's wrath and save the vast masses of the Greek population in Sais from retribution.

The corps marched west. The goal of their march lay two weeks' journey away, on the Libyan coast, beyond the vast Western Desert. It was the city of Cyrene. The unfortunate settlement, now desperately preparing to defend itself against the expected Egyptian attack, would gladly welcome any unit willing to come to her aid.

In every direction the troops now looked, they saw Libyan light cavalry on the horizon. Their scouts told them that beyond, to the east and north, were powerful Egyptian infantry units hoping to envelop them. Peleas's position was like that of a fly in a web, surrounded by spiders.

In the afternoon, the Greeks came to the last branch of the Nile, separating them from the Western Desert. Here, their path was blocked by a large unit of Egyptian and Libyan cavalry. Peleas, without the slightest hesitation, put his troops in battle formation, and they advanced on the Egyptians in a broad front, spears bristling and shields gleaming in the sunlight. But the enemy avoided confrontation: Egyptians evaded to one side, Libyans to the other. The road was clear again. The spider backed away from the fly.

The Greeks reached the water and began to ford it.

The spider web was broken.

Melicles and Polynicos walked behind the civilian carts.

"Melicles," said his long-legged companion to him, "as long as I live, I will bless the day I met you. Everything that's happened to me since has come thanks to you. You went looking for the passage, you found it, you broke in."

"Yes, but it was just an accident. We went together. It might as well have been you."

"No way. No such thing would ever have happened to me alone. But you are clearly under the protection of the gods. Adventure, danger, and fame follow you everywhere. Already back in Sais, when Anythe first told me about you, I felt that it had to be the case. And it is! Ah, fame! Ah, Melicles! Ah, glory!

"Yesterday was the greatest day of my life. Even my father looks differently at me now. And so do most people, it seems. And only I know that, in fact, I haven't done a thing! And this bothers me, Melicles! I do not deserve such respect."

"What do you mean? You were the first on the walls!"

"Hmm... Well, yes, that's true."

"And the whole army saw you there."

"That's also true, but..." Polynicos lowered his voice. "Do you know? I didn't manage to do any fighting at all!"

"What do you mean? I was there! I saw you! You were the first to jump on those guys!"

"Well, yes, I did jump on this fellow with my sword in hand, true. But – what happened then was that he – well – er – he took a step back, then two, and then – *boom!* – suddenly, the wall ended under his feet, and he fell headlong down to the courtyard! All I saw was his feet kicking in the air! And that was it! Because, you see, I, too, was unable to stop in time, lost my balance, and – well, I, too, went down! I grabbed the ledge, held on, and then spent the rest of the fight trying to clamber back up! By the time I got back to my feet, the Egyptians were gone!

"So, then I saw some Egyptians fighting in another section of the wall. I rushed there, and just as I closed in for a fight, these clowns just dropped their weapons and ran! And, well, you see, it was all over! My only chance of a proper fight! I didn't even get to cross swords with any of them!"

"Ha! But you certainly blew that first fellow away!"

"I didn't! Not me! It was he who fell! If I had at least touched him with the tip of my sword, I could claim that I had defeated him. But as it is!..."

"Well, you can certainly tell it that way. After all, you jumped on him. And he was running away from you. So, you caused him to fall."

"You think so?"

"Look. If he fell head down from that height, well, my fellow, that must have really hurt! For all we know, you might actually have killed him!"

"I suppose it's true," Polynicos fell into deep thought.

"So, you see, you can tell everyone that you knocked him down and hurt him."

Polynicos straightened up, his scruples removed.

They walked on in silence.

"Melicles!" Polynicos said suddenly in a slightly trembling voice. "Would you... like to be my friend?"

Friendship: that was another important word for the Greeks. It meant trust, mutual loyalty, help, compassion, support, advice, joint adventures, and joint struggle for the future. Without uttering a word, Melicles took Polynicos's hand and shook it. They looked into each other's eyes. Then they walked on in silence.

Hours passed. The troops advanced steadily. Melicles kept pace with others with difficulty. The exertion, sleep deprivation, hunger, and tension of the last several days had sapped his strength. The boy swayed on his feet.

At one point, Peleas, traveling on horseback, approached them. He was accompanied by Nehurabhed and Diomenes. He recognized Melicles immediately.

"Milesian!" he called out. "I offered a reward to your master, and he has refused to accept it. But he tells me that he was able to reach us in time only thanks to your courage and perseverance and that you deserve a reward. So, think about what kind of reward you want. You have earned it."

Melicles became confused and was silent for a moment.

"Come on, boy, don't be afraid to ask. What would you like the most?"

"To sleep," the boy said abruptly. "Commander, let me climb on one of the carts and sleep."

Peleas laughed.

"Fine! But that does not count! When you have had your sleep, you will come with Polynicos, son of Diomenes, and Eutychios the veteran to our purser. And he will pay you your share of the reward."

And then he rode up to the cars passing by and shouted:

"Hey there, children! Make room for our Milesian hero who is tired and wants to sleep!"

There was some scrambling on the carts; everyone wanted to welcome the famous hero. But Melicles carefully maneuvered himself onto Anythe's wagon.

"Are you comfortable, Melicles?" Anythe asked.

"I am in heaven!"

Soon, Melicles was lying down. He had eaten and drunk his fill. Anythe and her companion made him a snug sleeping bed. The boy lay motionless, staring at the beautiful head bent over him. Anythe was not veiled; in the haste in which they had been taken to the old Assyrian fort, she had not had the time to veil herself properly. And now, her head was covered with a hood which her Egyptian guards had given her. It was an unusual dress for a Greek girl, but she looked beautiful in any dress, thought Melicles. From under the hood, two curious eyes watched the boy with interest.

"Are you comfortable, Melicles?"

"I wish I could stay like this forever!"

Wanting to cover her embarrassment, she poked his arm with her index finger.

"The Milesian hero," she said.

And they both turned red.

Melicles did not take his eyes off her. Anythe's eyes narrowed as if from the glare of the sun.

"Melicles," she whispered after a while. "the commander said you're supposed to sleep."

"Yes, miss," the boy said obediently.

"Then close your eyes!"

Melicles closed his eyes. In an instant, deep, revivifying sleep descended upon him like a giant sea wave.

The next day was very important to Melicles.

First of all, he was richly rewarded by Peleas. Besides a gold ring, which he received – as Polynicos and Eutychios did – the treasurer also handed him a lavishly gilded, solid silver bracelet of great value.

Such bracelets were worn at ceremonial court receptions by royal dignitaries. This one had belonged to the commander of the Assyrian fortress, and now, by law of war, it became the property of the victors.

During the midday rest, he and Polynicos took their treasures to Anythe. There, they sat together, admiring their precious baubles. Diomenes stopped by, and Nehurabhed, and several soldiers. One of them, like Melicles, a native of Miletus, had been looking for the boy the whole day, wanting to talk to a fellow countryman.

And that was the second great event of the day. The soldier had only just returned from his home leave in Miletus. They fell talking and soon realized that he had once known Melicles's father, Lycaon the sailor, and that he also knew his mother and had recent news of her. Although he could not say much more than that, he was able to report that his mother was alive and well, and that she lived with her younger son and daughter in the house of her brother, a prominent ship carpenter, well known in the city.

The news confirmed what Melicles had expected. The news deeply moved the youth, his face changed, and tears began to well in his eyes. There were feverish questions and quick answers. The soldier even described the street where the carpenter lived: a narrow, dilapidated alley near the old port. Melicles now remembered the house he had known as a child: it was a proper house, though small, with a porch, a megaron, a second inner courtyard, and a warehouse in the back. He described some details. The other man confirmed them. And then they talked about the neighboring streets, places to eat, local specialties, about the port itself, about the workshops where the carpenter worked.

And then about other, less important things: about the big flat rocks by the port on which Melicles had spent his childhood days, fishing rod in hand; about the stairs leading down to the sea; about the fountain in front of the town hall and the natural spring on the slope of the mountain above the city. There was the best water in the world, and there, at all times of day, one saw girls with jugs on their heads, fetching water, and the little boys spied on them from the trees.

"Did you do that?" asked Melicles. "I used to do that too. And worse, one day, I got the brilliant idea of throwing fig peels at the girls. I got a proper flogging for that!"

"All great minds think alike!" the soldier burst out laughing. "I had the same great idea! And with the same result!"

"At this spring," he remembered further, "starts the water-carrying procession, when women fetch water on the feasts of *Eleuteriae* and *Didymeia*."[51]

"There is a wonderful view of the whole city from there."

"Yes! You can even see the sacred coastal road along which the processions go – all the way to Didyma, to the temple of Apollo."

---

[51] *Eleuteriae* and *Didymeia*: local holidays in Miletus

"Ah, yes, the priestesses in white robes, walking down among the trees and then along the processional road, between the statues of former priests. I have been told that there are plans to build a small chapel there, dedicated to the nymph of the spring."

"Maybe like the small temple with four columns which you pass on your right-hand side when you sail to Ephesus? Just as you enter the strait of Samos? Do you remember?"

"Yes, up on the hill. And next to it grow these huge ancient cypresses. You can see their tops over the crest of the hill even before you clear the cape."

"This temple has been there for ages! It was already there back in my day," interjected Diomenes.

"And on the other side of the strait, on Samos itself, there stand these huge sacred rocks of Poseidon, and among them is a little harbor. And there are steps carved in the rock, and above them stands this beautiful white house in a fruit orchard. Apples, figs, and plum. And this plum tree is found nowhere else, only there. Do you remember? It's absolutely gorgeous there when it blooms!"

"And now they are all about to bloom!"

"Yes! It's the most beautiful time of spring! It's nearly spring equinox. They will be holding *Eleuteriae* in honor of Dionysus[52] in the next few days."

"Temples decorated with wreaths of fresh leaves... And the games, and the stage performances, and a procession around the city."

"And in the evening, sailboats lit by torches will go out to sea, and you will hear singing all night, from all directions, as if the sea itself were singing."

There was a moment of silence.

The soldier sat with his head bowed.

"*Eleuteriae*," he whispered. "Do you realize it's *Eleuteriae* tomorrow? Melicles! The spring equinox is tomorrow! And here, in this country, there is no springtime here! One forgets to keep track!"

"Why did you leave Miletus, soldier?"

---

[52] *Dionysus*: Greek god of wine

"Ha! Don't ask me that! I had to. Never mind why. I was a soldier. I signed up here. The pay was good. I thought to myself: it doesn't matter where you live. But it isn't true, is it? It does matter where you live. And I can't stand it here anymore. It's almost as if the merciful gods arranged all this, this whole hostage thing and this mutiny, to give me a good shove, get me off my behind, and force me to go back to where I belong. If I cannot go back to Miletus, I will go back to Samos, or Colophon, or Ephesus, or Smyrna."

"And I will do the same," Diomenes said softly.

"Is it more beautiful there than here?" Polynicos asked.

"Ah, Polynicos!" Melicles exploded. "There are green hills, and white cottages among the vineyards, and the sea, you know, the sea! The vast, great, dark blue sea! And green islands, and sacred groves, and statues in the groves. And springs and nymphs at the springs! Ah, the gods can only live there; our gods, true gods are only there, Polynicos! And all the people there are your own – all of them!"

There was a moment of silence.

"And now the first apple trees are blooming in the gardens..."

Diomenes raised his hand to his eyes as if dazzled by the sunlight, turned on his heel, and walked away slowly.

### Chapter Twenty-Three
# The Old Mountain Lion

Another day passed.

The army continued to march west along the edge of the Western Desert.

On their left, as far as the eye could see, stretched an immeasurable sea of sand from which, from time to time, emerged flat stretches of dry, stony scree. And then came the dunes again, blown by the wind and shimmering in the super-heated air. There was not a sign of greenery: no trees, no palms, not even grass. No trace of any living thing. Nothing – hundreds of miles of total desiccated emptiness hammered by the merciless sun.

On the other side lay Egypt proper, the western end of the vast delta, green and golden, crisscrossed by long, straight rows of trees growing along canals and covered with the lush ripening crops. Stands of wheat and barley rustled with heavy ears of corn, rich meadows were full of grazing cows, armies of water buffaloes wallowed in shallow ponds, field hands were busy in vegetable gardens.

Here was the primordial border of two lands: the land of work, movement, and life; and the land of desert and death. The terrible kingdom of the murdered god Osiris[53] and the life-giving kingdom of the living god Horus[54].

Gradually, the army moved farther and farther away from the life-giving land. The area through which the road now passed was swampy, barren, and scarcely inhabited. From a distance, they could see the surface of some great shining body of water. At first, the travelers thought they had reached the sea, but it was only the western end of Lake Mareotis, the largest lake in Egypt over which, several centuries later, the famous city of Alexandria would be built.

Polynicos asked Melicles with disappointment in his voice:

"Don't you want to become a soldier, Melicles?"

"I will fight with you against the Egyptians."

"Yes, yes, I know. But then? Later? Will you not become a soldier? One of us?"

"No. I think not."

"What will you do, then?"

"I will be a sailor and a fisherman like my father was."

"A fisherman?

"Yes. It's smart work. And busy work. And noble work. You think, Polynicos, that a fisherman at sea is like these fellows here, on the Nile. But there, in Ionia, where one fishes at sea, one must know the kinds of fish and their habits, know where the water is deep, and where it is shallow, where it is warm and where it is cold, be familiar with the currents. One must read the weather and the wind – everything. A fisherman must know the sea like no one else. And a fisherman who has his own sailboat, and his own equipment, is widely respected. And my father had a sailboat."

"What happened to your father?"

---

[53] *Osiris*: Egyptian god of the dead
[54] *Horus*: son of Osiris, god of Egyptian kingship

"He died at sea, like a sailor. He died a beautiful death, Polynicos."

"Beautiful?"

"Yes... I mean... worthy and noble. My father – oh, I remember that day, even though I was still a mere child. I was just twelve. It was night. There was a storm. A terrible storm. I have never seen another quite like that. My father had seen it coming and returned early that day and was already with us on the shore when a cry went up that a boat was sinking in the bay.

"People were running along the shore, but no one wanted to go out to the rescue, nobody dared, the waves were just too high. Nobody, Polynicos. Nobody. Then my father, just him and his friend, an old comrade, a fisherman and a sailor like himself, set out. Just the two of them. And we never saw them again. The last thing I remember was my father's face. It was very stern. Concentrated. But also very calm as he pushed the boat down into the sea. He waved his hand to us to say goodbye. And that's the last I saw of him, Polynicos."

He fell silent.

They walked for a long time without saying a word.

"I didn't know your father was a hero," whispered Polynicos. And after a moment, he added: "It is a terrifying profession – to be a sailor."

"Yes. But it is also beautiful. It's wonderful, the most beautiful, the happiest in the world. To be a sailor. To have your own boat, obedient to your every command, faithful, reliable, beloved, and a few crew companions on the boat, and then, then the whole world is open to you. Do you understand this, Polynicos? The whole wide world! You can go wherever you want. The sea goes everywhere, and the wind will take you everywhere. Oh, Polynicos! Could there be greater happiness?"

"I don't know. I don't know the sea," whispered Polynicos. "I saw it only once, from far away."

"The sea is frightening, you say. But it's not. A wise sailor is not afraid of the sea. The sea will not hurt him. On the day he died, my father had returned ashore early because he had read the skies and understood that a storm was coming. The sea had warned him in advance. The sea is terrible, but it is not evil. You must be vigilant and respectful, and careful like a soldier on guard. And if you are on guard, your luck will follow."

Polynicos was perplexed.

"But adventures and dangers and fame are easier to find here in the army, in the life of a soldier."

"Not true!" exclaimed Melicles impetuously. "Think how much I have experienced on the sea and how much of the world I have seen while you sat here, stuck in the same military camp! A sailor's life is all about adventure and danger and struggle. At sea, one must beware of pirates and Phoenicians; and on land, when you dock in a strange country, you must be careful with the barbarians, to see whether they are friendly or hostile or whether they are perhaps planning an ambush. There are so many nations in the world, and every one of them is different. And you must learn how to get along with each. A wise sailor who has learned a lot and heard a lot – only such a sailor will survive and thrive. Yes, Polynicos. But the world is open to such a sailor. He will be able to reach everywhere – even to the Scythians who live beyond a great river in the north, a river as big as the Nile. And even farther north, where the land is covered with snow and rivers freeze solid like stone."

"I have never seen snow or ice," whispered Polynicos.

"Ah, of course you have never seen it here! You haven't seen anything, Polynicos! But back in Ionia, snow often falls in winter, and in Sicily, I saw a volcano, a smoking mountain; her peak was covered with snow, and it shone in the sun like a mirror."

"I haven't seen a volcano, either. I don't even know what it is," whispered Polynicos.

He was getting more and more depressed.

"It's just a really, really big mountain that smokes and spits fire and dust. When I saw that mountain, I was so impressed that I thought there was nothing grander in the world, but Nehurabhed, my master, said that in his country, mountains are even higher and even more terrifying. They are so huge that they reach above the clouds. The trees there are completely different, and the animals and the people. I have to go there one day, Polynicos. I absolutely must."

"From the bottom of my heart, I pray for a beautiful boat for you, Melicles."

"Yes, someday I will have her. Definitely! In the meantime, I will serve on the boats of other sailors. Everyone will accept an assistant who knows the sea and sailing, who has capable hands for work and can use the sword and has courage in his heart. I will go on distant journeys, to distant seas where no one has been before. Like the Argonauts[55], like Jason and his companions. O, Polynicos, would you like to go with me?"

Polynicos was silent – more serious and reflective than ever.

Suddenly, there were shouts in front of the column, and then a wave of human cries rolled over them until one and only one word emerged from the great uproar, repeated by thousands of lips:

"Thalassa! Thalassa!"

"The sea! The sea!"

And there it was indeed: just at the edge of the northern horizon and running its entire length from east to west, a narrow dark-blue streak, merging in with the sky above.

The boys grabbed each other's arms and stood silent.

A wind blew from the sea. Melicles breathed it in, filled his chest with it. He listened to its hum in his ears and tasted its salty taste on his lips.

"Well, Melicles," Nehurabhed said during one of their stops, "as of today, you are no longer my servant or disciple. You are free. Free. You

---

[55] *Argonauts*: mythical figures of Jason and his companions who sailed in their ship *Argo* to Colchis, a distant land on the Black Sea, to steal the fleece of a golden ram

can do whatever you like with yourself. It's difficult to say this, but we will have to part ways soon."

"Don't say that, my lord. I wanted to be with you for as long as possible. Didn't you say you were going to Ionia? I thought we might go to Miletus together."

"Do you want to go soon?"

Melicles was silent for a moment, sad and concerned.

"I don't know, my lord. If you please, I will stay a while longer."

"If I please? My boy! I have already told you that what you do is entirely up to you from now on! You could leave today. But why do you want to stay here?"

"I do not want to abandon them now, our Greeks, my brothers. Not now, while they expect to fight a war. After the war, if the gods let me live, I will return to my mother. But now..."

"This is a terrible war," said the old man glumly. "The Greeks don't stand much of a chance."

"All the more so, I will not abandon them in their misfortune. I want to fight alongside them. I want to see them through this difficulty. My friends are here, my lord!"

Nehurabhed was silent, thoughtful. From the boy's tone, he felt that his mind was made up and that no argument would help. He sighed heavily.

"Then... I, too, will remain here," he said finally. "I will remain here until the war is decided. I couldn't leave like this – without knowing your fate. And knowing the fate of these people."

He gestured in the direction of the camp.

Melicles looked up at him.

"Lord," he whispered. "I have wondered about you for a long time. Why do you take the side of the Greeks? Why do you spare no strength, health, or life to save them? They are not your people. They are strangers to you. You weren't doing it for money, and you weren't doing it for honors. Why, then? Will you explain it to me?"

Nehurabhed hesitated for a moment; his voice trembled slightly.

"I have been doing this for the Medes, my young friend. For my people."

"How is that?"

"Yes, well, it is not easy to explain, and you may not understand everything right away. But I will try to explain it the best I can. Listen, Melicles.

"We Medes and our fellows, Persians, have one mortal enemy – Babylon: Babylon and its terrible king Nebuchadnezzar, the ruler of the Chaldeans and the most powerful man in the world.

"No, not a man – a ravenous beast. He smashes mighty kingdoms like clay pots, razes holy temples, sacks populous cities, exterminates whole nations or drives them into slavery. He sows death and destruction like a peasant sows wheat. Desert is all that remains where he has passed. He has ravaged Elam, Syria, Judah, but none of this has slaked his thirst. He is even now on the prowl for a new victim.

"And he has long eyed my nation for this purpose. He has long waited to make us his next meal. His shadow hangs over my people like a storm cloud, like a suspended thunderbolt.

"Now, in the old days, Egypt was allied with Media. My king and king Apries were friends. Any aggressive move by Babylon against us, or against Egypt, might have exposed Nebuchadnezzar to a dangerous war on two fronts. After all, Egyptian troops were standing on the Euphrates, and our armies had destroyed Nineveh only twenty years ago.

"But now, everything has changed. The pharaoh's counselors have taken hold of him. They now rule Egypt, and they urged Apries to break his alliance with us and make a separate peace with Babylon. That's why I hate these men; I hate them because they deprived my country of an important ally, and by doing this, they put my country in terrible danger.

"Yes, Melicles! These are the same men who are now inciting the Egyptian people against the Greeks and preparing a war against Cyrene.

"I said that the Phoenicians stirred up the Egyptians and incited them into this unfortunate war. And that they did this by bribing the priests and the royal officials. And that is true. But behind them, behind these small greedy calculations of a quarrelsome merchant nation, another hand is hiding, a far more potent and far more sinister hand: that of Nebuchadnezzar.

"He is behind all this, the old mountain lion, wise, and patient and cunning. He subjugated the Phoenicians in the Levant, forcing their cities and kings to submit to his rule, but he leaves them a free hand to trade, and he supports their business ventures across the seas. The Phoenicians have traders and people and businesses everywhere. They have contacts. They have influence. They come and go as merchants, unsuspected of being Babylon's agents. But it is Nebuchadnezzar who wants to embroil Egypt in this stupid war. He wants to set against each other all the peoples inhabiting Egypt to weaken the pharaoh and occupy him with some unimportant nonsense while he attacks us, Medes, with all his might.

"Yes, Melicles, these are great and portentous matters and may be new and not entirely comprehensible to you. But in time, slowly, you will see how those great matters of state and high diplomacy affect the fates of small cities and even individual people.

"I have spent two years trying to prevent this war against the Cyrenians. I was in Carthage, in various Greek cities, at Delphi, with the highest council of your priests. I asked them to intercede. To help mediate the dispute. In vain. All in vain. In Delphi, I was told that the fate of the Greeks in Egypt was more important to them than the fate of the city of Cyrene. Sparta has an old score to settle with the Cyrenians and is happy for them to be wiped out. Syracuse trades with Egypt, not Cyrene. And so, I returned to Egypt with nothing.

"My last hope was to reach king Apries. The pharaoh was never a fool, and he was once a friend of the Medes and the Greeks. He had been reluctant to stir up hatred against the Greeks, and he has kept Egypt from this war thus far. I have been able to see him, but he is now a shadow of his former self. He is sick, tired, not entirely aware of things, in the hands of sly priests and his Chaldean doctors, who do not admit anyone to him, control what information reaches him and what information does not. He leaves the work of governing to his advisers, does not want to undertake the trouble of opposing them, and maybe even, in his old age, fears them.

"I suspect that he didn't even know about the plan to take hostages. And I'm almost sure that even though he agreed to disband Peleas's corps, he did not intend the complete abolition of all Greek units in the Egyptian army.

"And I know the whole thing will now cause a major shakeup in the Egyptian leadership, and heads will roll. But, so what? The war with Cyrene is now inevitable. After all, priests allege evidence of secret plots involving the Cyrenians. The Greek corps has mutinied. The pharaoh will either believe the priests, or he will pretend that he does.

"Despite all my efforts, I couldn't do anything to change the course of events. But I do not regret my efforts, nor its costs, nor its dangers. The case of Cyrene is a just cause and the Greek corps was in terrible danger, and now we have helped to save their families from certain slavery.

"And this... is important. If of all my projects and plans and efforts, I only managed this – to save these few thousand families from slavery, then... Then I think it is enough. It is good and mysterious and maybe even wise. Such was my fate – to accomplish this much. We can never know how matters will turn out, but we must always do our best, hope for the best, and never give up.

"Life is very mysterious, Melicles."

The old man pondered for a while, staring into space.

"Perhaps," he whispered, "perhaps saving these few thousand souls from slavery was more important than the fate of all great kingdoms of this world. I wonder... do you agree, Melicles?"

Chapter Twenty-Four

# Meet Me at the Thestis Well

Only on the fifteenth day after leaving Egypt and after marching day after day steadily between the desert and the sea did the column of troops and exiles reach the first settlement on the Cyrenian shore. This settlement was situated in a narrow green strip hugging a long white beach at the foot of mountains descending towards it in huge barren crags. The mountains were rocky, wild, burned by the sun, but they sheltered the settlement from the blazing heat of the desert.

The Greeks sighed with relief. They hadn't seen any human habitation for fifteen days – aside from a few tents of the desert nomads. For fifteen days, they had no place to hide from the midday sun. For fifteen days, they had been forced to drink rusty, brackish water drawn in a few oases along the way, scarcely enough to moisten parched lips.

But here, there were wells and even two small seasonal streams not yet completely dried up – and everyone could drink to their heart's content and the fullness of their bellies.

Peleas ordered to strike camp here, understanding that everyone needed a well-deserved rest. Besides, they were already close to Cyrene, only a day's march from here.

That same evening, a large cavalry unit and a dozen elders of the city of Cyrene arrived in the oasis to meet the rebel forces. They welcomed Peleas as a savior and looked with delight at the ranks of the heavily armed infantrymen, the peers of which would have been difficult to find even among the Spartans.

The next day came the moment of separation for the Greek exile camp. Women and children were to continue on to Cyrene, where they would be provided with food and shelter, and the army was to remain in place. After the conference with the Cyrenians, it was decided that this oasis was the best place to await the Egyptian army and give battle.

The families were hastily sent on their way because reports were already coming, brought in by desert nomad scouts, that light cavalry troops were following the Greeks and were only two days' journey behind.

It was a doubly sad day for Melicles because he had to say goodbye to two important people – Nehurabhed and Anythe. The old man, exhausted with the rigors of the recent weeks, the terrible experiences of the flight from Memphis, and the long march in the heat of the desert, was in failing health and needed rest. Besides, on Peleas's strict orders, only fighting men were to remain in the camp.

Melicles asked Anythe to look after his master, and Nehurabhed, in turn, promised to Diomenes to care for and protect his daughter. When parting, they all had tears in their eyes, and Nehurabhed held his young friend's head to his chest for a long time, unable to utter a word. Finally, the moment of departure came, and the long line of carts started west. The soldiers were now left alone.

The evening was sad.

The two boys sat moody, leaning against the wall of their tent.

"You know, Melicles," said Polynicos, "I really like that kid."

"What kid?"

"My sister, Anythe. I'm sad she left. I got used to having her around. Do you know what I would really like?" he asked, stretching himself dreamily on the sand, his eyes half-closed. "You know what? That you two might marry one day."

And then he added quickly:

"One day in the future, of course."

If, falling suddenly out of the blue sky, a thunderbolt were to strike Melicles on the head, his surprise could not have been greater. He sat paralyzed, mouth open, not daring to breathe. It was good that it was already dark, and Polynicos could not see the impression his words had made. Nevertheless, he was struck by Melicles's sudden silence.

"I know that you don't know much about her yet, not enough to like her," he continued after a moment, "but I am sure that if you do get to know her, you will like her. She really is a very nice girl, Melicles."

Silence answered him. Melicles tried to unblock his throat and swallowed hard. The paralysis persisted. Polynicos was perplexed.

"I'm sorry, my friend," he whispered, "I was just daydreaming. Have I upset you?"

There was a long silence.

"Why don't you answer me? Have I offended you? Why aren't you saying anything? Am I not your friend?"

At last, Melicles regained his speech.

"Polynicos, you are my greatest and best friend in the world, the dearest friend that I have ever had. But this is impossible."

"What is impossible?"

"Anythe will not want me!"

"She? What are you saying?! She watches you like a cat watches a saucer of milk! I mean, nobody asks a girl about such things, but to say that she doesn't like you is silly! Haven't you ever noticed how she looks at you?"

Melicles felt his tongue grow numb again.

"Diomenes will never allow it," he said with an effort.

"My father?" Polynicos thought about it. "Why wouldn't he?"

"Ah, Polynicos! I have nothing. I am a nobody. I was a slave only a year ago, then a servant. And your father is an officer."

"That's true."

"And I'm poor as a temple mouse."

"Well, not entirely! You have a gold ring and a silver bracelet, and your master has promised you a horse."

"Yes, but I don't know what it's all worth, and I don't even have any clothes, and who knows whether I will not have to help my mother. I don't know, Polynicos, how is it with her in Miletus."

Polynicos's face clouded over.

"Actually," he muttered after a moment, "we don't have anything now, either. We left so quickly that there was no time to bring any of our things. We are penniless."

Perversely, Melicles was pleased by that thought.

"That's true too," he said.

Polynicos saw no reason for joy in this, and Melicles, after a while, grew gloomy again.

"Well, your father is a *lochagos*, an officer, and he is respected by everybody. What am I? I'm a wandering tramp, Polynicos."

Polynicos tried to cheer him up.

"Nobody says it should be right now! But some time. Later. In the future. My father likes you. I told him that you and I have sworn to be friends, and he did not object. It even seemed to me that he was pleased. When the time comes, I will talk to him about it, suggest it as if it were my own idea. I will try to figure out what he thinks."

But Melicles sprang to his feet.

"No! No! No! No! No!" he cried impetuously. "Do not do this, on any account! Diomenes would laugh at me and send me packing. Maybe he will forbid me to see Anythe. Maybe, as you say, sometime later, in the future... Besides, it's hardly the time to think about such things now."

Indeed, there was no time to think about anything but war.

A great danger was approaching. Every day scouts brought news of the approaching Libyans. One of the most powerful Libyan kings, Adicran, who had appealed to the pharaoh for help against Cyrene, and the city's bitterest enemy, arrived with all his troops and was even now camped out a day's journey from the Greeks.

At the same time, additional Greek forces arrived every day.

The eagerly awaited main army arrived from Cyrene on the fourth day, commanded by its king, Battos the Second. His army numbered about four thousand men. However, apart from perhaps six hundred *hoplites*[56], young, vigorous, and well-armed soldiers, who could really equal Peleas's men, many very young and very elderly people were among them, and many had had no war experience. They all volunteered in that terrible moment to defend their homeland, all wanted to fight to protect their loved ones, and all were ready to lay down their lives rather than withdraw from the battlefield, but it would take a lot of time to turn this chaotic group of volunteers into an effective fighting force.

Feverish work raged in the camp.

Untrained youths were incorporated into units of older soldiers on the idea that they would be led by example and that, surrounded by veterans, they would be less likely to break.

Melicles and Polynicos were again assigned to the unit commanded by Eutychios, but this time, they did not bewail it: they now knew that every unit could turn out to be useful, and the unit's action in Sais had covered it with glory.

There was a great deal of work. Apart from exercises, the soldiers had to dig ditches and surround the camp with fortifications, preparing for the arrival of the enemy, which was now expected at any

---

[56] *Hoplites*: Greek foot soldiers who fought in heavy bronze armor in tight formations called phalanx

moment. Meanwhile, three weeks had passed, and the main Egyptian army was nowhere to be seen.

This delay turned out to be very fortunate for the Greeks because every day, new men and new supplies arrived from Cyrene, and soon, volunteers from overseas began to arrive.

They mostly came in small groups, such as just twenty men from Mantinea in Arcadia, but from Corinth and far off Samos, larger units arrived, each of two hundred well-armed and trained *hoplites*. The soldiers from Samos especially attracted attention with their gorgeous uniforms and splendid armor, and with the person of their commander, the young, handsome, barely twenty-year-old Polycrates, who became from day one the favorite of the entire camp.

Only a hundred *hoplites* came from Syracuse, but the help offered by the city was perhaps the most crucial. A large contingent of the Syracusan fleet arrived at the port of Cyrene to protect it and the army from the direction of the sea and to guarantee supply lines. The fleet also stood ready to cover any retreat in the event of defeat and to evacuate any sick and wounded from the camp.

Unfortunately, the possibility of defeat had to be taken seriously. The Egyptian army had a great numerical advantage, and the ratio of forces was staggering. The sense of dread, however, did not deprive the preparations of energy or enthusiasm. Everyone knew that they had to win. Each new unit, each new soldier, was greeted with joy.

To cheer the troops and evaluate them, a review of forces was staged. On the hill stood the chiefs: the king of Cyrene, who was at the same time the commander-in-chief of the entire army, Battos; Peleas, second in command, along with his deputy, the *taxiarch*[57] Aristarchos; and other commanders of the allied forces: Polycrates of Samos, Iphitos of Mantinea, Gorgos of Corinth, Eumedon of Elis, Deinomenes of Syracuse.

Long lines of troops marched before the gathered commanders. All eyes were on the brilliance of the heavy-armed ranks of Peleas's infantry. Soldiers in bronze helmets and armor, carrying large oblong

---

[57] *Taxiarch*: a high military rank

shields, marched with a steady step, their metal shields and spears flickering in the sun, the earth shaking beneath their feet. The main *hoplite* ranks of Cyrene presented themselves as gloriously, but all paled next to the splendor and richness of costumes and speed and efficiency of maneuvers of the soldiers from Samos.

After the review of the forces, the priests from Cyrene addressed their solemn prayers to the gods for victory in the coming fight. A dozen oxen and a hundred lambs were slaughtered in sacrifice to immortal Zeus and to Apollo, the patron god of Cyrene. At dusk, by great fires, the priests cast auguries. There was a solemn silence. Everyone waited with bated breath to see what the priests would say. The omens turned out well.

At the same time, another news cheered the hearts of the soldiers. A messenger from Cyrene arrived reporting that a detachment of two hundred *Spartiates* arrived that morning. It was not a large force, but the very name of Sparta had a magical draw because a superstition was widely held among soldiers that no defeat was possible in a land battle in which *Spartiates* took part. The Spartans also brought with them the blessings of the Great Council of Delphi and the prophecy that the beloved city of Apollo would not be destroyed.

This lifted the morale of the army and delighted the elders immeasurably, for it testified that Delphi, respected by the whole of Greece, had convinced Sparta to give up its initial hostility and lend its force and prestige to the defense of Cyrene.

The next day, the Spartans arrived by land and the Syracusan fleet by sea.

Melicles went down to the shore looking for the Syracusans, curious to see if any of his acquaintances were present. His expectations proved justified. Walking along the beach and looking at the ships, he suddenly heard his name, and a moment later, fell into the crushing embrace of Kalias.

Kalias had arrived from Syracuse with arms and food for Cyrene. In Cyrene, he met Nehurabhed, and, learning from him that Melicles was in the camp, he followed the Syracusan navy in his galley – in part to see Melicles, in part to do a little trading, but mainly to be at the center of events and see for himself the splendid army assembled from the entire Greek world. As always, curiosity, garrulity, and greed drove him on.

Melicles assumed that Kalias would fight alongside them, but he was mistaken. Because of Sotion's continuing sickness, Kalias was now the ship's first commander and could not leave his post. He dragged the boy with him on deck, received him hospitably, and questioned him about his adventures. With great pride, Melicles showed him his Sais prizes: the ring and the armband. Kalias clicked his tongue, smacked his lips, examined the jewelry against the light, pushed it right up to his eye, tapped it with his knuckles, weighed it in his hand, and the young soldier's entire gain from the conversation was to learn the value of his prizes.

The value was considerable, but the boy was only interested in whether it was enough to buy a sailboat. Having learned that, as things now stood, the value of his prizes came at most to half the value of a small sailboat, he grew sad and lost further interest in his treasures.

Then they went ashore because Kalias also wanted to see Diomenes. But before they found him, before they got through the crowds, there was a sudden commotion in the camp; officers were seen rushing around mustering their men, and soon, the terrifying, hoarse voices of military trumpets drowned out human voices. The trumpets were sounding the alarm.

Melicles bade farewell to Kalias and rushed to his squad. Polynicos, who had just arrived straight from his father's tent, reported in a voice trembling with excitement that there had been news of the entire Egyptian army on the move.

The long-awaited battle was upon them at last.

The fifteen thousand-strong corps of the Egyptian infantry had finally arrived, joining the Libyan mercenaries and the army of the Libyan king Adicran. Together, the united Egyptian-Libyan force numbered around thirty thousand men. The Greeks were putting in the field fewer than eight thousand men against them. The odds were almost four to one: four enemies to each Greek. Given their crushing numerical advantage, the Egyptians felt certain of victory.

That very same day, first skirmishes took place in the surrounding hills, and before evening, the Greeks saw ahead of them the vast Egyptian army. The army spent the whole night in a state of readiness. Everyone felt certain that the next day would be the day of battle and that it would probably decide the outcome of the war.

But the day of the decisive battle was delayed. Libyan cavalry made several approaches to the Greek fortifications, but the ground, which the Greeks had intentionally cut with numerous ditches, made it difficult for the cavalry to maneuver and broke their ranks. The Greeks easily pushed back the scattered units. The whole day passed in such skirmishes. The Greeks hardly suffered any losses, while the Libyan losses were significant.

The next day went much the same. The Libyans, having learned from experience, approached more cautiously, but there still were no major clashes. Egyptians, who had at least appeared on the horizon in battle formation the previous day, this time did not even leave their camp and remained behind the crest of the hill all day. In the evening, the cause of the enemy's strange behavior became clear.

Libyan spies, coming from tribes opposed to King Adicran, reported that the entire Egyptian army and most of the Libyans had set out in a circular movement, through the desert, hoping to reach the valley of the River Thestis, cross the Cyrenian hills, and from there to descend onto the defenseless city – or at least to cut it off from the main Greek army.

There was no time to waste.

With nightfall and in complete silence, the Greeks also left their camp and marched west to intercept the Egyptians. They left only a few hundred men behind them to disguise their departure by burning huge fires and making a lot of noise.

The entire Greek army, now numbering around seven thousand men, moved under cover of darkness. The forced march through the rocky country lasted all night and all morning. Only around noon did the first columns reach the mountain passes between the Libyan Desert and the city of Cyrene.

Upon arriving, they discovered that the passes had already been occupied by Egyptians. However, it was only a vanguard unit, and it quickly retreated. The Greeks swiftly moved into the mountain pass. As they took defensive positions, right there before their eyes, only a few thousand paces away, the entire Egyptian army appeared, lining up hurriedly in battle formation.

Behind their ranks lay the open desert, and only a few whitewashed Libyan houses indicated the location of some underground water source. The settlement was called Irasa in Libyan, and the natural spring around which it was located was sometimes called the Well of Thestis.

And here, in this wild, abandoned, empty wasteland, the long-awaited decisive battle took place, a battle whose fame was to resound in the entire known world for decades afterward and which the Greek historian Herodotus was to record for posterity and call The Battle of the Thestis Well.

The battle started around noon and lasted until late at night.

The fortunate circumstance for the Greeks was that the Egyptians were unable to make full use of their greater numbers in the narrow pass. The mountains on the two sides of the pass were neither high nor very steep, but the rocky slopes were littered with massive piled-up boulders and crisscrossed by steep crevices, making them completely impassable for the cavalry and not much use for infantry. The Egyptians, therefore, were unable to surround the Greeks and had to crowd in as many men into the narrow pass as they could fit, with the rest of their army remaining uselessly in the back.

Ferociously, time and again, the crack Egyptian regiments threw themselves against the Greek phalanx, trying to push it over the pass and down towards Cyrene. But all their efforts to rip apart the wall of Greek shields, to open even the smallest crack in it, were in vain. The old Cyrenian *hoplites* and the glorious corps of Peleas closed their shields together and stood steadfast. A wall of corpses grew up around them. A couple of hours had passed, and the lines held unmoved.

A dangerous moment came about two in the afternoon when, in the middle of the hottest hour of the day, the Greeks attempted the common maneuver of relieving the front ranks and letting them rest while replacing them with fresh men, all without interrupting the fighting. But the fresh men were not experienced veterans. They were mostly the irregular volunteers; they had had little training in this difficult move and could not hold their line as well. Seeing this, the Egyptians threw their best units against a section of the volunteers and managed to break a wedge into the Greek front line.

Things were starting to look bad for the Greeks, and their line began to waver when Diomenes, who fought with his squad on the left wing and seeing the danger, lunged with a handful of his men to help shore up the volunteers. Polycrates himself rushed in from the back of the field with a small group of officers; shouting, cursing, and threatening, he rallied the wavering line, and then, jumping off his horse, he himself grabbed a shield and stood in the first rank, fighting like a simple soldier.

The volunteers, burning with shame, recovered from panic and rallied. The rank held. And then, the terrible, death-dealing *Spartiates* struck from the right side upon the penetrating Egyptian wedge and, as it attempted to retreat against their own ranks (which were pushing upon them from the back), they crushed it underfoot; the wedge swayed, shuddered, then broke. Hundreds of the best Egyptian soldiers lost their lives while trying to retreat.

Melicles and Polynicos fell into the crazy whirlwind of the fight in that most dangerous moment of the battle. At first, they were stunned by the inhuman tumult, the crush of bodies of men squeezing shoulder to shoulder and chest against chest. When, however, the Egyptian wedge had been crushed, they regained their senses and began to act more lucidly. Bearing in mind Eutychios's instructions, Melicles restrained his fury and did his best not to get too far ahead of his comrades and not seek individual glory in fancy hand-to-hand duels. Battles were won by massed formations of soldiers acting in unison, Eutychios had explained, and not by individual heroics.

But Polynicos, finally hearing the sound of his own sword, fell into a frenzy, and once he managed to cut down one of the Egyptian soldiers, he no longer heeded a thing. He chopped and chopped in wild abandon, slipping carelessly beyond the line of the Greek phalanx. It was all the more dangerous because, in this sector of the front, their unit faced the best of the Egyptian veterans. And so it happened that he caught an unexpectedly treacherous blow of a spear to his head. He staggered and fell, lifeless, to the ground.

Melicles scooped him into his arms and dragged him back beyond the line of the fighting ranks.

Here it turned out that Polynicos was dazed rather than wounded. The bronze helmet cushioned the force of the blow, and the youth only had a huge bruise on his forehead. After recovering from the daze caused by the shock, he sat up and, in a still trembling voice, asked what had happened. Melicles, having made sure that there was no need to worry about his friend, left him in place and jumped back into battle. There was no time now to take care of the bruised.

Hours passed. The terrible fight continued. Soldiers' hands fainted from constantly dealing blows, from holding up their heavy shields, their chests short of breath, the heat burning their heads and thirst burning their insides. Melicles was still fighting in the front ranks, his hair matted with sweat and blood, his helmet dented, his shield hacked. Trembling with exertion, he fought on and kept pace with Eutychios's veterans.

As evening fell, the Egyptians began to withdraw. First, the Libyans withdrew, relieving the wings of the Greek army. Then, the main body of the Egyptian foot began to slowly retreat. The sun went down beyond the hills. Then, in the valley below, in the Egyptian camp, loud trumpets gave the signal for a general retreat. The Egyptians withdrew in good order, leaving the Greeks in command of the battlefield.

The battle was over.

The Greeks did not have the strength to follow the retreating army. Exhausted soldiers threw themselves on the ground where they stood, took off their helmets, unfastened their armor, and wiped sweat and blood from their foreheads. In front of them, barely a thousand paces, the Egyptian and Libyan armies were settling for the night's rest.

They, too, were exhausted. From this distance, in the light of the fires of their camp, the Greeks could see rows and rows of the enemy lying down on the ground, like a field of freshly reaped grain.

Nightfall found both armies in the same places where they had been at noon.

Suddenly, the commander-in-chief, king Battos, appeared on the field, among the men. He had the other commanders with him.

"Soldiers!" he shouted in a loud voice. "The fight is not yet decided! These Egyptian scoundrels were about to lose, so they withdrew instead of seeing the battle to the end. They will now rest and have another try at us tomorrow. So, tomorrow, we will have to start all over again. Let us not give these dogs a break. Tomorrow will be harder than today. We don't have water here! Do you understand? And they have it there in that little village. So, by Zeus and by all the gods, soldiers, get up! Get up and stand in line! Not tomorrow, in the heat of the day, but today, in the cool of the night!"

The men began to struggle to their feet, cursing and grumbling.

"Water, water," parched lips whispered. Of all the commander's words, this one was paramount in their thoughts.

Then Polycrates appeared in front of his soldiers – youthful and lighthearted as usual.

"Come on, boys!" he exclaimed in a cheerful, upbeat voice. "There is nothing for it... let's go and drink their water tonight!"

The joke worked. There was laughter in the ranks. The soldiers rose, armed, and began to form a line.

"Water!" roared thousands of parched throats.

Within a few moments, the Egyptians, already getting ready for the night, saw with horror row upon row of enemy troops descending upon them, emerging out of the night.

But the Greek commander did not strike evenly all across the length of the entire phalanx. He had observed that the Egyptian encampment was divided by a narrow ravine and decided to use this to his advantage by concentrating his attack on one part of the camp first. He gathered his best men on the left flank and concentrated his attack on the right side of the Egyptian army.

The battle flared up again, and a terrible clash ensued. But this time, the battle went differently. The same Egyptian regiments, which had held up so well against the Greeks all day, could now not bear the first blow and began to give way. Like the Greeks, the Egyptians were exhausted, and the swiftness of the Greek attack left them too little time to form defensive ranks. Confusion ensued as they struggled to assemble, and the Greek phalanx descended upon them with full force. All day, the Egyptians had fought upwards, and now the Greeks were striking down on them again. They were now pushed back; they wavered; their ranks not so much broke as never quite formed.

Some Egyptian units on the left wing tried to get over the ravine to aid them, but the Greeks had already seized the edge of the crevasse and fiercely defended the passage.

Other Egyptians tried to go around the gorge to aid the right wing, but by now, it was too late. Nothing could stop the phalanx.

A wild elation seized them. The old veterans suddenly sensed that moment in battle when the balance suddenly tips irrevocably one way, and victory becomes inevitable. Push, push, push! Another quarter of an hour, one more terrible effort! The whole Egyptian right wing suddenly burst and disintegrated like sand blown by the wind.

The Egyptians went into full panic mode. The darkness was almost complete now, as was confusion. It was now too dark to see, command, and carry out orders – too dark for Egyptian and Libyan reserves to counter-attack. Under the cover of darkness, the Greeks began to cross the gorge to seize the opposite side of the camp. A terrible fight ensued, but it was brief. Seeing that the camp was lost, the Egyptians tried to retreat into the desert, but the retreat was disorderly and turned into discriminate flight.

The rising moon illuminated the immense mess and gave the Greeks enough light to slaughter the few enemies remaining in the camp.

The Libyans broke up into small groups and fled to their homes in the desert. The Egyptians found themselves in unknown terrain, parched, hot, dry, without food and water. They, too, scattered into small groups and attempted to find their way back to Egypt, but many were lost in the desert. From the entire Egyptian corps, fifteen thousand strong, only a few hundred reached home.

The news of the victory reached Cyrene the next day, causing a frenzy of joy in the city. People did not want to believe their good fortune. They fell into each other's arms, knelt, and kissed the ground and the steps of their temples in thanksgiving. The city, on whose doorstep destruction and death had stood only the day before, now breathed a huge, joyous sigh of relief.

And the glorious news spread across the shining sea, to the whole world, to all allied cities, all corners of the Greek world, awakening great pride in the victory everywhere. Divided into scores of countries, into hundreds of independent cities, separated by borders and quarrels and wars, the Greeks now saw, for the first time in five hundred years, proof of their immense, combined strength.

And when, several decades later, the threat of Persian invasion hung over Greece itself, when the world's largest empire struck at the very heart of the Greek world, the Greeks remembered how the tiny Cyrenian settlement had fought off the great might of Egypt, and the memory comforted those preparing the desperate defense of the homeland.

And upon Egypt, which had been so sure of victory, the news of this inconceivable defeat fell like a thunderbolt from a clear sky. Riots broke out among the population, and the Egyptian army mutinied. The same conspirators who had incited the unfortunate expedition now proclaimed that the pharaoh Apries was responsible for the defeat. His reluctance to pursue the war energetically led to its inept execution and indirectly resulted in the destruction of the expeditionary army.

The rebellion was led by the pharaoh's closest advisor, Amasis, the chief of the household staff. The weak, wavering pharaoh Apries was abandoned by all except for the Greek regiments headed by Symonides. They remained loyal to the old pharaoh to the end, but even they could not save him. Apries lost his kingdom and, a few years later, his life.

Pharaoh Amasis I, the leader of the rebellion, ascended the throne. Everyone now awaited a resumption of the war and a thorough settling of accounts with the Greeks. But the new pharaoh was one of the smartest people of his time. He realized well the immeasurable weakness of Egypt and the utter worthlessness of his allies, the priests. He understood that Egypt could not manage without the Greeks, without the tax income derived from their businesses and the strength of the Greek mercenaries.

And contrary to all expectations, except for the first few years while he was still working to rid himself of his old advisors, his many years on the throne, almost half a century, became one of the longest periods of harmonious cooperation and coexistence between Egyptians and Greeks.

### Chapter Twenty-Five
# This Piece of Junk?

The day after the battle, Greek troops followed the scattered enemy and reached the former Egyptian encampment where they had first skirmished two days earlier.

The Egyptians, retreating in disarray, had abandoned most of their supply train. The Greeks found in the camp hundreds of carts, tents, ladders, chains, ropes, and siege machines prepared to capture Cyrene, as well as grain, flour, oil, dates, and animals. All that had now fallen into their hands.

Peleas's troops, marching in the vanguard, were the first to arrive in the abandoned enemy camp and quickly scattered around in search of booty. Melicles followed the others, looking around curiously. And then he saw her: right there on the beach, lying on its side, lay an abandoned sailboat. She must have shattered many days ago. There was a gaping hole in her bottom where she had hit underwater rocks, her mast broken and numerous gaps shining among her dried-out planks.

A few soldiers were stripping her bare.

Melicles walked over to them and examined the boat carefully.

"What are you doing?" he asked the soldiers.

"We're gathering firewood. We will roast a horse," they answered without interrupting their work. Melicles ran his hand over the ribs of the unfortunate vessel.

"Beech! Real beech wood, the best, from Cyprus," he whispered and turned to the soldiers.

"It's a pity to break up this boat."

They looked at him suspiciously. They were old soldiers of Aristarchos; they had spent their entire lives in military camps, unfamiliar with sailing boats. They did not know the value of the wood, and they needed fuel.

"It's a waste of a good boat," the youth repeated. "Look, the whole skeleton is healthy, ribs strong, the keel is intact. Any carpenter would pay well for this boat."

One of the soldiers shrugged.

"So what? We can't carry her on our backs."

And they continued their work.

Melicles pursed his lips. A sailor's son and nephew of a ship carpenter, he watched the scene in dismay. Finally, he couldn't bear it.

"Who let you hack this boat?" he asked in a trembling voice.

"Aristarchos himself gave it to us. Come on, kid, get lost," they growled at him. They were getting angry.

Melicles went to Aristarchos.

He approached him timidly because Aristarchos was a high-ranking officer, a deputy of Peleas himself.

"Is it true, commander, that you have given these soldiers this boat?"

Aristarchos looked at him in surprise.

"Yes. These are my soldiers. They said they needed firewood."

Melicles wanted to say something else and stuttered. But Aristarchos was already gone.

The boy turned back to the broken boat as if dragged there by magical power. He stopped nearby. The soldiers glared at him. At that moment, one of the planks, torn off with a strong hand, broke free with a groan. Melicles gasped. It seemed to him that the boat was crying, calling to him for help. He approached the men again. He looked again at the broken bottom.

"What do you want?" one of the soldiers growled.

"Maybe he needs his behind whipped," replied the other.

But Melicles had made up his mind already.

"I will buy this boat from you," he said firmly.

The soldiers laughed contemptuously.

"What will you give us for her? Your rocking horse?"

Without saying a word, Melicles removed from his arm the armband he had received as his Sais prize and put it on the side of the boat. The armband sparkled beautifully in the sun. The soldiers looked at it. There was a moment of silence. The soldiers exchanged glances.

At that moment, Polynicos, who had been looking for Melicles for a long time, approached them.

"What are you doing here?" he asked.

"I'm buying this boat!"

Polynicos's eyes widened in disbelief. One eye, actually, because the other was still completely swollen from the blow and covered against flies with a patch.

"You're buying this boat?"

"I am!"

"This wreck?"

"Yes, this wreck."

"And you're giving your Sais prize for it?"

"Yes!"

And so the deal was struck. The soldiers assumed Melicles was a little confused, perhaps had had too much sun. But why not take advantage of this opportunity? The beautiful armband went into their hands, they passed it around. Melicles only asked that they leave him all the wood and the tools with which they had been breaking it.

Polynicos wrung his hands.

"And what are you going to do with this piece of junk, Melicles?" he asked, kicking the wreck with his foot. "You can't take it with you."

"Yes, I can!" he said.

There was a stubborn resolve in his voice. His eyes flashed like those of a hungry wolf who had just got hold of a bone and meant to keep it. Polynicos had never seen him like this.

"What are you going to do with it? How do you get this to Cyrene?"

"I will fix it, patch the bottom with boards, and I will sail it along the shore."

"This holey sieve?"

Melicles said nothing and began to work.

Polynicos stood there for a while. Then he tried to help Melicles, but it was no use: his head hurt him every time he leaned forward, and the unbearable swelling was annoying him dearly.

A group of soldiers, colleagues from the veteran unit, stopped by. Eutychios himself came too. They had learned about the strange trade from their comrades in the detachment of Aristarchos, and they came to see Melicles's purchase. They shook their heads sadly.

They felt sorry for the boy because they had learned to like him.

Melicles walked over to Eutychios.

"*Lochagos*," he said boldly, "will you release three or four men from your squad for a day?"

"Yes. Today is a day of rest."

That was the usual practice in those days, to grant soldiers a day of rest on the day after battle.

"Well, then," said the boy, turning to his companions, "who will help me repair this boat? I'll pay you for your work."

There was a moment of astonished silence.

"I'll pay you!" the boy said firmly. "Look! I have here this ring, my Sais prize. I am giving it to Eutychios for safekeeping. When we get to Cyrene, I will sell it and then pay everyone as promised."

Eutychios took the ring but shook his head reluctantly.

"I'm not sure about this, Melicles," he said.

Polynicos took his sore head in his hands.

"O, gods!" he groaned. "Now the ring, too!"

He was completely depressed.

Several men volunteered, and feverish work began. Melicles took command of his assistants. Planks were cut to size, leveled, cleaned and smoothed, and nailed in place. The boat's skeleton was intact; only the outer skin needed to be fixed. The mast was broken, and oars were missing, but the rudder was still there.

Soon, another soldier joined the working group. He was old and hunched over; he looked quite sluggish. Melicles hesitated to accept him. He did not know if the man could be of any use.

"I was a sailor once," the old man said.

And he was accepted immediately.

Gradually, the beach grew deserted. Soldiers returned to camp, where the commanders were apportioning war booty.

Melicles turned to Polynicos:

"Polynicos! If you are able to walk, go to your father and claim our share of the booty. We deserve the same as the others."

"Of course."

"And ask them to give us a tent, even a small one. There should be a lot of tents."

"What's the tent for?"

"Why, for the sail, you dummy!"

"I don't know if they'll give us a whole tent, just for the two of us."

"Ask for a tent for the three of us, then. It will be easier to get a tent for three shares of plunder than two," said the old sailor.

"What do you want in return, soldier?"

"That you accept me as a companion on your boat. As your helmsman. That's all."

Polynicos set off

He began to take heart. Maybe this was not such utter madness after all.

After a while, he returned, dragging a heavy canvas behind him. Melicles inspected it carefully.

248

Hours passed. Melicles did not rest and did not let anyone else rest, either. But his companions did not complain. He paid them well and was entitled to their labor. And the boy's enthusiasm was contagious and infected everyone. They needed to fix this boat – just to spite those who made fun of them. And they must hurry: the army was to break camp the next day. Until then, the boat had to float. They redoubled their efforts.

Soldiers gathered around them again.

Some of them laughed; others looked serious. However, those who mocked were without exception men who had seen nothing of the sea. Like the troops of Peleas, most of the mercenaries had spent their entire lives on land. But the Cyrenians who had lived with the sea rooted for the boy. More and more of them stopped by. Some offered advice; others pitched in with tasks.

Through Eutychios, Melicles obtained more wood planks from the camp. The old *lochagos* looked at the boy with increasing admiration. In his eyes, Melicles suddenly matured. With a serious, focused face, he seemed much older now. He managed everything quickly, he decided boldly. And his companions, who liked him but had treated him a little like a kid, now obeyed his instructions unquestioningly.

A strange change occurred around the boy within a few hours, and everyone noticed it – everyone except Melicles himself. He couldn't see anything around him: he cared for nothing but his boat.

At one point, Eutychios and Diomenes stopped by. Eutychios beckoned the old sailor aside.

"What do you think?" he asked, pointing to Melicles. "Can the boy make something out of this piece of junk?"

The old soldier looked at him with his aging eyes.

"This boy is a sailor's son," he said finally.

"Did he tell you that?"

"No, but it shows. He is a son of a sailor. Or of a ship carpenter."

But Diomenes was not convinced.

"It's all right," he said. "Leave him to it. But we're leaving tomorrow morning. Get it done by then."

"We will!"

The next day, as the soldiers left the camp on their way back to Cyrene, Melicles's boat was already on the water.

Melicles and the old sailor had improvised a temporary mast and were now hanging the sail they had stitched from a yard arm they had fashioned from a wagon axle.

Other soldiers looked at them curiously. No one laughed anymore. Seeing, however, that the boy must still bail water seeping in through the planks of the hull, they assumed the boat would not reach Cyrene.

Polynicos wanted to go with Melicles, but Diomenes forbade it.

"Once I learn that this wreck can float and this puppy can sail it, I'll let you accompany him. Until then, no!"

Polynicos insisted, and there would have been sharp words between them, but Melicles intervened and dissuaded his friend from going.

"You will be no use to me on the boat, with your sore head and your one eye. You can't even bend down; how will you help us bail water?"

It was true, and Polynicos stopped insisting. They parted ways. The army marched out west. But not only Polynicos, but also Diomenes and Eutychios, and many soldiers, kept gazing over their shoulder towards the sea, looking for the lonely sail swaying on the water.

Then they went around a promontory, and the boat disappeared from sight.

In the evening, the army camped at their former fortified camp.

Polynicos and Diomenes sat on the shore, looking anxiously towards the sea in the east. Polynicos bitterly reproached his father for not allowing him to go with Melicles, for ordering such a hasty departure of the unit and not having left any men to guard the boat.

Diomenes explained that the decision had not been up to him and that he could not risk men from his unit to guard some boy's wreck, even if the boy was their friend. But he now wondered if it might not be better to send a few riders back along the shore to find out what had happened to the boy. The sun was already starting to go down, and there was still no sign of the boat.

Suddenly, Polynicos, who had very keen eyesight, stood up.

"They're coming!" he shouted.

Indeed, the silhouette of a small sailing ship had rounded the cape. The ship tipped a little to one side and went slowly, but it was moving closer.

"Is that the boat?"

"Yes! Yes! You can see the short mast, the broken mast! It's a giveaway. That's her!"

The soldiers now also noticed the sailboat and pointed it out to each other. Eutychios came ashore and stood there, looking at the boat.

"Brave boy," he said appreciatively. "He set his heart on it, against everybody, and he succeeded. I believe he will bring this boat to Cyrene."

Diomenes nodded.

"Yes," he said. "He'll grow up to be a real man someday."

"Commander," replied Eutychios. "I believe you are mistaken. He is a man already."

And then he added:

"Didn't you see him at work when they were repairing the boat?"

"Yes, I saw it. I am glad, Polynicos, that you two have become friends."

"And will you let me accompany him from now on?"

"What can I say? I guess I will have to."

After Eutychios left, Polynicos had a long conversation with his father. From time to time, they looked out over the sea. Against the darkening sky, the tiny silhouette of a small sailing ship wobbled and swayed, swayed and wobbled, and all the time, came ever closer.

Only late at night, in the bright light of the moon, did Melicles's boat land in the tiny port where the Syracusan ships had stood just a few days ago. Polynicos and Diomenes were waiting for her. Melicles came out wet, wobbly on his feet but joyful and with fire in his eyes.

Polynicos grabbed him halfway.

"Father has said I can now go with you!" he exclaimed.

"Yes," confirmed Diomenes. "I didn't know you were a sailor, Melicles, or that you knew so much about boats. I thought you had lost everything with that purchase and that you would fail. I was even angry with you for getting all hell-bent about this boat. But I was wrong. I admit it."

Melicles smiled proudly.

"Well, it may well have gone otherwise. If there had been a bigger wave or a stronger wind, it would have been much harder."

"I wish to help you now, young man," said Diomenes. "Especially if Polynicos is to remain your companion henceforth. Do you have anything you want to ask me?"

"Yes, commander. I would like you to release this soldier from service and let him stay with me as my helmsman."

"He's not my soldier. Eutychios will have to decide that. But I am pretty sure that Eutychios will release him. As it is, most of our soldiers will be released because tiny Cyrene cannot support such a large troop of soldiers for long."

There was silence for a moment. The old sailor went ashore in search of his commander. Melicles did not leave his boat. He bent down and examined the carpentry.

"Everything looks fine," he said finally. "We'll be in Cyrene by tomorrow night."

Diomenes gave him a sharp look.

"Do you mean to arrive there before us?"

"Of course! I will cut right cross the bay."

Diomenes watched the young sailor for a long time as he bustled about with ropes and sail.

"Listen, my man," he said slowly, thoughtfully. "Polynicos mentioned one more request from you."

Melicles shuddered, blood rushed to his head; he felt his heart leap into his throat.

"What did you say, Polynicos?" he stuttered in a strangled voice.

Following his example, Polynicos was busily checking how much water had gathered at the bottom of the boat. He checked slowly and thoroughly and then rechecked and did not say a word.

"He mentioned Anythe," Diomenes finally broke the silence. "Is it true?"

Melicles lowered his head like a culprit.

"Yes," he whispered.

"How old are you, Melicles?"

"Eighteen."

"Hmm. And maybe you're not even eighteen, and Anythe isn't even fifteen. You're still both children.

"But listen up, my friend. Yesterday, I told Polynicos that I would not let him join you on your boat until you proved that you could handle it at sea. You convinced me, and so I agreed to let Polynicos travel with you.

"So, now, Melicles, I will say this: let us see. If you can sail, if you can rebuild this boat, if you can work hard and make a living – if you can do these things as well as you can fight and as you stand up for your friends then... then we will see. I need to get to know you better, get to know your family, to see how you get along in life. And then, yes – then – well…"

He put his hand on his shoulder and looked him in the eyes.

"I want you to know, Melicles, that I wish and hope from the bottom of my heart that you succeed. Do you understand me, Melicles?"

Melicles looked up at him.

"I think I do, sir. Thank you. But… you said, when you get to know my family. How can this happen? As soon as I fix this boat in Cyrene, I will sail it to Miletus to see my mother. But you?"

Diomenes interrupted him:

"Well, my friend! I, too, will go to Miletus. Or nearly to Miletus. We will go to Samos. Prince Polycrates has offered me the command of the port in Samos. And I accepted. So, we will set off at about the same time. And thereafter, we will be constantly close, half a day's journey by the sea. Isn't that right, Melicles?"

And when there followed a sudden silence, he added with a strange smile:

"Yes, my boys. I would like to see once more, in my old age, this tiny temple with four columns on the mountainside, on the right side as one sails from Miletus to Ephesus, just opposite the strait of Samos."

### Chapter Twenty-Six
# Anythe Again

And Melicles succeeded in everything!

He managed to sail the boat to Cyrene – and arrived there before the army. And then he managed to refurbish it and even put in a new mast (with the help of his friend Kalias). And then he managed to sail it clear across the Mediterranean Sea, all the way from the shores of Libya to Ionia.

As he sailed, he remained within sight of the great Samian galley on which Nehurabhed, Diomenes, and Anythe traveled. In good winds, his sailboat overtook the galley and, going ahead, showed the way. In poor wind, it fell behind, but always the three travelers on the galley could see it on the horizon: the silhouette of a small sailing boat, guided by the hand of the young sailor.

Diomenes did worry constantly about his son, who was inexperienced and traveling under the command of "that puppy," as he called Melicles. And when, during the crossing from Crete to

Rhodes, the tiny boat fell behind far enough to disappear beyond the horizon, there was some consternation. People on the galley started to worry, all the more so that soon, the weather turned bad and strong wind and high waves hit the galley. The storm was not dangerous for the mighty sixty-oar galley on which they were traveling, but how would the small sailboat deal with the gale and mountainous waves?

The storm had passed, a day had passed, the second day had passed, the Samian galley rounded Rhodes and approached the Asian shores, and the small sailing ship was still nowhere to be seen on the horizon.

Anythe sobbed, Diomenes was silent and angry, and Nehurabhed tried to comfort them with his account of the boy's resourcefulness during the great storm between Carthage and Syracuse. But in Halicarnassus, the first great Greek port on the Asian shore, their worries were dispelled. Melicles's boat, whole and undamaged, caught up with them again with its entire crew safe.

It turned out that the severe storm could not have threatened them because it could not have found them at sea at all. Melicles, with the skill of a true child of the sea, had sensed the coming of the storm, and after consulting with his steersman, decided not to risk the fragile boat in the coming squall. He turned back to Crete and came into harbor before the storm hit. Only after the storm passed did he set off again. Then, taking advantage of the strong wind, he arrived in Halicarnassus barely a few hours after the Samian galley.

Diomenes, having heard the story, gained respect for his sailing abilities and stopped calling him "a puppy" – even in his private thoughts.

"I am glad that Polynicos learns sailing from such a great master," he said with playful solemnity.

And then, at last, the day came when, off in the distance, Melicles saw the familiar hills above Miletus, then the well-known port, the city, and above it white farmhouses among the green vineyards. And then he found the stone steps familiar to him since childhood, leading upwards towards the old town and a narrow street near the port.

And then...

Polynicos, who was following Melicles and unable to keep up with him, stopped at the entrance to the house. Melicles rushed inside. After a while, a sudden, prolonged, joyful scream reached Polynicos's ears. Polynicos hesitated for a moment, then walked through the small porch. Before him, in the tiny courtyard, Melicles was standing, hugging his mother. A little boy and a smaller girl were cuddling up to him. They were crying and chaotically telling each other something through their sobs. Polynicos stood for a long time, confused, not knowing what to do with himself. Melicles saw him at last.

"Mother! Here is my best friend!" he called, gesturing for him to approach. And then, leaning down towards his mother, he whispered in her ear: "Just remember, Mom, I am eighteen. It's very important."

His mother looked up at him with teary eyes.

"What are you now, my dear, that is so important?"

"Eighteen."

"Ah, yes, my child, as you say."

It is midday.

A hot summer day.

Melicles and Nehurabhed are sitting on the stone quay in the harbor. The marina lies in front of them, farther out lies the bay and farther yet, the sea. The water in the marina is barely swaying, sparkling in gold on blue, touched from time to time by a warm gust of wind. Galleys and fishing boats in the marina sway, too, slightly, as if drowsily. The closest of them all, right under their feet, has been freshly repainted and has a large, clear inscription on the side: "Anythe."

And Anythe herself is also on the boat. She comes every few days from her father's house in Samos to stay with Melicles's mother, who is now sitting next to her, repairing the net. She comes to learn her future job as the bride-to-be of a sailor and a fisherman. But the girl became drowsy in the heat and the steady rocking of the boat and sleeps now at the rudder, with a slightly open mouth, a wave of her golden hair covering her face, her arm resting under her head. She is breathing calmly.

And the water of the marina also breathes calmly, as if asleep. It licks the shore lazily, sloshes from time to time softly under the side of the sailing boat, and caresses the girl's cheek with a gossamer-fine sea mist.

"And so, Melicles, now we must part. It's hard. But it has to be."

"Can't you stay any longer, my lord?"

"Alas. I was only supposed to remain in Miletus for a few days, and I am here already in my third week. It's time to go."

"But will you return one day, my lord?"

"I will."

"Soon?"

"Maybe. I will be sad without you, my young friend."

"You must return, my lord. Return and stay longer. Think how nice it would be. And Anythe adores you. And Diomenes and Polynicos love you. And my mother."

"Yes. I will try. Perhaps I can be assigned a mission to Sardis. Or to Delphi. Then I will at least have to pass through here and see you and yours."

He gave Melicles a sad look and then continued:

"You Greeks are a terrible nation. Whoever has known you once must keep coming back. Yes. Maybe it's because you alone have learned the most important thing."

"What is it?"

"Life. You alone know how to live. And that is great art."

Melicles smiled.

"Life is beautiful," he said.

Nehurabhed shook his head gloomily.

"It could become beautiful... someday. Someday, when people finally learn two great arts: how to live and how to rule."

"Yes, my lord. Indeed, it must be great art to rule, to rule a great state, a few nations at once, like your king," whispered Melicles.

"No, my young friend. That is the smallest art, although people think otherwise. To govern twenty nations, to conquer half the world requires little wisdom and is not really worth the effort. Given enough luck, any trickster can do it, provided that he has no soul and no conscience. But to rule just one city, but wisely and in such a way that its people can live in peace and contentment – that is wisdom, Melicles. The only true wisdom worth learning. And among all the rulers of the world whom I have met, I only met one who could truly be called wise: Solon the Athenian. The only one. May it please my god to grant me again another meeting with him someday."

There was silence.

The old man became lost in his thoughts and his memories. And Melicles abandoned himself to watching his boat floating before him. His faithful boat, his trusty boat, ready to obey his every command. He smiled happily.

"Oh, but life is beautiful," he said.

"You said that once before, you know. In Taranto."

"Yes... But I didn't have Anythe then."

Nehurabhed did not know which Anythe the boy meant: the boat or the girl.

Perhaps he meant both.

*the adventure continues*

# WIND FROM THE HOSPITABLE SEA

*Melicles, Kalias, and Polynicos return for an encore performance in another bestseller from the same author.*

In extraordinary times, twelve-year-old boys must act like men.

Greece 562 BC. For insolvent debtors, the price of bankruptcy is slavery. When his mother and siblings are seized for unpaid debts, little Diossos must run to fetch help. He must cross mountains, forests, and stormy seas, brave wild animals, slave catchers, pirates, and the power of the state. He has a month to achieve his quest, only days to grow up.

The Heroes of *Out of the Lion's Maw* return for an encore in this classic tale of high adventure, full of white-knuckle twists and turns, cliffhangers and last-minute escapes, engaging characters, and sparkling humor.

Continuously in print since 1946 across Eastern Europe, the book has been compared for its tempo and style to *Treasure Island* and *The Three Musketeers*.

Come, see what has delighted millions of readers for three generations.

## TRANSLATOR'S SPECIAL REQUEST

Translating and publishing this book has been a labor of love for me. I grew up reading it and I have always wanted to be able to share it with my American friends. And here it is.

It will not make me rich, but if you liked the book, would you please recommend it to a friend? And give it a review? As you now know, the book deserves to be known and our reading friends will thank you.

## ABOUT THE AUTHOR

Witold Makowiecki (1903-1946) was a Polish agricultural engineer. He had to abandon his profession for health reasons and, during World War II, under German occupation, took up writing for the young. He is the author of two popular adventure novels set in the ancient Mediterranean. His books, written in the swashbuckling style, have been translated and have remained in print in Eastern Europe ever since their original publication in 1946. Here, they appear for the first time in English. Each book is a stand-alone volume, but the appearance of several characters connects them.

## BY THE SAME AUTHOR

*Out of the Lion's Maw* (2022)
*Wind from the Hospitable Sea* (2022)

## ABOUT THE TRANSLATOR

Tom Pinch is the penname of a translator and a publisher based in Luxembourg.

## ABOUT THE PUBLISHER

Mondrala Press is based in Luxembourg and is dedicated to publishing English translations of Polish classics: the greatest books you have never heard of.

Made in the USA
Coppell, TX
31 October 2022

85540102R00163